MRS. PORTER'S LETTER

Mrs. Porter's Letter

Vicki P. McConnell

Illustrated by JANET FONS

the NAIAD PRESS inc.
1982

Printed in the United States of America

First Edition

Cover design and title page by Tee A. Corinne

Interior drawings by Janet Fons

Typesetting by C & H Publishing Services
              Shelburne Falls, Massachusetts

Printing by Rose Printing Co., Inc.
              Tallahassee, Florida

Library of Congress Cataloging in Publication Data

McConnell, Vicki P.
    Mrs. Porter's Letter

    I. Title.
PS3563.C344M7   813'.54   81-22483
ISBN 0-930044-29-0   AACR2

Mrs. Porter's Letter *is dedicated with love and devotion to Maurilyn Denise, my storm's eye.*

WITH SPECIAL THANKS TO:

The real Audrey Louise, for her karmic friendship and the porcupine stories

To Cyndi, for sending me gloxinia

To Janie for taking calls at odd hours and for journalistic research

To Roberta for early editing and continual support

To Martha for final editing

To Ronnie for adjusting horizons

To Janet Fons, for sharing with my words her special talent at illustration

IN SPECIAL MEMORY OF Sara M., The Dancing Queen

ABOUT THE AUTHOR

To quiet all rumor-mongers, I am still Gingerlox. *I first published with Naiad Press in 1977, a novel:* Berrigan. *In 1979, I self-published erotic poetry titled* Sense You.

It is not irony but destiny that one of the names in my family is Dyche. My birthplace was Kansas and I grew up there as a tomboy, kibitzing play-by-play for many years on football benches with my coach-father. My mother had been an amateur actress, painter's model, and avid reader before me; hence my degree in Theatre and English. Not destiny but irony, my combining parental influence to teach a year in a rural Kansas high school: Speech, English, Volleyball, Basketball.

I lived in Oklahoma after I taught school and it was there that my dyke evolvement really began. Unlike most of my friends, I was a bar dyke politicized, rather than a Feminist making the logical choice of Lesbianism. My evolvement progressed when I moved to Denver, with N.O.W., and Lesbian collective Diana's Grove.

Few of my current friends believe in my shyness; some even suggest I should be a stand-up comic. I have a weakness for Geminis and velour shirts; I use my motorcycle for therapy. I have always had dogs but through consciousness, I am now open to cats and to an appreciation for meditation and other rituals which wax cosmic. The Spirit, She does move and shake each of us toward our own contribution.

Nyla Wade is only beginning in this book and I have imaged her in at least four more plots, the second of which is already in the works and logically tracks her to Burnton, Oregon, and to her possible Lesbian partner for future adventures. I think we need the "Nora and Nora" of Dyke Detectives and my spirit has been moved to take up that challenge.

VICKI P. McCONNELL

CONTENTS

ONE

Ahead of Her Time

"That's no work for girls," said the principal, waggling his limp moustache. "Don't try to be ahead of your time, Nyla Wade."

It was my first job interview and I haven't liked them since. I was a senior in high school and had applied to plant grass on the new football field. I wanted to tell the principal as he refused me that his eyebrows were plenty bristly and would have been better suited under his nose. But that's the problem with interviews: you can't really say what you mean. Honesty shows your inexperience. Lying would suit if I could do it better. Rather than give you a try, too many of these limp moustaches tell you what's decent work for an experience totally foreign to them, this "being a girl." The ignorant judge the inexperienced with a lecture on the unknown.

My feeling for job interviews hasn't improved over the years. Not when I interviewed after I finished my journalism degree, making the rounds of the local newspapers, or when I married and wanted some part-time writing. Now when I want to free-lance and start my life in a new direction, a job is not just for experience but is essential. I find myself once again prey to pronouncements about being ahead of my time or behind in my experience or having just plain missed the boat while I was a wife. There are different faces now but the philosophy is the same; shades of that principal have followed me all my life.

Yet today I got lucky. I met with the Public Relations chief at Kinter Paint Company. Kinter is the company featuring TV ads where a koala bear dips her delicate feet into a paint can and leaves prints on the front door of a house. When the homeowner opens the door and sees the prints, he looks around and spots the koala sitting up a tree. A voice says: "Need your house painted? Kinter's the best. Koala us or we'll koala you." Then the bear winks.

Kinter has a company newsletter called *The Brush Stroke* and the p.r. chief wanted to talk to me about editing it free-lance instead of the agency he'd used before. We met just before lunch. He had a ruddy face that didn't spell instant doom and his eyes didn't go for my hemline first thing or travel to my breasts on the pretense of admiring my pockets. I relaxed. We babbled over my resume and he said he took his sophomore year at the college where I graduated. He asked if Dr. Walter Peistermeister was still the faculty sponsor for *The Clarion,* our college newspaper.

"He is," I said, letting my portfolio slouch.

Give me a deadline, I thought to myself. Dare me to miss it. There isn't an agency in town I can't outdo today. Especially if it means I don't have to sit through another job interview. I kept this bravado to myself, behind my teeth, hoping it wouldn't spill out when I smiled. I didn't want to seem like a woman too eager for a job. I wanted the p.r. guy to see a woman he'd choose for the job because she didn't jump at his cues. I hoped to hell he didn't think I had to and I hoped to hell that I *didn't* have to.

"So what do you think, Ms. Wade? This is going to be a mixed bag: some editing, some artwork, and layout. An eye to good p.r. And of course, you have to like the bear."

"The bear?"

"Gigi, the koala in our ads. She is to Kinter what the arches are to McDonald's."

I haven't been wearing Eau de Eucalyptus for nothing, buddy. I coughed because I could see that delicate little bear dipping her feet in the paint again and I didn't want to snicker at this crucial moment in the interview. I mean, the sacred bear, the sacred arches and all, were serious business.

"I'm sure I can handle it. Mixed bag, bear, and all."

I sounded very confident. I felt my own spine made of the steel of competence. I let him see a woman who expected success. I didn't let him see a woman who wanted to shout "Hot Damn!" immediately.

"All right, then, Nyla, I'll give you a crack at it."

We discussed the regular features, the use of stringers' stories from the company. I would do copy fitting, editing, and rough layout. I could search out my own features when I wanted to. The printer would call me with the blueline and then we would go to press. No question of decent work for this girl, no hints at my being behind my time. Saved from another waggling moustache!

"I look forward to my first issue," I told him as I was leaving. "I have the deadline schedule, of course."

"Of course."

His ruddy face closed with a satisfied smile. As we shook hands, I didn't notice if it was my whole hand he took or just my fingers, the way men do sometimes, afraid they'll squeeze too hard. What I knew was that I was getting a grip on myself, with power again, my life in my own hands.

Hot Damn! I was a grown woman skipping out of the parking lot of Kinter Paint Company, with a job! I wound up my trusty Mustang. I can always find her in a parking lot because the "T" is upside down in the middle of the other letters. Faithful, though: she never breaks down for more than forty bucks a repair job.

I headed for Sivu's Sundae Shoppe to celebrate. Sivu was serving as always, shaped like an ice cream cone himself. His face was dark as a Greek olive and when he said, "Chocolate Chip?" he was talking no minor mocha majesty.

As I settled into one of the comfy booths, I considered that Sivu's had been my perennial mainstay through my life in Denver: love and lust, marriage and divorce. I don't remember the love and lust as much these days as I remember marriage and my divorce. I sat in Sivu's for hours after my day in court. Eight weeks ago this Friday. The judge was not impressed with my do-it-yourself petition. There was no humor in him. No pity either, not one tear when I listed what I had taken from my marriage: a loveseat and my underwear. Mike didn't show up. No humor in him either, I guess. But nothing changed in that, he was always the absent husband. No alimony, no goodbyes. Not even pocket change for a Sivu's sundae. That was the day I knew for sure I was on my own.

Full of my success and chocolate delight, I could bask in sweet finality. No more interviews for awhile. I would set myself up an area to write, to cut and paste. Get plenty of paste! Sharpen the blue pencil. Reread *Principles of Editing.* Real work! Life can surprise, alright. But the blue pencil is law!

TWO

A Shrouded Piano

I shifted and fussed and reshifted. I tried to set up a place to begin work on *The Brush Stroke* but there was no way I could take myself seriously as a writer while I was trying to write on a TV tray overloaded with pencils, pads, and reference books. I hadn't done layout for some time, so I was latining a rough board to practice; with every letter that I tried to press down, the tray wobbled precariously. And the light was all wrong. The only lamp I had salvaged in the move was an old high-intensity jobbie from Mike's dorm that overheats and smells of burning dust.

I made circles around the apartment and each piece of furniture in it. I now had a room of my own, a whole apartment to myself and real work, but I couldn't quite get started. I helped myself to a scotch. This is a clean space I live in, with just enough of me in it. I built the bookcase myself, to sit solid, showing every book spine clearly. The loveseat where I sat alone to read F. Scott Fitzgerald was by the coffee table, a garage sale stray, so no guilt about heel-marks. My bedroom maintains the ascetic. There's a queen-sized bed, and the bureau Mother shipped me from Milwaukee. She worried that I would dress out of cardboard moving boxes and always look rumpled everywhere I went.

The TV tray just wouldn't do and I knew it. I was eager to get started, even if it meant breaking through my bare bones efficiency atmosphere. Nyla Wade, Woman About to Write, deserves a desk. A real desk, an extravaganza purchase, the desk of a lifetime from which great literature could be cast.

Now I couldn't go shopping for such a major purchase alone. I needed a companion, a friend with good taste and patience for how fast I look and how quickly I move on to the next store. A friend who would celebrate with me when I found exactly the right desk and it cost too much but she wouldn't say a word about the price. She'd just stroke the wood and look wistfully at me and say, "Oh Nyla, it's *you*. I feel your first novel just hovering in the darkness under this roll-top."

The novel was my secret dream, not sightable just yet but in some private hinterland, definitely not on the same horizon with Kinter's *Brush Stroke*. Yet there was a friend who knew of the novel. She'd been through my college years with me and she loved to shop: Audrey Louise Landry. I was sure I could find the perfect desk to launch my career if only Audrey Louise would help me search.

Saturday, a perfect day to find a desk: from my bay window, I felt a breeze and saw rare grey in the summer sky, light and air playing in cool shadows. It was no small coup getting Audrey Louise for the whole day because her husband, Joel, and their three small sons were entirely dependent upon her constant presence. Audrey Louise and Joel got married the same year Mike and I did. We probably would have had a double ceremony except that Mike and Audrey Louise never liked each other. She wanted her attendants to wear burgandy, too, which I thought was gaudy as hell so we made our marriages in separate ceremony. Audrey Louise missed a period in college before I did, but would not read the Planned Parenthood brochures I brought to her at the dorm. I got the word *abortion* out of my mouth only one time; she let me know that was the last time she wanted to hear it. A few years later, when I joined a consciousness-raising group, I asked her to come along. She told me, "I'd like to join, Nyla, but I don't have any extra time. Maybe when Mark starts walking."

Of course when Mark started walking, then Tony was teething, and her oldest son, Sam, became cranky whenever she went anywhere. So I left her the books the group was studying. I knew she'd peek into them eventually. I told her all about the meetings. She'd laugh and say, "My lord, I never thought of that!" or "Good god, Nyla, you mean you really talk about orgasms right there in front of everyone?"

Feminist was a word Audrey Louise let me say to her; it was not like the short-lived try at discussing abortion. She mostly let all the ideas fly around her. She wasn't obvious or in a hurry about claiming any for herself.

Audrey Louise was the one person who didn't ask me assinine and probing questions right after the divorce. She's always been able to look directly at my intrigues and pull one side of her mouth up and say, "Absolute nonsense. It'll never work. Not one chance in a million. You're crazy to try this. It probably isn't good for you. You sure you want to? Okay then, let's go!"

When I opened the door to Audrey Louise on our precious grey summer Saturday, she hugged me and then immediately started talking as she surveyed my apartment.

"Have you tried Chaney-West yet for this desk? But no, you aren't the High Tech type. What about Billton's, Nyla? Maybe not; everything they have is overstuffed."

"Not to mention overpriced. I'm not in the market for a sofa or a chair. Just a desk. But not just any desk."

Audrey Louise began clucking as she walked around and touched each piece of furniture, few though they were. This clucking was her way of comforting or commenting, but you usually had to ponder which translation to choose. She took a rapid scan of my bedroom, my disaster area around the TV tray, and then turned back to me.

"Spare is spare, Nyla Wade, but spartan is too much. You need a nice velour bedspread and some cheery towels in that bathroom. My, it *is* small. I swear, a sofa would be a help. We could put it over there . . . "

"Just a desk, Audrey Louise. And maybe a special lamp if I see something unusual. But that's all. I'm not in the chips yet, you know. I didn't get my fortune made for me in alimony."

"Well, you should have," Audrey Louise said, disgruntled, and then she went to the window. She always got disgruntled about Mike; she was my advocate of You-Got-a-Raw-Deal where he was concerned. She stood at the window a few minutes, letting the shadows silver her hair. I was about to ask, "Are you ready to go?" when she said, "You feeling okay about doing this newsletter thing? I mean, I know you're a good writer. I've known that for a long time. But looking for work takes its toll. And Mike wasn't exactly supportive. It amazes me that you still have it in you."

"What?"

"The desire to write."

Before I could tell her that I finally knew the desire to write came entirely from myself, before I could testify to the support and encouragement in this independence by my C.R. group, Audrey Louise began pulling me by the arm to the door.

"I've read those 'sisterhood is powerful' books you gave me, so your C.R. group was probably good help to you. Not that you didn't have it three-fourths figured out already. Now if *I'm* any sister to you at all, I know that the Nyla Wade of ole Psi Chi has always been a Woman Writer underneath. With a spirit needing a desk — *today!*"

Audrey Louise had six places in mind for us to start shopping for the desk, insisting that we walk up and down every blasted aisle in every store. When I protested, she persisted. We saw feathers and bamboo, circular beds, plastic lamps, washers with fifty-nine cycles and a computer print-out to prove the rinse was precise. Forlornly included with some lawn furniture was a silver painted tree, each silver painted leaf eye-shaped and looking at me. I kept looking for an end to the aisles.

The few desks we found were not suitable: too shiny, no real wood in them, no scratches to prove a previous labor. "Nonsense for six hundred dollars," Audrey Louise pronounced, pressing her hands in the center of one of the desks to feel it give. It was made with no weight to it, a backbone of glued strips, nearly black wood with no reflection in it. It reminded me of Mike's eyes, showing no reflection of me when we made love, just his irises black and swallowing into privacy.

I lost track of time. We wandered from modern furniture to antiques, past pens and barrels and baskets full of wooden brushes, pictures of someone's dead relatives, and at least a thousand white flowered dishes. I finally sat down under a sign reading "Aged but not Ancient." An Illingworth gramophone was playing in front of a wall covered from floor to ceiling with Coca Cola trays. In front of me were stacked six old iron red mailboxes. Suddenly I wanted to laugh and take one of the mailboxes home so I could use it to mail myself nonsense notes.

"Your heart isn't in this, Nyla Wade," Audrey Louise hummed at me as I sat ensconced in a white enameled barber's chair.

"I've seen every drop leaf table in Denver but not one decent desk. Not one."

"Well, I've shot my wad. I don't know where else to go."

She sighed and pushed her mouth into a half-moon shape. Then she raised her eyebrows at me, waiting for me to decide our next move. I thought of the silver tree we'd seen with its leaf eyes and hoped I would see a final place for us to try.

"Let's go one more place. Then I'll treat you to Sivu's and you'll forget about everything. Ice cream is an aphrodisiac, you know. You'll go home and make Joel grateful."

Audrey Louise laughed and pushed at my arm. We headed down the sidewalk not sure what last shop we'd find. I looked across the street and saw a sign reading "The Gravy Boat." The front windows were cluttered from top to bottom. A Howdy Doody doll waved with a small motor behind his arm. Something about the windows, the dark shop, struck me strangely. I got Audrey Louise by the elbow, fairly dragging her across the street.

"This is a thrift store, Nyla, for petessakes. It's closed anyway."

A sign on the door read: "Illness in the family. Store open by appointment only." I peered past the sign and Howdy Doody. There was someone sitting between two open curtains at the back of the store. I didn't realize I was rapping loudly at the window until Audrey Louise caught hold of my hand.

"She's coming, Nyla. She heard you already."

The lady who unlocked the door could well have just risen off one of the shelves to shake hands. She might have been a porcelain ballerina fifty years before; she was dressed out of the open trunks on the floor.

"May we come in and look around?" I asked, putting out my hand. Her eyes paled the delft we'd been skirting all day. The hand she offered was small, nearly colorless the nails. She waited for me to shake lightly or vigorously, her eyelashes dropping down, her shy mouth only a little open.

"It will be all right, I think. Usually Thomas, my brother, shows people through. But he's been quite ill lately."

She didn't take her hand out of mine and I was bending over to hear her and see that perfect face, so there we stood for a moment. I felt a movement or shifting of some layer around me. I knew I wasn't imagining it because Audrey Louise had entirely quieted. The old lady moved aside to clear the door. I stepped on the threshold and the wood crackled.

There were two narrow aisles amongst chaotic piles of every imaginable relic. Audrey Louise stopped at a fringe-topped baby carriage. In front of me was a hand-made dollhouse with a tiny radio, an organ, and a miniature chamberpot inside it. Elsewhere, dishes were stacked over and under everything. Clothes and curtains hung or were stuffed over half open boxes and crates of still more items. There was a bronze horse rearing up on hind hooves, and a ceramic kitty. I could smell dust and possibility. I wanted to turn the room upside down so I could find what I felt sure was here for me. But everything seemed to be sitting on tables or chairs. No desk visible.

"Nyla, come quick!"

Audrey Louise was in a far corner near the curtains where the old lady sat delicately eating a sandwich. She had found a floor lamp for me to look at, elegant wood with a peach-colored fabric shade.

"It's beautiful!" I knew at once I wanted the lamp to keep the bookcase company, or brighten the bedroom.

"Can we plug it in?" Audrey Louise whispered. "To see if it works?"

I looked down the wall behind her but with no hope of locating a plug-in amongst the paraphernalia piled everywhere.

"Here's a bulb."

The lady made no sound joining us from her spot between the curtains. Audrey Louise startled with a small jerk that I noticed only when I felt her arm harden next to mine. We screwed in the bulb while the lady deftly found a plug-in behind one belabored chair. The light glowed through the peach shade, thin as a pinned wing over velvet.

"My mother used to keep that lamp in her parlor," the lady said. "She had lots of suitors to call after Father died. I thought most of them were too young."

"I like the lamp very much," I told her. Our voices were getting lost in the dollhouse, deep into the crates with their hidden contents. The shop was getting darker.

"I'll look up the price for you."

We all stepped in one motion toward the curtains. The lady opened a ledger carefully. I saw then the room behind the tiny office. There was a wardrobe in sight and a bureau.

"Why don't you put your furniture out here in the main area?" But I knew as soon as I asked that there was no more room for even one additional ceramic kitten.

"Thomas doesn't really like the larger pieces. We inherited some. Others were here when we rented the store. You may look."

Again she moved aside for me to pass her. I had to scoot along through the office the way you do in a movie theater, sort of sideways and keeping your knees out of the way. As I passed the lady, so passed a new aspect in her face: portent, a curtain drawn away. When she looked at me without shyness, I noticed her white eyelashes. I almost expected her to delay me, to hold me for a moment again with her slight, cool hand. I could feel now more than ever Audrey Louise's close silence at my back.

At the entrance to the back room, I felt along the wall for a light switch. All I could make out in the dim shadows were huge shapes of all sizes. Audrey Louise put her hand on my shoulder.

"The old lady passed this up to you."

In the darkness, Audrey Louise handed me a long-handled flashlight. I heard the lady say, "There's no light back there. Thomas has been meaning to fix it."

I scanned the room with the flashlight beam. The chaos continued here, connected by the tunnel of the office from the front room to the back. Overloaded boxes were stacked on most of the pieces of furniture: more clothes, and rugs draped over whatever had been inherited or abandoned.

"What's that at the back?" Audrey Louise asked. I shined the beam back to where she indicated.

"Looks like a piano or something. With a shroud over it."

"That's a tarp, Audrey Louise. Shrouds are for funerals."

"Maybe the piano died."

"Funny way to bury a piano."

Audrey Louise took the flashlight from me and ventured forth

11

with no fear. She scanned over the tarp as we approached. I caught a glimpse of something "footed" when the light hit the bottom of the tarp. Footing furniture was the old-fashioned penchant for carving clawed feet on the legs of chairs and tables, a lion's noble paws for the distinctive men of those past days. I only heard the swish of the tarp when Audrey Louise lifted it. We both coughed and the flashlight reflected a small swirl around us of falling dust. When she dropped the beam back on our discovery, we were looking at a roll-top desk.

"There's something on this, a little sign or something."

Audrey Louise pointed the light on a tiny sign. Hand-lettered were the words: "Don't roll. Works fine." Audrey Louise giggled and I shooshed her, taking back the flashlight. Slowly I ran the light over the desk. A light golden wood, it had gold clasp fittings and filigree around the key. Four drawers were on the left side, a small door on the right. I wanted at once to roll back the top. It might not be my novel hovering in that small enclosed darkness, but whatever it was beckoned unbearably.

I turned the key, put my hand on the top of the desk to give it a gentle push. Audrey Louise looked back toward the office. The old lady was standing watching us but she made no protest as I carefully opened the desk. It rolled smooth and soundless, which surprised me. No telling how long it had sat under its shroud; I expected the oil to have long since rusted in the track.

The flashlight revealed to us a gold oak desk with swirling scallop to the wood grain. There were six compartments under the top: three small drawers, two letter shelves, and a tray for pencils. The roll top reminded me of the bottom of an old-fashioned skirt: something pleated and protective, and yet underneath, the strong loins of a pioneer woman. There was no question that I wanted to burrow in between those skirts and be my own pioneer, give my heart to words, whether they were mine, Kinter Paint's, or the ones left behind to me by Fitzgerald.

"I don't believe you made a beeline for this store, Nyla, and here's the very desk you were seeking."

I put the light up between Audrey Louise and me. Our heads were wreathed in dust, surprise, and excitement. A smile as quiet as the dark shop passed from Audrey Louise's face to mine. Behind us, our blue-eyed observer commented, "Thomas thought

that was a beaut. Thought it would be a sure sell. But he's had trouble. Buyers noticed it every time. They'd be ready to take it and then they'd notice. Just walk away shaking their heads. Guess that's why he covered it up and put it in the corner."

"What? They noticed what?"

"The flaw. We could have dug it out, I suppose, and had the spot refinished. But still, it would have shown itself. The flaw."

Another layer moved around us in this strange, cluttered space. I felt it move and jangle my heart with a shiver.

"What flaw?"

"You'll see it. In the back corner, just under the tray."

I wanted to stamp my feet at Thomas for not fixing the overhead light so I could get a better look at my desk. Mine already, *my* desk. I focused the flashlight beam on the back of the desk's writing surface, sliding my hand over the top, the smooth luxuriant wood. So there *was* something hovering underneath the roll top. A flaw she called it. I had to lean way in to find what she meant by the flaw. Audrey Louise moved behind me and I could feel her body against mine as we both strained deeper into the mystery of the desk. And then we saw it, embedded at a slight angle above the surface of the desk.

I stood up sharply and ran the beam over Audrey Louise and then the old lady. Then I bent back again to look at the flaw. Someone had stabbed an ebony pen into the shoulder of the desk. It had been broken off at the bottom of the ink barrel so that the silver point went in an inch or more into the wood. There were three sharp shards left to the pen barrel, sticking out of the wood like a tiny hand signaling that moment when someone was angry or hurt or struggling and struck out with the pen. Who owned this desk? Who wrote here? Who opened and closed the drawers and locked the key? The indelible silver painted tree and its eye-like leaves came to mind. Would I need such special eyes to see the answers to this flaw, this desk left behind by all those fastidious antique buyers who closed the top down between innocent skirts when they saw the secret?

Audrey Louise squeezed my arm. "We can borrow Larry's truck."

I didn't want to leave. I was afraid someone might dig the pen out and sand over that sign before I came back. I put the light on those three sharp black spears of the broken pen again. To me the flaw was the very beacon I had hoped to find.

THREE

Twenty-Four and Still Holding

"Keep your end level, will you!"

"All right! Quit griping."

For the second time, Larry tipped the desk too far and the three of us did a keystone cops backpedaling routine to keep from toppling out of his truck and into the street.

"That's better. Now we've got it. No sweat."

He made a sucking noise through his front teeth, like spitting backwards. Robert Redford does it sometimes during moments of high suspense. Larry did it, no doubt, because he's probably seen every Redford movie at least three times. Larry is Audrey Louise's baby brother, twenty-four and still holding at that age ever since I first met him.

"Hold 'er steady. Easy, easy now." Joel directed us from my apartment building doorway. He had bad back syndrome so he could only supervise. "Not so far to the left, Audrey Louise."

Larry got to the edge of the truck bed and stepped down to the street.

"I'll support this end by myself and lift while you girls move toward me with the other end."

Audrey Louise and I were groaning and straining but Larry could hold up one entire side of the heavy desk alone and wait for us. He gave that sucking noise again. "No sweat."

"Be careful, honey," Joel consoled from the doorway, being sure to rub his sacro apologetically.

We weaved with the weight of my pride and joy, first to one side of the truck, then to the other, as if the desk itself were heaving back against us.

"Are you two fighting back there?" Larry joked. He loves to laugh at his own jokes. Audrey Louise was finding the effort of the move unfunny.

"This is ungodly heavy, Nyla. Only for you would I risk lowering my pelvic floor with this lifting. I'm a mother, for godssakes. What I do for friendship."

I couldn't help starting to laugh. It was contagious. Audrey Louise giggled, snickered, then let out a full roar of laughter as we both pushed forward against the desk. I felt my fingers losing their grip on the desk's edge. The full weight of the desk teetered onto Larry. The desk went out of my hands completely and my legs hit the side of the truck and strained further. Audrey Louise bent over laughing, while I flapped my arms to keep from falling over backwards. Larry meanwhile had become a gruesome grimace, his biceps bulging, as the weight of the desk bore down on him.

"Do something!" Joel screamed, running from the doorway and trying to push a shoulder up against the desk to help Larry.

With a loud crack, the desk hit the tailgate and rested there at an awkward angle against the side of the truck and Larry's shoulder. Joel danced around him, still trying to find a wedge for his own shoulder.

"I told you we needed a goddamned dolly, Audrey Louise. I fuckin' told you that!" Larry was sucking and cursing and straining, his hefty thighs muscle-hard as he held up the desk.

"Shit, we still have the stairs to go!"

We couldn't stop laughing at Larry and this impossible treasure that would not be simply moved from under a tarp and into my living room. A spotlight at least was demanded, and some fanfare. If nothing else, the threat of it toppling all three of us as we tried to deliver it to its new home.

"I wasn't sure you three would still be speaking by the time we got this up here." Joel appraised the disheveled movers as he stood with one hand on the desk, one on his hip. Audrey Louise was stretched out face down on the living room rug; Larry slumped over one side of the loveseat. I had my back to the bookcase and was downing my second scotch, a double.

"We did it, though. Here's to success!" But no one was toasting with me. Joel tried to be energized for the rest of us.

"This is a fine piece of work here, Nyla. Worthy of a Virginia Woolf, yes? We'll expect great things from you now."

"I hope not, Joel. She was a sufferer. I expect this desk to harbor the joy I get out of writing, not suffering. I've had my fill of that for awhile."

"Audrey Louise told me about the flaw. I'd sure like to get a look at it. Could you unlock the top?"

I didn't like his question. There was something lurid about it, as if he wanted a peek at a nasty nickelodeon. And Joel wasn't like that. I just didn't want to share yet. I wanted them the hell out so I could piddle in my space and do a little dance around the desk. Maybe even begin to write. Write my special first words in between those special skirts. The grand lady had arrived amidst my other furniture. If I was to be her mistress, we needed some time alone together.

"I'd like to see if there's any damage from the fall."

Joel and I inspected the back of the desk; I hoped he'd forget the front and his wish to look at the flaw.

"You act like it's a kid with a broken leg. At most there's a pinch in the wood near the base. That's all. No sweat." Suck, scratch, stand: Larry at twenty-four. "You got any more beer?"

Thank god Audrey Louise stopped wanting me to marry her brother. At first her approach was the "for my own good" ploy: "You're separated. You need the company." Then she tried coaxing my vanity. "You'd have pretty babies together." We sulked at each other through July after she asked me why I never dated him and I finally told her.

"He's a jock. He rearranges himself too much. What the hell would I do with a jock?"

"Maybe you should switch types. *Bed* instead of *head.* The college professor type sure didn't work out."

Stubborn stalemate and no speaking for weeks. I picked up the phone to call her at least twenty times, knowing she was doing the same thing on her end. Finally she called me after her Labor Day family reunion picnic.

"My god, Nyla, you're right about Larry. I never noticed before. But he does it all the time. He did it at the reunion softball game right in front of everyone. Shifted his balls right up there on the pitcher's mound!"

If only Larry were more like Audrey Louise. He has her argumentative nature, her one track focus at times. But not her softer, conciliatory side. I'm sure he's never read a single Fitzgerald. I can hear him say, "Tender Is the Night? Wasn't James Garner in that one?"

"You want to go bowling, Sis? Come on, Joel, let's throw a couple of lines. It's Saturday, you got the time." Larry sucked and downed the last of his beer, crushing the can automatically when he finished.

"Whatdya say, honey? Will the sitter mind? Nyla can pair off with Larry and we'll team score."

Audrey Louise clucked an unidentifiable but authoritative tone from her prone position. Joel caught his cue.

"What am I thinking? I can't bowl with this back of mine. You'd have to peel me out of the alley after the first frame. Besides, Nyla probably wants to tidy up around here. You know how women are: they always like to fuss with new things."

Joel always loved to tease me; my feminism provided him with fertile ground for his deviltry. He never failed to irk me, even though he was trying in his way to be understanding that I was ready to be alone.

Joel helped Audrey Louise up; she groaned again to remind me of her sacrifice. They started down the stairs. Larry hung a moment at the door. I motioned back to the desk. "She sure was a beast to get up those stairs. Thanks for helping, Larry. And for loaning me your truck."

"No sweat." For once, no suck in of air. He kept his eyes on the floor. I started to say, "See you sometime?" but caught myself. I had to unlearn that, making offers only out of politeness.

"Call again sometime, Nyla. Nice to see ya." He thrust one thumb up in the air at me and then bounded out and down the stairs. Still holding at twenty-four.

Alone with the desk, selfishly alone, I could have worn a path around it, touching it here and there, feeling the new authority in the old wood. I welcomed this solid memory with my own enshrining, hoping it would soak up the inspiration I intended. I probed around the back; there was a deep scratch and a gouge out of the wood. But it was just a jostle scar worn for the move to a new home.

Standing in front of the desk, I was full of the sight of it, the presence, as if the space of the room were shimmering with reply. Attentively, I pulled open each drawer, then pushed it back. I dusted the pencil tray. With no one looking, I rolled the top three, four times, just to hear the wisp of sound in its movement. This was all the sanctuary I needed, my small retreat from all the Larrys and Joels and Mikes. From the divorce and the fear of starting over. I knew my command was there in that writing space, with that venerable golden oak. There were no commands from outside of me now.

From its corner, a summons: those small, sharp spines of the broken pen. I ran my finger around the flaw, the wound of the pen, and wondered if the desk would yield up the cause of this trauma and whom the blow was meant for.

FOUR

A Scarlet Orchid—A Hidden Love

As easy as that: my initials on the blueline layout and Kinter goes to press. I came home after my quick trip, on time, ahead of deadline. My copy so painstakingly laid out for my first issue has now been dismissed as all part of the printing process. I should have taken a swing by Sivu's for a "success sundae." I wished for some secret admirer to have left me a note: "Congratulations on your deadline!" But there was no note. Only a double scotch which I poured for myself. I leaned back into the pillows on the bed for a very quiet celebration. Then . . . something . . . moving behind my eyes. I didn't call for it but there it was. A flower . . . a scarlet flower blooming. Closing and opening, in and out like film slowed down and then speeded up. I opened my eyes, closed them again. It was still there, someone else's dream. What the hell? I must have missed my Vitamin B for the week. This must be some leftover stress that didn't surface as I was trying to beat the deadline. Some stress: a flower moving oddly and staying inside my head. It's an orchid, I think. Maybe I've read about it or seen a painting somewhere. But why this uncanny growth? It blooms, then pales, reblooms, its petals pulsating.

I closed my eyes and tried hard to make the flower dissolve into black blank space. But it persisted. My feeling of stress climbed some invisible thermometer in my head until I was sure the mercury would pop its vessel.

If there was an award for felicity, Audrey Louise would deserve it. She came unexpectedly at exactly the right moment, ringing my bell and bustling in, clucking madly, sending the peculiar flower vision to a far garden. I breathed an incredible sigh of relief as she said, "These things are important but you don't exactly toot your own horn so I took the liberty of scanning your calendar last week. I happened to notice this was your first deadline week. So happy first success! You did make it, didn't you? Or am I too early? Oh of course you made it. Give me a scotch and tell me word-for-word everything they said about your work at that paint company. Koala Somebody, aren't they? And here, open your present. Everyone needs a present now and then for occasions such as these."

I couldn't get to the scotch quickly enough or to my gratitude for her timely arrival, her caring interest.

"I was having this weird feeling just when you rang the bell."

She refused to take me seriously.

"Horny, you're probably horny. Now, my gift isn't exactly an obvious writer's present or anything. I hope you don't mind. But I saw it over at Van Awson's. That place is a faggot's paradise, I swear. Just overdone with feathers and tapestries. But this sort of leapt out at me, you know?"

"Audrey Louise, you know I'll love it whatever it is. I'm bloody grateful to see you." I hadn't given her a kiss in a long time.

"Don't overdo, Nyla Wade. It's just a silly present!"

Beneath the wrapping paper was an elegant pillow embroidered with a stately unicorn in bright, cheerful colors. No quavering orchid but an irresistible creature that made me grin.

"You still like them, don't you? I remember you were crazy for unicorns in college."

"Yes I was, and you never gave me one then. You said I was too trendy and the preference would pass. I like the pillow very much. Thank you. Thank you, Audrey Louise."

"My goodness, Nyla, more hugs and kisses? You *are* getting too lonesome just mistressing that solemn ole desk and your serious words. Let's do get you out and about some soon. Now I've got to run. I just wanted to . . . oh you know, be supportive."

"You have saved my day once again in our long life together. Give the boys a tweek for me."

She wouldn't sit still for any more of my affection.

"They're over at Grandma's tonight. Joel has his own tweek in mind. See you, love!"

At the door she clucked at me again. "That's a pillow, see. But not for a bed. For a couch, see. You need a couch and we *are* going to shop for one soon."

The curious flower did not float back into my mind after Audrey Louise left me. I was relaxed enough from her visit, in fact, to doze off on the bed until someone in the building slammed the lobby door hard enough to jolt me awake. It was past midnight and pitch black in the apartment. The bulb in the one lamp I always leave on had burned out. So I felt my way to the living room, groping for the old dust-burner lamp on the desk. I never could stand to sleep in a totally dark place. As my hand touched the metal shade of the lamp, I had another flash of that orchid, its eerie bloom like a mouth crying out. I grabbed the lamp with both hands but it tumbled down onto the floor. When I righted it and hit the switch, hoping to push the flower out with the darkness, the lamp clicked on, blue grey, then off, then a puny amber. Smelly amber. Burnt dust again. But at least a little light.

I pulled at the large bottom drawer of the desk where I'd put a package of 60-watt bulbs. The drawer came out halfway and stuck. I jiggled the drawer but it wouldn't slide; when I pulled harder, it still wouldn't budge. When I slid it back, it didn't seem to catch up against anything. Again when I pulled the drawer out, it came only partway.

Reaching back into the space between drawer and desk, I felt the back of the drawer and the track. Nothing: no nicks in the wood, not a jutting nail or a loose bearing. As I pulled my hand out, something scratched the top of my fingers lightly. Thinking it might be a sequestered mouse, I jumped and managed to rake my hand badly against the top runner of the upper drawer. I could feel a nasty pain over my knuckles but no blood. And still the drawer stuck.

I prayed that whatever had scratched me was either dead or at least skeletal. And let it be of this world and not the nether. I was more than cautious as I inched my fingers back into the space again, walking them along the drawer's edge until I reached the back. I began to feel up behind the top drawer, until I had nearly my full arm inside the desk and I was turned sideways for as full a reach as possible. Perhaps we unlodged something when Larry dropped the desk? There are no mice in this desk, I told myself. But if there is anything in here with a ferocious bite, it will get my whole arm, right up to the shoulder. I felt a corner of something, like cardboard. It was bent and slid back out of the way as the drawer moved in but blocked the drawer when it moved out. I pulled on it but it wasn't just a small piece of something. I wondered if it was some lightweight backing material in the desk and if I pulled too hard, the whole desk would come apart, as if hinged, and fold over me.

I gave the corner of it a yank and something large and flexible snapped away from the desk up near the top drawer. I let it fall. Carefully I slid the drawers out and put them on the carpet. I had to reach once more into the innards of the desk and pull out whatever I had unloosened.

I half expected to pull out an old magazine or catalog of some sort with a cover of faded scarlet orchids printed on it. But the packet was in fact an envelope, banded tightly to keep the contents within it. It had been pushed quite flat from the pressure of the drawers against it. Someone had taped it in the desk to keep it from being found. That was clear by the double layers of dusty, peeling tape which bordered all four corners of the envelope, and the fact that it had been taped in such an odd place.

Pandora's box having no good reputation, I was not entirely eager to rip into the envelope. It was covered with a powdery, sticky coating of dust. There was no label or initials or writing of any kind on the outside. It didn't look like an envelope for school work such as a child might have. It was more distinctive: for legal papers, perhaps? Someone's handwritten will, leaving an unknown fortune? Perhaps the envelope held a manuscript of some kind, a spectacular story from a secret talent. Blackmail notes, by chance, or pictures of a victim compromised? It was probably just someone's Past Due notices or an old insurance policy. Or pressed flowers brittled over the years and stuffed between pages of love notes. Possibly I would find the pressed and powdered petals of a scarlet orchid?

It was hard to touch the envelope; the dust rubbed off with the feel of caterpillars as I removed the bands and lifted the flap of the envelope. What seemed to be within were several small packets of letters, tied up together. They bore only a return address on the outer envelopes, but no name. I thumbed through one packet and pulled out one letter. It was addressed to Cybil Porter and signed, "Love, W. Stone."

Thumbing through a second bunch, I saw they were the same as the first, all to Cybil and in chronological order by post date. Signed by the same W. Stone and all sent to the same address in Rochester, New York.

I had chanced upon letters taped out of sight inside a desk. Was the desk Cybil's then? Could she be traced? Was she still alive? Some quandary overtook me, a resistance to reading another person's private mail. Especially this, so private, it would seem, that the letters had to be hidden. And yet, I had found them and must, in order to understand their value, read at least some of them.

With eloquence and passion, W. Stone had loved Cybil Porter. I found myself wishing as I read Stone's letters that some time in my life, I would receive this kind of love. It was not clear to me why, but W. Stone wrote with an underlying sadness that convinced me they were lovers who had to live apart. Sentiment was layered with sensuality: a longing for the physical, a sustenance by the spiritual, conflicted by their distance from each other. But these were storybook letters. W. Stone was indeed a rare and generous lover.

After sitting cross-legged and engrossed in the letters for more than an hour, my legs had gone stiff. One knee buzzed as the circulation ebbed. When I stood up, the leg buckled and as I caught my balance, the other foot scattered the third bunch of W. Stone's letters. There among them, I spotted one different, in an envelope not yet fully addressed and not yet sealed. When I opened the envelope, I found a response from Cybil, one never sent to W. Stone. All the other letters were Stone's; here was the second voice in the pair, sharing a love bonded by obvious passion and separated by an unnamed distance.

"Dearest: when I look at the calendar, it hardly seems a year since we were together. My days go by so rapidly, keeping pace with Spencer and Lawrence. Time slows only in those minutes before I fall asleep and am thinking of you.

"Lawrence: such a large name for this small treasure, my son. He reminds me of you in his poses, his lithesome streaks from room to room, and even in his awkward falls and the smile that follows them. It is as if he understands a faux pas may belong even to the beautiful.

"I think of you often these days when I am alone with Lawrence. At this age, his love is simple and his joy complete. He embodies now what we shared when we were first together: our innocence and discovery. Our pleasure then was the taste of freedom for which we were both so lonesome.

"I don't ache as I used to about you, missing you so dearly. But the feelings are always close, near my heart, letting me know their strength has not diminished. I hope someday to help Lawrence understand us and what comfort he is, what special and unique help. As we both know, none of it is simple and all of it can seem impossible to understand.

"Spencer and I have traveled less since Lawrence was born. But I really lost my desire for trips just after my time with you. There was nothing to travel to except you and only duty to come back to, though I love my family. I'm sure Spencer is unaware of our relationship. He did see that I changed when I returned from my 'vacation,' gained a vitality and happiness that I didn't have when I left. He could never imagine you, could never begin to comprehend what we shared. Despite all that goes on around me, you and I are the most private and sacred aspect of my life. You and I, our 'us,' is a secret I intend to keep, a joy I intend to celebrate. I have nothing to confess about it; I am alive and will be for the rest of my life because of you.

"Although we are both obsessed with another meeting, I fight hard not to count on it, not to subject either of us to disappointment. It may be possible. I want to say it *must* be possible. But if we can be together again, it must be planned with ultimate discretion. Not to protect Spencer, but the two of us. For we are ahead of our time, you and I, with our connection for each other. And that carries with it great danger and risk for a love already burdened by difficult conditions.

"So we go on as The Porters of Kingston Row. Spencer

has always had more energy for this life than I have. He takes the pace and the frivolity in stride, while I still have to work at it. For him, Porterfield is home base. To me, it is still another family's fort in which I am allowed to wander. How different life can seem to two people looking at the same thing. When Spencer looks at Lawrence, he sees his legacy, the son born late to both of us, a miracle we did not expect. I look at him and see you and the hope that I will see you truly, soon, in the same room, close as breath upon my face. You, whom I shall always love. Yours, Cybil."

A mystery from within the desk had revealed to me another woman ahead of her time. I felt as if Cybil Porter had reached out of time and touched me, her letter a clear voice in my life. Not just a ghost's voice but as real as her own had been in the days when she and W. Stone were corresponding. Closer than breath upon my face I felt the presence of these two lovers and their history together, "under difficult conditions." In the darkness with the letters and the desk, I was not alone: the three of us were there, with revelation.

FIVE

The Emerald Eye

I should have stayed at my desk and worked on the new warehouse story for *The Brush Stroke*. Kinter has been after the acreage for months. I reviled myself all the way to South Broadway on a return trip to The Gravy Boat. But no matter how hard I tried to write at the desk, all I could think of was the letters and my probe in the darkness: my hand deep inside the mystery, myself unnerved by the uncovered secret and the revelation of what went on between two lovers. Was the broken pen part of it? I wondered about my part in it, the past passion that felt so immediate and evoked my sore spirit. Was the vision of the flower part of it? That scarlet monster pounding its petals against my thoughts: if only it was somehow predictable! I toppled a whole mountain of green bean cans in the store yesterday when that flower flapped into view like no friendly creature. What the hell is it? Where in hell did it come from? And how do I send it home?

No speck of Nellie Bly in me today. "Dubious concentration": that's what Dr. Peistermeister would label my writing attempts, just like he did when I was in college. Though I stared at the warehouse story for hours, realigning sentences and focus, searching in vain for that elusive "journalistic flow," all I could think about was some way to trace my desk back to Cybil Porter. In the midst of my distraction, Audrey Louise called me, excited to report that after so many years of mothering, she finally has time to take a Women's Studies class two nights a week. It's ironic that when I am full of questions about the desk and the letters and sighting an abominable cosmic blossom, unable to concentrate, unable to write, unexcited by Kinter's story, I am also surrounded by everyone else's excitement. I love irony as much as I love job interviews.

At the turn off of 14th Street onto Broadway, one of W. Stone's lyrical passages came to mind to comfort me:

"We watched the dancers that evening and I wanted desperately to hold you in my arms and dance with you. But we couldn't take the chance. Yet I could feel the weight and touch of you: electric, a strong current between us. It was all I could do to keep from reaching out and taking your hand. Our waiting was worth the small tortures, though, when later we had our own night of dancing alone together on your terrace. We were naked in the moonlight and humming our music to each other. I suppose anyone looking up could have seen us, but all I could see was moonlight glancing off your temple and wreathing your ardent mouth."

I was able to park right in front of The Gravy Boat. As I walked from the car to the shop door, I tried to ignore my heart sinking: there was no light visible in the window. I know I looked ridiculous pressing my face against the glass door, still holding its sign about illness in the family. For a moment, I closed my eyes and conjured the dim space inside the narrow office, conjured too someone sitting just behind the curtain. When I opened my eyes again, I looked and saw no one there. Perhaps the little stooped lady could be rummaging in the back. As I pounded on the door, willing even for a ghost, there was a movement at the curtain. I stopped pounding; there appeared a white hand holding the curtain, with no attached body in sight. I reconsidered wanting the ghost. The hand went up the curtain nearly to the top. With a snap of movement that startled me, the curtain opened. It was not the old lady I saw then. There was a tall, thin man standing there, almost as tall as the narrow doorway. And he was so white: his skin, his hair, even his eyeballs seemed entirely white, with no color in them. He was looking at me, and just standing in the doorway.

"Hey, hey! I bought the desk! The one with the flaw! Please, I must talk to you." I rattled the door in my excitement. Still the old man stood motionless in between the curtains. Maybe I was crazy. Maybe he wasn't there at all. There was so little light and so much dust. He became some part of the frozen time inside the shop.

Then he moved, coming toward me. I was only partly crazy. I had stood there long enough to convince him to come to the door. He only opened it part-way; his voice was tremulous.

"May I help you?"

"Oh yes, yes. I bought a desk here several weeks ago. Are you Thomas? I'm Nyla Wade. I think it was your sister who sold me the desk."

His eyebrows were so white they disappeared. But there was no befuddlement in the eyes that watched me. Closer up, I could see his eyes held the same delft blue coloring as the old lady's. When he spoke again, his voice was firmer.

"You bought the desk? The one with the flaw?"

"Yes. I'd like very much to talk to you about the desk. Just for a few minutes."

I expected him to open the door wider for me to enter. Instead he kept it partly closed and asked, "Is everything all right?"

Before I could answer, I felt an odd tingling at the back of my neck, as if someone had quietly come up behind me. Sagging against the door, my knees buckled and my mind whirled. It overtook me before I knew it. Thomas grabbed my elbow. All I could say to him was, "Do you see it? The flower . . . "

I wasn't the fainting type. So I don't know for sure if I fainted but I couldn't remember anything between the time I was on the sidewalk at the door and when I came to, sitting in the tiny office of The Gravy Boat. With worry tracking every fold in his face, Thomas was dabbing at me with a wet paper towel.

"Better?"

"I don't know what came over me."

"You've had some trouble with the desk, haven't you?"

"What do you mean?"

"Did it . . . fall on someone?"

How on earth could he have guessed about Larry dropping the desk? My neck tingled again. I talked fast, hoping to keep that gargantuan floret at bay.

"No, no one was hurt. But we did have some slight trouble getting the desk off the truck. We dropped it but only the desk was damaged. Just a small gash in the wood at the back. Tell me, do you know who owned the desk? Who sold it to you? Or could you find out? I . . . "

There was clearly a tingling in Thomas too. He pulled his lips tight together, raised his translucent eyebrows and began muttering, his eyes roaming to the cluttered outer room.

"Only the desk this time. No one hurt. No one hurt . . . lucky."

He was not with me at that moment. His eyes scanned the dark outer room, straining, hunting. I couldn't hear him breathe. Again I wondered if he was really there with me or if I had made him up as an alternative to that damned flower.

"Your sister said a lot of people passed over the desk because of the flaw. Do you know how the pen got into the desk that way?"

Thomas stood up abruptly and left me without answering, disappearing into the stacks outside the curtain. I heard a platter rattle. Then he returned, holding the ceramic kitty. He began running his ivory white hands over its ears, petting the old cat.

"Your sister said you'd been ill, Thomas. Are you feeling better?"

I hoped perhaps a little small talk would make us both feel less edgy.

"I am out of the hospital and glad of that. But I feel . . . "

We both looked at the cat simultaneously, sure it had just purred slightly. I wished Thomas's sister was here. She was so much easier to talk to.

"I have been sick for a long time."

"Do you think you could tell me, Thomas, who sold you the desk? I'd like to contact them. To find out something about the history of the desk."

"You should leave well enough alone."

His comment surprised me, especially when he set the cat down and began fumbling with a huge ring of keys. After a moment, he selected one to unlock a cabinet. I recognized the ledger he pulled off the shelf.

"Sometimes she writes in the seller's name," he said, distracted, not speaking to me at all. He searched the pages with one fine, long, white finger. "She's ill now, you see. As if we take turns with our infirmity." He did not disguise a quiet anger. "There is still so much we would both like to do. Do you like the lamp with the peach-colored shade?"

How did he know about the lamp? Did they discuss me and my visit? And how was he able to pull events about me from thin air?

"That lamp was one of Mama's favorites."

"Yes, your sister told me."

I wished Audrey Louise had come with me. I felt jerky suddenly, a hint of hysteria drying my throat. But just then Thomas found the date the desk was purchased.

"There is no seller's name written here. Just the date she bought it. About two years ago."

No name; Thomas went on to other entries from that day, reading them quietly to himself, oblivious to my disappointment. No name; still at square one.

"Is there anywhere else you can look? Anywhere else she might have written the name?"

We passed a shiver between us when he looked up at me; I knew my flower might return at any moment and Thomas's own spooks to him. I should have bolted out that damned shop door and forgotten the letters and the desk and the flaw. Thomas and his sister, already too ghost-like for comfort, were too close to the edge of passing.

"Look somewhere else? No, I don't think so. Faye might know where to look. But I can't call her. She's on oxygen, you see."

Faye, of the porcelain skin and eyes the color that faded with an era. Knowing her name comforted me.

"Are you sure, Thomas? Don't you keep files of any kind?"

No diplomacy in Thomas, as he shook his white hair.

"Too old. Files been around here forever, as long as some of this stuff. Not in order. No. No, you need Faye to get you a file."

"Oh please, Thomas, won't you look? This is very important to me. All I need is a name. An address. Anything, even a phone number would do. I'll help you look. Just tell me where."

Whether suggesting fortune or doom, my request transformed Thomas. He squared his shoulders with a gentle push and swept one hand toward the door.

"Please wait outside the office. I'll look."

No persistent fainting stranger rifling my files, thank you. Wait outside. His manner was clear. So I waited, standing in one place with all the indistinct shapes of dishes and clothes and doll carriages shuffling in the dense air of the outer room. The bronze rearing horse was no longer in the window. Someone had shut off the switch in Howdy Doody. And yet I was sure if Thomas took too much longer, the tables where I was would begin to dance, dumping their burdens into heaps, clattering like graveyard bones to a sinister tune. I decided never again to adventure here without Audrey Louise.

"I think I've found something for you."

My hand was shaking when I reached for the piece of paper Thomas offered.

"Randolph Porter sold us the desk. That's his phone number Faye copied onto the receipt. Found it by luck in the Bill of Sale box. Dusty box. Nothing in order. But no telling if that number is any good now."

Thomas gave me a look of concern but I barely noticed. The phone number was my first exciting clue.

Driving home, I prayed for no more visions of the flower. I was lucky. *Lucky:* Thomas said it was lucky no one was hurt when the desk fell. How did he know about that? Just a lucky guess? I hoped I was lucky with the phone number for Randolph Porter. I couldn't get to my desk fast enough when I got home. I reached for the phone to dial, but then decided I wasn't ready, wasn't prepared with succinct questions. I gave myself a minute. What did I want to know about the desk and what should I ask first? I wanted to get myself a scotch. Better yet, I wanted to call Audrey Louise to tell her all the news. Writing, especially about Kinter and their precious warehouse acreage, would have to wait a little longer.

"Thomas sounds very weird to me, Nyla Wade. You should have taken me with you."

"I know, I know, Audrey Louise."

I didn't tell her about the flower right away, or the letters. I was afraid she'd just tell me again that I was horny, or decide that this time I really had gone off the deep end. What I needed more than anything was for someone to sympathize with me. Unfortunately, Audrey Louise wasn't reading my mind.

"Not to change the subject, honey, but I thought of a great idea today. You do up some little ads for your free-lance writing on cards and I'll post them on the bulletin boards all over campus. I mean, why not? It's free advertising and you'd get some work to add to the paint company newsletter."

"Okay, okay. But let's get back to this desk business. I need to tell you some things."

"Have you met a new man? Someone who came into The Gravy Boat while you were dealing with weird Thomas?"

"No! Everything in my life does not revolve around some man. Now remember the last time you dropped by my apartment? With the pillow? I said I'd been having some strange feelings . . . "

"I knew it. You've guessed my surprise. You've sensed it."

"What surprise? Don't tell me you've already bought the couch that goes with the unicorn pillow. I can't afford it, Audrey Louise, really, I can't."

"Oh come on, it's not that! It has nothing to do with a couch. Can we have lunch tomorrow? I have news for you about someone from your past. It will explain your strange feelings and then you'll be all reassured. Don't worry about a thing. Holy shit! The casserole is smoking and Sam has tied a cape around the beagle. I must rescue the dog before the boys launch him off some pinnacle. Pardon my abrupt parting, love, but chaos impends."

Our conversation was all too short for me. I hoped when I could tell Audrey Louise about the flower that it would go away. She's been magic in my life for so long, I was just sure she could do something about my visions. But I could tell her tomorrow at lunch and balm myself in the meantime with scotch. I drink too damned much of the stuff, I know. I drank less before the divorce. I probably wanted to drink just as much but never did in deference to Mike. It was one of the few points I ever conceded to him, but he would say I rarely conceded to anyone. He knew so very much about it, like everything else.

After I talked to Audrey Louise, I felt restless and fidgety. I wondered if it was too late to try calling Randolph Porter. Looking up the area code of the number Thomas gave me, I found I had a Virginia number. Two hours time difference: ten p.m. No one goes to bed that early in the East. Somehow I had the impression that the Porters were eastern rich. All of W. Stone's letters were addressed to Porterfield on Kingston Row, and that sounded to me like an estate of pomp, circumstance, and considerable wealth. A good reporter doesn't let her imagination get away from her. As I dialed, I hoped Virginia gentry didn't retire early.

I was so sure Randolph himself would answer the phone that when a woman's voice greeted me, I was speechless for a moment.

"This is Louise Porter."

She had a mellow accent with the slow, round tones of the South. I thought of marmalade.

"May I speak to Randolph?"

A second surprise: a peal of laughter from Louise.

"Is this long distance? No one around here has called him Randolph for quite some time. Are you one of his college friends? He's out in the field right now but if you'll wait, I'll go ring the buzzer out there. If he's anywhere near the equipment shed, he'll answer on the field telephone. But it might take a minute or two. Whom shall I say is calling?"

"Tell him it's Nyla Wade." Oh wait, I thought, he won't recognize my name. But should I tell this woman about the desk? I wasn't sure so I said, "Perhaps I have the wrong number. Do you think there's another Porter in your area?"

"No, probably not. At least not another Randolph. Randy Porter is my son. I'll see if I can get him on the field telephone. I could just have him call you back; you're wasting your money on this call if I can't reach him out there."

At least Louise was asking no prying questions.

"That's all right. I'll be pleased to hang on. Do try and call him. I'll appreciate it a lot."

While Louise Porter put me on hold from Virginia, I tried to collect myself. I assumed all the Porters were rich but Louise sounded very down to earth. She probably thought I was one of Randy's girlfriends from college.

"Hello? Are you still on the line?"

Static crackled around a young man's voice.

"Yes, hello. I'm still on the line."

"I can't hear you very well. Hello?"

"Hello. There is a lot of static, isn't there?"

"This is a field telephone. Very rudimentary. You there?"

"I'm here, yes, hello. You are Randolph, that is, Randy Porter?"

"Yes. Can you hear me?"

There was a steady barrage of static, then the line cleared for a moment.

"I can hear you. I'm calling about a desk you sold to a Denver antique dealer. It's a roll-top . . . " Again we were interrupted by what sounded like lightning flashing over the line.

"Denver? You're calling from Denver?"

Randy didn't sound like he knew about the desk at all. Perhaps Thomas had given me a bum steer. Inadvertent but entirely the wrong direction.

"Are you still there? Hello?"

"Yes, Randy. My name is Nyla Wade. If the line stays clear a moment, I'll tell you about the desk."

Several minutes passed; there was only a little static and I was able to explain to Randy about the desk, Thomas, and The Gravy Boat. While I didn't mention the letters or the flaw, he still seemed puzzled. He explained that he was tired; he and his father had been harvesting very late into the day. One of their field hands had a sick child so Randy had come in from his school to help out.

"We have to get it all done this week before I go back to school. I'm a law student at Columbia."

"But you don't remember ever being in Denver or selling a desk?"

"Not at all." There was a pause. "Gee, I'm sorry. I'd like to help you."

"Is there a member of your family named Cybil?"

"Sure. She was my great aunt by marriage, Uncle Spencer's wife. Why?"

I needed a story to keep this boy talking, but I couldn't think of one fast enough. "I . . . uh . . . found her name engraved in the desk."

"Maybe it's coincidence." He wasn't taking the bait easily.

"Possibly, but this desk is an extraordinary antique. It may belong in your family even if you didn't sell it in Denver. Is there anyone else who might know? Your mother, perhaps? I spoke to her earlier and she seems most cooperative."

For a moment, there was silence again on the line from Virginia.

Either I had the wrong Porter or Randy was considering how willing he was for me to talk to anyone else. If I had the right Porter and he wanted the sale of the desk kept quiet, drawing in the rest of the family would blow his secret. I was banking on that chance. Randy finally chuckled through the crackling receiver. "You must be some antique nut, lady. Maybe I can call you back tomorrow when it's easier to talk and I'm not so tired. Maybe I'll remember something about the desk."

I thought Randy might be giving me the slip.

"Are you sure you'll have time tomorrow? With your work and all?"

"I'll have time. I get up at 4:30, but I come back in for breakfast about nine. That would be 7 a.m. your time. Will you be up?"

"I'll be up. Seven sharp."

"Seven sharp then. So long."

I barely slept from the time I hung up the phone, dreaming repeatedly that I wouldn't awaken when Randy called me back. Over and over in my dream I heard the phone ringing but I couldn't come out of my sleep to answer. I finally gave up trying to stay in bed at 6:00, made tea, and tried to gather my thoughts so I could ask Randy what I wanted to about Cybil but without sounding too curious.

At seven sharp, Randy Porter called me back. He did, in fact, know about the desk but because the phone in his parents' house was on the same line as the field telephone, he had avoided telling me what he knew.

"Party line-itis, if you know what I mean."

He assured me his mother was not the eavesdropping type but he had some guilt about selling the desk and didn't want to take a chance of her overhearing our conversation. Randy had been in Denver two years ago and had sold the desk. He didn't remember Thomas, Faye, or The Gravy Boat, but he was able to verify that my desk had belonged to his great aunt, Cybil Porter. The desk had been in the Porter family for years; Cybil used it in conducting family business.

"I wasn't thinking too clearly two years ago when I sold the desk. I had made a quick trip to help out a friend. I needed money fast but I couldn't involve the family. At the time, my great uncle

William in Rochester, New York, called me to say he was settling some of Cybil's affairs. She had asked that her desk be left to me. I was surprised because I had only visited her twice and hadn't been able to attend her funeral. I set out for Colorado, stopped by Rochester to get the desk, and hauled it on a trailer. Then I met up with my friend and we agreed selling it would be best. If I hadn't been so strung out at the time, I never would have sold it. That's a grand old desk you got there, Miss Wade. Cybil kept that desk in the main study where she liked to work."

"Yes, the desk is quite an inspiration. It would be perfect for a lawyer but now it's perfect for a writer. I'm sorry you had to sell the desk, but not sorry I was able to buy it."

"Miss Wade, my parents don't know Uncle William gave me that desk. And he doesn't know I sold it. I'm sure they'd all be upset to know I let such an heirloom go out of the family. Why my uncle waited so long to settle Aunt Cybil's wishes in her will, I don't know, since she died in 1970. He's very closed about the family. Perhaps because he's the only surviving relative in his immediate family. He didn't talk much about Cybil. She was sixty-eight when she died, but she never showed her age. Some of the other women in the family were jealous of that."

Yes, yes, still a woman ahead of her time, fit for dancing on a moonlit terrace.

"What about her son, Lawrence? Can I contact him?"

"Only at Crestlawn, buried with his parents. He was only thirty-one when he was killed in an accident, hunting with Uncle William. Uncle Spencer died in 1942."

"So as you said, of Spencer and William's immediate family, only William remains?"

"Yes, that's correct. Their sister, Dorothy, was my grandmother. Her husband died in World War I and she took back the family name when she inherited the Virginia farms. That's why my father and his family are also Porters and we've lived here since. I'm somewhere between the Porters of New York and the Porters of Virginia. I love the farm, but I'm studying law like Uncle William."

"You know a lot of family history, Randy. You have a good mind for detail."

"That's what Uncle William says. That's why he encouraged me to go into law."

After some additional brief conversation about the family, Randy signed off with a slight trace in his voice of hopeful entreaty toward me. I didn't know quite how to reassure him that I'd try to keep his secret about the desk if I could. *If I could,* unless I needed William Porter to help me find W. Stone and to do that he'd have to know I had the desk.

I took some time to ponder our conversation before I headed for the library to do some research on fountain pens. I thought maybe I'd find some clue to the one stuck in the desk. For hours I had this twinge in me, sort of like a knee cramp. I regretted that Cybil Porter was dead. There was so much I wanted to ask her. The son that should have survived her did not. Only Spencer's brother William survived from Cybil's time, to hold the family business in Rochester, the seat of Porterfield on Kingston Row. I gathered from several of Randy's remarks that Cybil's nearly thirty years' reign in Rochester after Spencer died went against William's grain. Randy didn't come right out and say the word *feud,* but he intimated that. Cybil must have been some steely woman. If that flower appearing to me had anything to do with Cybil Porter's life, maybe it was the gloomy symbol of William Porter's long suppressed anger toward his sister-in-law.

The library yielded to me, its stacks a sanctuary since childhood. I used to think about the irony of these books: Frankenstein nestled with unicorns; bats flying from page to page as well as faery's dreams. I could have an adventure any time I wanted to as a child: with Jason and the Argonauts, with Joan of Arc, with a Hobbitt. When I wanted to know about fountain pens, a new book had just arrived by Cliff Lawrence: *Fountain Pens— History, Repair, and Current Value.*

It's hard to imagine a fountain pen being more than just a way to write a letter or pay the bills, unless you're a writer or pen collector. The lush color photographs and drawings in the book made me want to become a collector at once, to fill the drawers of Cybil's exalted desk with Duofolds, Ripples, and White Dots: lapis, and the hard rubber ones in red and yellow. I especially liked the Lady Patricians Sheaffer made in 1936: filigreed bands and gold nibs in jade and shimmery gray. I put the polaroid picture I'd taken of the flaw up above the book, so that as I turned each page I could scan it and the many photographs for similarities. But it was hard to pinpoint how old the pen was or even to know if it too was a family heirloom and well predated Cybil's own era.

Alas, there was no nib in the book that matched the pen in my desk, or what could be seen of it from the snapshot. So I checked the book out for further study and went to meet Audrey Louise for lunch.

"Try something new for once, lovey. Amaretto sour. You can drink scotch at home any ole time."

Audrey Louise pushed the drink toward me as I took off my coat to join her.

"Is that class you're taking Women's Lit or Assertiveness Training?"

"A little of both." She winked and sipped. "Ummm. You're going to love this."

It was nice to finally just sit down and rest my eye on her familiar soft face. No phone call to await. No pen nibs to scrutinize. Only my friend willing to share an adventure. I took a sip of the Amaretto sour.

"You're right, Audrey Louise. This is a good drink. I might just chug this one so we can have another."

"Oh we can, we can. I put the babysitter on extended retainer for the afternoon."

"Whoever she is, she must have a helluva store of stamina."

"There isn't just *one*, Nyla Wade. No woman alive including me could stand those boys for long. I have to cultivate babysitters by the droves, and schedule them in shifts."

We both snickered and she reached over to push at my arm in a way that always makes me feel young when we're together, like schoolgirls continually finding out how silly the world is. I was ready for my second Amaretto sour; Audrey Louise ordered two more.

"So do you want to hear my surprise? Or have you guessed it, with all these cosmic sensations you've been getting lately?"

"Don't tantalize me forever, Audrey Louise. I haven't guessed anything."

"Then you'll never guess who I ran into on campus."

"Norman Mailer. And he wants you for a weekend in the Adirondacks."

One of the truest joys in my life is to hear Audrey Louise guffaw. She cuts loose with no shame, no sense of volume, and with the purest appreciation for cacophony.

"God no, Nyla, I don't mean anyone famous. I said it was someone out of your past. But you won't believe it."

"Okay, who?"

"Well, maybe you won't remember. Never mind. Let's just have another drink and forget it."

"For godssakes, Audrey Louise, who is it?"

She leaned toward me over the table and said in a simmery voice, "Arthur Quaid."

"Arthur Quaid!"

His name rang a little too enthusiastically as I remembered what he was like in college ten years ago: sandy haired, with the proverbial sensitive poet's face and long, exquisite hands. Romance ran out of his lips on rainbowed ribbons and I had loved and lusted for him from afar.

"Ah, I see you *do* remember him, Nyla. He's in town. He asked about you. And he's *available.*"

Audrey Louise enjoyed drawing out every syllable of her last word.

"I thought he went off to Stanford to become the Boy Wonder of twentieth century poetry."

"He did. A sonnet writer, wasn't he? Moors and indigo mood and all that, as I recall. Now he's back here for a semester guest lecturing on something."

"I'm sure his students are all the richer for it."

My second Amaretto sour disappeared. I ordered two more and they were both for me.

"You can be such a tight ass, Nyla Wade, I swear."

Audrey Louise tried to get one of my drinks and I protected them with my arm.

"What's that supposed to mean?"

"It's been several months since your divorce. It wouldn't hurt to have coffee sometime with Arthur Quaid, would it? It's not a major commitment. I could even ask him over for dinner. We'll mask it as a family gathering."

"That masks nothing and we both know it. That looks *more*

like matchmaking than anything else. Besides, maybe even having coffee is a major commitment to me."

"Have you given up sex altogether?"

"I thought we were talking about *coffee!* About having *dinner.* Now I see we're talking about sex, which I suspected we were. But of course, *that's* no major commitment."

"You know what I mean. You aren't seeing anyone. You're just holed up at that desk all the time."

"Look, Audrey Louise, some of us recuperate slower than others. Me, I have to nurse every wound until the last wrung tear. I'm generally not happy about what happens between men and women these days. I'm not sure how to remedy it. I'm not even sure it can be remedied. I just don't have anything to give again, not yet. And I'm not sure I want to anyway. Not to Arthur Quaid or anyone else. Right now I feel like there are only two things that stay for sure in my life: my work and my friends."

Audrey Louise cranked up her lip and clucked at me. I didn't respond to her news of Arthur Quaid the way she wanted me to, but she didn't want to fight with me. I tried to change the subject.

"So how's your lit class coming? I'm glad you're taking it. I think it's very Willa Cather of you."

"It's all right."

She refused to laugh at my joke. Her clipped tones were intended to chastise me. I kept trying to cajole her.

"Is Joel okay about your taking time off from the boys?"

"He doesn't mind."

"What about Sam? And the other boys?"

"He's fine. They're all fine. They have TV."

"I see. All is perfection except for your tight ass friend, Nyla Wade, who will not even think of giving poor Arthur Quaid the time of day. Give me a break, Audrey Louise. I might surprise you. I might call him. But at my own pace, my own time."

She sent a look my way that only mocked a mean look. Then she softened slightly. I wanted to keep that change of mood on my behalf.

"Besides, if I don't, the next surprise you're liable to bring me is a vibrator."

Audrey Louise didn't fail me; her roar of laughter spread out over me like the shawl of our friendship. "Nyla Wade, the things you say!"

We decided to eat light and keep drinking. I ordered a salad called "nutty cheesey" and Audrey Louise had one with shrimp.

"Did you bring me those ads I asked you to write up?"

"Oh Audrey Louise, no one at school needs a free-lance writer."

"Are you kidding? The term paper racket could make you your first million. You never know where opportunity knocks. Did you write the ads or not?"

"Yes, I did. But only because I knew you'd give me unending misery if I showed up without them."

"Fine. To prove what a stubborn shrew you can be, you may give me a commission on the first job you get when someone answers one of these ads."

"You're on. Here's to your commission!"

We began our first of many toasts for the afternoon.

Audrey Louise listened intently to my tale about the flower, the letters, the phone call from Randy Porter as we drank well past the salads and the afternoon. Finally I asked her, "What on earth do you think that flower means?"

"Don't start squawking at me now, Nyla, but the color and the movement of that flower are definitely sexual images. Maybe a symbol or sign perhaps of that connection between Cybil Porter and W. Stone. But even more important, well, you know I never put much stock in stuff like this, but it just seems from what you've told me that you were somehow meant to find those letters. That flower is some kind of weird clue about all this. There's more here than meets the eye. I don't blame you for being fascinated. Just be careful."

"We aren't talking murder here, Audrey Louise. We're talking about hidden letters and a broken pen point."

"We're talking about the private business of a rich family. A Kingston Row family with farms in Virginia and an estate in Rochester. With a hunting accident in the family. And what sounds like a matriarch who had an affair. An unpopular matriarch with a brother-in-law with no love lost for her. You can bet he may have known about the affair and wouldn't want the rest of the world to get wind of it."

"Whoever knew about it is probably dead. And maybe no one

else did know about the affair. It's most likely that Cybil hid those letters herself and no one ever saw them except her."

"Until now, that is." Audrey Louise gave me a grave look over her drink.

"The pen point in the desk was probably an accident too."

"Listen, if Cybil was the only one to see those letters, why didn't she send the one she wrote to W. Stone? I bet she had to bundle them all together and stash them in the desk quick. And if that pen point was only an accident, well, isn't this just a family *full* of accidents? The hunting accident, for instance: Spencer's only heir with Spencer's younger brother, a man who was jealous of his nephew's mother. His place at the pinnacle of Porter power robbed from him by Spencer's widow: that's ripe with questionable motive."

"Audrey Louise, you have more trouble with your imagination than I do with mine!"

"Okay, Nyla Wade, but don't do anything foolish. You may think you're sifting through dead ash and find yourself one live fire. Be careful. And if you decide to do anything at all, call me first."

"You'll be the very first to know anything I find out."

"Promise? No more trips to The Gravy Boat without me?"

"Double promise. Now let's order two more of these fine drinks!"

My excess at lunch turned into nausea by bedtime; I paid dearly for my spiritous midday lark with Audrey Louise. Even chamomile tea didn't soothe my vindictive stomach. I laid out the back page of the next *Brush Stroke* issue, finally able to take a look at the warehouse story. But I kept feeling worse and then worse still. If I'd just had scotch, I could be snuggling my own dreams contentedly, but I'd had to try something different. Thumbing through the books on pens again, I tried to be confident that time would pass and my gastrionics abate.

I was surprised to find that the price of a Mont Blanc pen would nearly pay my rent and the price of a 1944 Eversharp 64 would easily satisfy the phone company. If only I didn't have bills to pay, I could buy these two gorgeous pens to sign my checks. The pen I thought most beautiful was called The Lucky Curve. It had a sterling silver design in the shape of snakes. And even more impressive, the snakes had emerald eyes. I never used to like snakes at all until I read about their use in the early Isis worship ceremonies as a symbol of female power. It's easy to see why women don't like them these days: the power has shifted and snakes are a much-abused image. The Lucky Curve was popular in 1898. *1898:* the date waved a flag to my memory, despite my nausea. Thomas had estimated the age of Cybil Porter's desk for me at around 1890. If the pen had been passed in the Porter family with the desk, my lord, was I looking at the very same kind of pen that was embedded in the desk? I ran to get a magnifying glass and the Polaroid snapshot, to move up closer to the light. Then I thought to hell with this! I'm trying to compare the snapshot when I should be looking at the pen point itself!

By the light of Mike's old dust burner, I held the photograph in Cliff Lawrence's book up close to the pen point. The Lucky Curve barrel was black steel with a Victorian overcase. All I could verify from the shards left in the desk was that they too were black. I could see so little of the actual pen point: even if the snake design carried down over the nib. Because that portion was buried in the wood, I couldn't tell anything really about the nib's design. The only answer to the problem was unthinkable: to dig the remainder of the pen out of the desk, taking a chance of breaking it off further or even being unable to dig it out at all. But if I could and I was still unable to tell anything, then there would be no restoring the flaw and its special magic.

Should I try to know a little more or let sleeping dogs lie? Should I call Audrey Louise for her advice? Should I write to William Porter, reveal Randy's indiscretion, and just say, "Hey buddy, what the hell is the story on this desk anyway? And this pen? Did you shoot your nephew? Did you try to blackmail Cybil about her affair with W. Stone? Is this a Lucky Curve or just a regular Eversharp Skyline?"

For once I didn't wait or call or delay for an outside opinion. I had to make my own decision. Screwdriver in hand, heart in mouth, hammer at the ready, I began the delicate operation. Was I meddling with something terminal or could I give the patient a new breath of life? My head was pounding.

Easy now, don't stop once you start. Strong pressure but don't gouge the desk unnecessarily. Don't dig into the wound any further than you need to. God, they didn't make this wood to soften with age! I thought I might faint—from my headache, from the strain of tampering with the desk. I gained an edge with the screwdriver and the fragment of pen began to move. The pen was rammed in farther than I thought. The barrel was not broken right at the nib but higher up. Centimeters at a time rose up in the lamp light. And then I saw the top of a silver curl, a definite swirling, like snakes . . . I kept pushing, a great weight of effort for this tiny bit of pen. I felt my leverage giving out on me. My elbow ached. Perhaps I should have used a screwdriver with a longer handle. I stopped to throw off my sweater, so hot I felt I'd been in a sauna. I blinked, began again, the weak amber light and the dusty smell now more than ever unbearably irritating. Then, chipping away the last small but stubborn chunk of resistant wood, staring at me as dust burned acridly from Mike's infernal lamp, staring at me from the wound retorn, from the deep inches of the desk's mystery: one emerald eye.

SIX

The Graveyard

Before and after I dug out the pen point, the minutes eluded me. I didn't keep track of time or the whacks of scotch that came and went, but dispensed with none of my sadness or curiosity. The flaw was gone, unreplaced by any answer. Replaced by a definite clue, yes, but one that held with it more questions. Did Cybil Porter use this pen with its emerald eyes to write of W. Stone: "I don't ache as I used to about you, missing you so dearly"? I ached, about the operation completed but no sure prognosis for the patient, about the past for W. Stone and Cybil, lovers apart by strong circumstance, about myself, not so divorced from my own feelings as I thought, not missing Mike at all dearly but wishing again for someone sometime to ache for me.

I was a little drunk when I peered hesitantly into the bathroom in case the orchid was lounging in the sink. I was a little sorry for myself when I looked into the mirror, no emerald eyes on me, no silver-painted leaf eyes either, just Nyla Wade looking back at herself, up too late and querulous about tampering with the flaw. That the scotch could not distort. No answers for any of us in that mirror, so I succumbed to sleep.

When I picked up the phone that jangled me out of my nightmare, I was barely holding the receiver and saw fuzzy numbers on the clock-radio: 4 a.m.

"Nyla Wade?"

A woman's voice, low and steady: I didn't recognize her. Or was it a young man?

"Yes. Who is this? Cripes, it's four in the morning."

There had better be a good reason for a call at this hour. But there were no reasons offered. No answer, only silence. No breathing, no click of relief. Just silence. Was I awake or still in the nightmare? Still drunk?

"Who is this?"

Woozy though I was, I managed to sound emphatic. The caller waited, still quiet, as if we were both in the same room and not at all connected just by telephone wire. Silent, waiting. It took me at least two minutes from the time I picked up the receiver to slam it down. And then I was alone in the dark bedroom. The desk lamp was on in the living room. But there around me it was dark, too dark all of a sudden, for me to focus the familiar shapes. I snapped on the bedside lamp, slightly reassured by its golden shade and soft light. No one was with me except my imagination. No threatening flowers, no silent strangers. Why in hell didn't I say, "Yes, this is Nyla Wade. Haven't you heard of me? I train killer dobermans in my home and I live with an Army sharpshooter team. We're kinky, yes, but dead accurate. Want to come for tea?" But I didn't think of anything flip or funny or bold to say. I just heard that awful silence that reminded me of every psycho movie I've ever seen. The killer calls from a phone booth nearby and while you hold the receiver, he slips into your house and slashes you to pieces. Maybe it was just someone picking numbers at random, some sadistic insomniac who wanted to ruin my sleep. Or some kids playing a prank.

I had been dreaming I was in a greenhouse to get Audrey Louise a cactus plant. No one seemed to be there: no counter, no clerk, no bell to ring for service. There was a door at the far end of the narrow building; the light shaded blue-green on the green plants. I remembered distinctly in the dream that I was delighted to find a whole table of blooming gloxinia. They're a large flower but fragile, with a short season. If you pluck one bloom, sometimes the entire plant will wilt overnight. But what blooms: pink and purple, edged in blue-black, silky to the touch with millions of soft pink hairs all over each leaf. A distinctly female flower, with its softness and vulval colors. Mike thought they were obscene: they embarrassed him. I sent him one once at his office and he was furious with me. I decided if there was no cactus in the greenhouse, I'd get a gloxinia for Audrey Louise. She'd love the colors, the feel of the leaves. She'd probably want to wallpaper her bedroom with them.

Still no one came in the back door of the greenhouse. I went to have a look; perhaps they were just out of earshot.

"Hello?" I called. No one was on the other side of the door. "Hello? Anyone there?" I called again. In the dream, I felt the way I had when I stepped into The Gravy Boat: some odd attraction not entirely comfortable. A noise behind me made me turn toward a mini-orchard of unusual trees: hybrids, and they had leaves like a jade plant but bore textured oblong berries. I said to myself, "Makes you wonder about fruit cocktail." I heard the noise again. There was a quivering from the trees, as if they had all turned in one direction at the same time. It must be the odd light in the greenhouse, making me hallucinate, I thought. If only someone would arrive to help me make a simple cactus purchase.

Then it wasn't just a movement I imagined but a rustling noise that turned into a loud thrashing, as if the leaves on the small trees were being hacked off. And then above the trees, its stalk snaking up by some terrible magic, its leaves thrashing the trees below it, appeared a headdress of scarlet blooms, the pistils like mean eyes upon me. Perhaps we never hear their voices when we pick them as little children, their shrill shrieks when we casually pull flowers out of the ground. This one now had a voice all right, one that seemed to be not shrieking but snarling at me as it moved over the trees, moved toward me. I couldn't move away. But I must move. Where? Backwards, toward the door. Other stalks began to rise up too, more angry scarlet flowers, humming at me in a cruel whine, so huge their blossoms, their pulsating blossoms. Finally I found my feet and made a mad dash for that door at the back. As I flung it open, from out of nowhere a man jumped into the opening, blocking the light of my escape, his arms against the wall on either side of the door. I didn't know him; he had grey hair, wore a grey wool suit with a watch-fob. I wanted the hell out of that greenhouse.

"Get out of my way! Don't you see them? Who are you? The flowers!"

"Give it to me!" he shouted back at me over the whine of the attacking foliage. "I know you have it."

"What, for godssakes?" The orchids were upon me in full march.

"The emeralds!"

The grey-haired man took a step out of the doorway toward me; he barred my free passage forward and the legion of scarlet pedicels were at my back. I had the pen point in my pocket. I was afraid to reach for it; he would know for sure I had it with me. It was as the flowers were within grasp of me that a door beneath me gave way and I fell away from them in the dream, fell sideways in my bed answering the phone call at four a.m.

I had too much to drink with Audrey Louise but I didn't deserve either my lurid nightmare nor the distressing phone call. There ought to be tighter controls on phone books. When all else fails, blame AT&T. I had to get out of bed and walk through the apartment. Check the doors and windows. But I couldn't move. I was sure I was going to be grabbed at the bedroom door with a chloroformed towel and that would be the end of Nyla Wade, another victim of metropolitan living, another female crime statistic. Funny how they don't mention that in most violent crimes, the assailants are men. But that voice on the phone: it sounded like a woman to me at first. What the hell did I know? Get those feet moving, Wade. There's only a little space to cover in this apartment if you're going to get it, so get it now instead of lying rigid and terrified in your bed for the next endless hours until morning.

At the door, I took a deep breath and then pounced through the entry into the living room, shouting "kee-eye!", followed by my best shot at a karate kick and punch. There was no towel in the face, no hint of a stranger lurking. I was shaking and I pulled a tendon. Whoever called me like that deserved no less than fifty lashes and a quick boil in oil. All my security was invaded. Who had I hurt to deserve such fear? I was minding my own business in my city, trying to rebuild my singular life. I didn't want to think about how often I was in danger. I didn't need some bored fool dialing right into my bedroom to remind me.

The doors and windows checked out safely. I wanted to sit in the bay window and take some comfort from the moon. But that call had ruined any chance of that for me. I'd just worry someone was watching me, to snipe me from the trees or to testify later that I had invited rape by sitting in my neck-to-toes flannel robe in the moonlight. My private walls and my locks and guards and caution and awareness did not keep me invulnerable. The phone call wasn't the only thing keeping me up. Too many questions had been unsettling me for days since I had found those letters. My dreams day and night were plagued by the scarlet flowers. And now this stupid phone caller. What's the matter, Nyla Wade? I knew it wasn't post-divorce blues anymore or career doubts or lack of love. Someone somehow was sending me a message about all this but why in hell couldn't it come by peaceful carrier pigeon instead of late-night phone maniacs and disagreeable greenery!

I watched the sun's light cross the living room floor from my bed some hours later, still angry that I hadn't been able to go sit in the window to see the sunrise. I didn't move until past ten and I was pouting. The phone rang again. Should I answer? Do those weirdos call in the daytime? Maybe it's one of those places selling magazine subscriptions or someone giving away a free rug shampoo. Or best of all, maybe it's Audrey Louise with some story about her boys. I chose to give AT&T another chance.

"Nyla? This is Steve Raymond, Kinter Paints P.R. How's your morning going?"

I sighed with relief: no weirdos on the line.

"Should I get worried, Mr. Raymond? You said you'd only call if there was a problem."

"Not at all, not at all. That was just interview talk. I've got a special request. We've closed the deal on our warehouse acreage and there's an interesting angle to it I think you can add to your story. I know you can find a way to write the thing up right. The site we've bought used to be a graveyard. A very small one, located just outside Fleming, a town since eaten up by metro zoning. The town's still there but they'll be moving most of the graves into a large area just north of the present location before we start building. While we could stick to straight news on this, you know, use a township grid and some black and whites of the graders, I thought we might do some p.r. on Fleming's history and Kinter's cooperation in helping relocate the graves. Ride it just a little more for interest, you know? More like a feature. What do you think? I'm not asking for whitewash now, Nyla. We can go either way."

"Not whitewash but high gloss anyway, I guess. You do want a coating of something on this, don't you?"

He hesitated a minute. I'd read him right and he was surprised at my insight. But at least there was no awful drop into darkness for the moment he was silent. Not like the scary silence of last night's phone call.

"I want all the facts but as little friction as possible. The newsletter is, after all, our p.r. vehicle. We haven't done anything wrong but people are very touchy about graves. Superstitions can crop up everywhere."

"I get your meaning, Mr. Raymond. Are you sending a photographer?"

"Yes. He can meet you out there or swing by and pick you up."

"No women photobugs on your staff?"

Again he hesitated and I expected the tone of his response to be nettlesome. I knew I was pushing a little.

"Jamie is already on another assignment." His tone was entirely complacent.

"I see. What's the fellow's name you'll be sending?"

"Dean Medino. Shall I have him pick you up?"

"No, I can find my own way."

"Audrey Louise? This is Nyla. Yes, yes, I'm fine. Well, I had an obscene phone call last night and that wasn't so fine. What did they say? Nothing. Okay, it wasn't obscene in that sense unless you call the effect of total invasion into a place you thought was safe obscene. And I do. Anyway, more on that later. I'm running out the door to visit a graveyard. Stop that laughing, Audrey Louise, and listen to me. No, I haven't been hired by an occult newsletter to cover graveyards. I'm going out there for the paint company. What? No, the koala will not be at the graveyard. Audrey Louise, will you be serious for one moment because I'm about to make you very happy if you'll only let me get a word in edgewise. This is *my* phone call, after all! Thank you, that's better. Now I really do have to run but I'm free Saturday evening.

What are you up to? Fine. Invite Arthur Quaid to dinner."

Steve Raymond didn't tell me that some of the roads to Fleming were only partially paved. I'd be going along fine reading my directions and suddenly disappear into a pot hole only to re-emerge at the Brighton city limits with a junction of six frontage roads, none of which fronted Fleming. So much for the efficiency of metro zoning.

Perseverence and no dubious concentration were what led me finally to the warehouse site which Steve also failed to mention was not marked. I expected at least a few small billboards of Gigi, the precious winking koala, saying, "Coming Soon— Kinter's the Best." But there were none, nor were there any graders in sight when I pulled off what could only loosely be called "the main road." I began to get the sneaking suspicion that Raymond had thrown me a straight ball so I wouldn't notice a curve. No whitewash, he said. Yet there were no signs that the graveyard was going to be moved. Maybe whitewash was exactly what he had in mind.

The photographer had arrived before me; I knew his car by Kinter's parking sticker. But he wasn't anywhere in sight. There was a knoll above me and out in front of the knoll was a long expanse of meadow. Aspen flourished on the slight rise of the land. But where were the tombstones? The warehouse shouldn't be hard to build but it was a shame, I thought, to clutter up the meadow. It was surprisingly level for being a graveyard. I figured someone had already moved all the markers. There were no sounds of the city out here, or even of the country. A small wind lured the aspen leaves to their matchless tremor. No sign of graves, no feelings of ghosts: this place seemed like a portal opened between too much life in one place and the place of no life, the burial ground kept at a distance. There was no phone ringing out here with a stranger's voice. I felt completely alone but unafraid.

W. Stone and Cybil Porter were suddenly dancing before me across the peaceful meadow, not naked in moonlight, but definitely gossamer amidst the quiet trees. I smiled at my romantic self that conjured them; now they were my secret friends and despite rumors of feud and peculiar accidents, despite their possible connection to my pestering orchid, what their love was comforted me with its persistence and possibility. I did not think of their romance as the same kind I was used to, not of the ilk I read about alone in my loveseat. There was a different, more caring feeling about these two.

"Hallo!"

The shout echoed out of the trees behind me. I jumped at the sound and then saw a tall, slender man walking down out of the aspen. He had his hand out as he approached me, and a camera around his neck. In six years of dating, courting, marriage, the phases of man and woman living together, Mike never once could open himself this way to me. Just put out his hand and walk straight up to a decent emotion. He always seemed to hold a part of himself back when he reached, even when he needed comfort.

As the man approached closer and saw my quizzical look, he was unable to see as I did the shadow of Mike walking behind him, turned slightly, guarded. Mike's shadow sent my loving dancers away from the meadow with a quick, dark breath of memory.

"Has shaking hands gone out too? I assure you I am not the type who tries to open car doors for women."

He wasn't handsome but his hair wound around his ears in an attractive, unruly way.

"I'm Dean Medino." He stayed pleasant though I had yet to respond to him. "Of course my friends insist on calling me Dino. But I'm not Italian. You are Nyla Wade?"

"Yes." We did shake hands and Mike's somber shadow faded.

"Glad to meet you. I was just getting some shots of the tombstones."

"Where? You don't mean up in the trees?"

"Of course. Where else?"

"But why are they going to build a warehouse in the middle of an aspen grove?"

Dean squinted at me, waiting for me to catch up to the obvious. I made the eventual deduction.

"Ah, but then the aspens won't be there, of course."

He squinted into the sun. "Of course."

"So they'll tear out the trees and put up the warehouse. Then they'll tear up the meadow to move the graves. Why not leave the graves and put the warehouse in the meadow?"

Busy with his lens cap, Dino remarked, "Why not skip the whole thing? Leave well enough alone. Put the warehouse on a freight car and ship it to Toledo. Well, that's the plight of corporate planners. They have to do something with all their need to reorganize nature." He focused the camera, adjusted the meter setting. Then he motioned toward the aspens. "Shall we?"

We crossed an age-greyed wooden bridge that leaned over a long dry creek bed. I began to see the tombstones from the very edge of the trees, a few at a time in small groupings, almost a part of the trees and the overgrowth. There were iron fences around some of the family plots. At the beginning of the path into the graveyard stood a pyramid-shaped monument, with a carved curtain over the top. Even a drawstring with a tassel on the end was carved, as if I could pull it to reveal something within the stone.

Walking among the other stones, Dino and I separated. As he moved farther away from me, crunching through the leaves and snapping branches, his camera clicked an eerie noise in this place. I began reading the names and noticed the dates. Still walking, amazed at the embrace of nature around the stones, gradually I grew disturbed to discover how many of the markers were for babies. Miranda Crockett, four years old: there was a tulip on her gravestone that reminded me of a Judy Chicago design. Eddie Reed, three years old, eight months, eight days. His plot was thick with thistlebrush. Tessie Fowler, four months. Dave Powell, two months, six days. And more. I stopped at one baby's grave: there were four aspen growing, one at each corner of the small plot to make a natural four-poster for the child. Only the canopy was missing.

I noticed some graves without stones. With just small rusted shovels stuck in the earth at the head of each plot. Dino crunched closer again.

"There was a smallpox epidemic. It got a lot of the children." He pointed to the shovels. "Some went so fast they didn't live long enough to be named." He brushed a twig from his shoelace and then patted some dust off the stone under the four-poster. I couldn't believe Kinter Paint Company was going to rip up this natural setting and move all these babies into a meadow that had probably been undisturbed since before any of them died. Just to build a warehouse, an unbeautiful utilitarian metal building. Graveyards were supposed to be spooky; this one only felt sad and all I could think about were the bulldozers and graders. Some war: the dozers versus thistlebrush and babies' ghosts.

There was a cement vase overturned near one of the graves. I righted it on its base, hearing how loud the stone-on-stone sounded in the trees. Dino went out of sight again, camera silent now. There was a flirtatious breeze circling the aspen and the stones, more like smoke than wind. I thought of one of the antique shops Audrey Louise and I had gone into. We'd seen a stuffed two-headed calf and she thought it was awful. They also had a coffin with a sign on it marking it as a stage prop. Of course Audrey Louise had to open it and when she did, she let out a scream. For indeed there was a skeleton within the coffin, complete with a tangled red wig. I couldn't visualize such skeletons here in the Fleming cemetery. No screams or scares among these stones and gentle souls.

At my feet was a family plot more recent than the smallpox victims. The husband died in 1957; his wife in 1958. She could only hang on one year more. I've hung on since the death of my marriage; so many times it seemed like a year, like ten years. Cybil Porter survived Spencer by almost thirty years. But she had a second love to soothe her heart: W. Stone. I remembered Stone had written to Cybil about death in one of the letters:

> "It isn't good to think on dying, I know, but if you go first, save me a place like that small lake at the spa. The one with the friendly geese and goldfish where we'll be in the arms of nature, and you'll be in my arms. That way death won't be fearsome; it will be like our special place, with grass offering the perfume of spring and a few hidden places to lay down. You'll be there with me forever, as if you were a season yourself."

W. Stone's words wooed my memory away from the sad infants' graves. Cybil hung on because when Spencer was gone, she had another hope in her life. I was sure her gravestone was magnificent, but not amidst knotty trees and craggy bush like these Fleming souls. And what about W. Stone? Had he a plot somewhere too or did he live in a one-room walkup or a home for the elderly? Was he in a wheelchair, a victim to a weak hip and silenced now with age? How old would he be? Almost eighty?

The wind sinuated at my ankles, moving my pants leg slightly, almost a small tug. To do what: stop the bulldozers? And then it occurred to me: what if there was no tombstone yet for W. Stone? What if I knew where he was? I had in my possession a letter his lover wrote him which he never received. Rightfully, the letter was his with a message now after all these years that might seem a dear comfort. A letter that could provide a renewed sense of Cybil as delicate and compelling as the wind in this graveyard, as the perfume of spring grass. Maybe that's it, Nyla Wade. Delivery: of the letter and the memory of an old lover. We all end up as old lovers one day, waiting for some sweet signal from the past, something we didn't dream or mumble to ourselves. Something real: a kind of delivery.

The last stones I saw were three together, small arched limestone markers, humped up on the grass with just one word on them: INFANT. I swallowed hard, saying some silent goodbye to them all, as I caught up to Dino back at the cars, out of the aspen and back into reality.

"This is some place, isn't it?" he said, surveying the meadow and the aspen grove. I liked the moment of sunlight across his forehead and his hair. I liked that he didn't loop his thumbs in his belt or suck in air and say "No sweat."

"Yes, but I still can't believe what they're going to do to it. Or why the Fleming people will allow it."

"This is all past history to them. Most of these children died in the late 1800's. I think the epidemic struck in '95. Money washes over past history pretty fast these days."

For a moment standing with Dino in the middle of honored memories about to be bulldozed for the sake of the dollar, it wasn't the baby ghosts or the four-poster or capitalism versus morality that I was thinking about. It was my bedspread. The one with "no flair" as Audrey Louise had said, not in the design on top or with me alone underneath it. I looked at Dino again and credited that he was thankfully not Mike, Joel, or Larry. He was somewhat like I remembered Arthur Quaid when I first saw him. But what also struck me was that despite Dino's pleasantness and his appealing hair, his sensitivity for this odd graveyard full of infants, not for one second would I consider peeling back my bedspread to invite him in. Was it just that I couldn't bear to go through all the re-acquainting and re-educating? It felt so impossible to start again. Maybe I was re-educating myself and I didn't know it before then. Well, I was sure Audrey Louise would have said that a grave-yard was no place to be questioning one's sexuality, so I shook hands with Dino and headed home.

The drive home was better than the drive to Fleming; I didn't take even one wrong turn. Luckily, I didn't feel any of the tingling which lately seemed to signal the incorporeal orchid. Why couldn't it be gloxinia instead? I know that gentle crimson bloom could never snake its way into a nightmare. Snake . . . silver snakes with emerald eyes on a Lucky Curve pen. Made only a few years before Cybil Porter was born and used by her at my grand desk as she ruled at Porterfield on Kingston Row. Randy Porter said she died at sixty-eight in 1970 so she was born in 1902. The desk and the Lucky Curve pen must have belonged to some one of the Porters before they became Cybil's. So the desk was not of her time but weighted with the time of previous Porter history, and the pen was another family heirloom. Cybil ruled a fortune that was not hers by blood for thirty years; she herself had felt it clearly and written it to W. Stone when she described Porterfield as "another family's fort, in which I am allowed to wander." I wanted to see clearly through the dusty window that opened into Cybil's past. It was the only way I could think of to find W. Stone and deliver the letter. What I knew, with some discomfort, was that the way to find the key to the pen, the desk, the past for Cybil and W. Stone, rested in William Porter.

I was restless when I returned from the graveyard. I couldn't conjure W. Stone and Cybil to dance through my living room. I couldn't get geared up to start the graveyard story. Steve Ray-mond was careful to call it the *warehouse* story. So far I couldn't decide if I should give him a piece of my mind or not. Maybe the best thing was to just put it all to bed: all the thoughts about every-thing. Heavily dose my weary mind with Sleep Aide and wake up tomorrow, oblivious to the intermediate hours. Snuggle under the thin bedspread and friendly sheets, the slight dent in the bed just for my supple cheeks. Why have I never had a lover who sent me gloxinia and appreciated my supple cheeks? Lousy karma, I guess. You'll have to try something different soon, Wade. There is always comfort in bed, though, even alone in it. Cocoa, Lillian Hellman's latest bestseller, and my own bed. It felt so safe.

Bone-jarring: two nerves vibrated against each other in a sharp pain up my breastbone as the phone shattered my warm safety. Surely not again: it was too early for a weirdo, only nine o'clock. Second ring. Third. Fourth. Persistent bastard. Six rings. What if it was Audrey Louise firming up Saturday night? Of course. She'd think I was taking what she used to call my "three chapters of Fitzgerald constitutional." I refused to let my hand shake as I lifted the receiver.

"Hello?"

"Nyla Wade?"

Definitely a woman's voice and I didn't recognize her. The nerves vibrated again as I squeezed my eyes shut and hoped this was not the same person who called me before. I hoped she would tell me she'd seen my ad at the college and ask me to give her a hint on how to research a feature she was writing on the return of penny loafers.

"Yes, what is it?"

Silence again.

"What do you want? Do you have the wrong number? Maybe there are two Nyla Wades . . . "

Before I could finish, she hung up. Again I had only silence for company, the silence of questions and instant fear because I knew there was only one Nyla Wade in the phone book and this was no common mistake in dialing. Why was she calling me? Why wouldn't she say who she was or what she wanted? How did she know my name? Maybe she worked with a psycho. She called while he crowbarred the door. Damn it! The cocoa was cold and so was the bed. I shivered even after I put on my robe and made the rounds. I got so bold as to open the front door into the hallway and check the stairs. Fear was a thorough antidote to Sleep Aide.

I opened the bottom drawer of the desk and pulled out W. Stone's letters to Cybil. I slipped off the rubber bands which replaced the ribbons that had fallen apart and thumbed through the postmark dates. The letters started in May, 1937, running through September, 1969. Postmarked first from Atlanta, then Columbia, South Carolina, and the last few years from Jacksonville, Florida. Thirty-two years of faithful correspondence.

If I had the nerve to call William Porter, what would I ask him? "By the way, did you know W. Stone?" Could I ask him anything without seeming too snoopy? "How long was the desk in the family? Whose desk was it originally? Did anyone besides Cybil use it? And what about the pen? Or did one of those private Porter skeletons put it so violently into the desk? What did Spencer die of and how old was he? When did Lawrence die? Where were you when the accident happened? Did you like your nephew, Mr. Porter, or did he remind you too much of his mother?" I'm starting to sound like Audrey Louise. No sleep and these phone calls are getting to me. Everything I want to know really hinges on two questions and I don't think I can ask William Porter: who is W. Stone and where can I find him?

I didn't get to retire early like I wanted to. All I did was wear myself out thinking of all the questions unanswered about the letters, the desk, and the pen. Questions unanswered about why a paint company would destroy a meadow and an aspen grove for the sake of a warehouse. I even began to question their treatment of Gigi when she wasn't in front of the camera. I wished . . . wishing is always dangerous when it involves someone else . . . I wished I had an escape from all the questions, someone to snuggle with. Not just my quiet and faithful thin bedspread. It wasn't powerful protective arms around me that I needed, but someone warm, generous, and enfolding. Like those hidden places in the grass that W. Stone wrote about, holding Cybil in his arms. It wasn't mother love either that I needed, something much less threatened than that by unspeaking, holding intimacy. I needed a comforting bosom all right, but I didn't dare yank Audrey Louise from her own private snuggle to come across the city at this hour.

Mike was never a snuggler. Sometimes he even kicked, the few times he dreamed. Not a hard kick from the hip but a short snap at the knee, a knee-jerk. Pushing away even in his dreams. He was warm when we had sex, but he was not warm because he stayed close. I remember his heaving shoulders; it was the only time I ever saw him show much energy. I could have done without it. And I usually did better by myself. Remember that, Nyla Wade, for future reference. Better . . . by myself.

SEVEN

The Melon Eater

Another Saturday: I sat in the bay window defiantly brave in the sunlight. So how do you find a missing person, when you don't know his first name or what he looked like? When all you know is that he lived in Jacksonville, Florida, in 1969. When you can't ask about him of people who might have known him in New York. Suppose William Porter knew of the affair as Audrey Louise suggested? That was my worry: that he knew and wanted proof and that was what had prompted Cybil to keep her letters hidden. Yet they came to Porterfield in the first place; the envelopes clearly bear the Kingston Row address. Could Cybil have guaranteed that every day she'd be first to see the mail? Or was there some aspect to W. Stone that would not have given away their affair? In thirty-two years of letter writing, someone was bound to notice, including Spencer and William, so there must have been something that kept them from being suspicious. And if that was true, wouldn't it be acceptable then to ask William Porter about W. Stone? Yet how would I explain even knowing that name? No way to tie it to the desk unless perhaps I said some note had been left in it, but I hated the thought of having to reveal Randy's secret about selling the desk.

I was still at first move. If W. Stone was known in Rochester, could he be traced there without William Porter's help? School records, tax reports, a bank? But again, no certain first name. Suppose I could find out where Cybil went to school? If they knew each other in school . . . but the connection could be one in a million.

If William was too much of a risk at the moment, I wondered, could I call Randy Porter again? Tell him I found a note from Cybil to W. Stone in the desk. See if *he* knew Stone. Randy might be cooperative, might not balk at a mention of a note. I could say it was jammed into the corner of one of the drawers. I could even say someone in the antique store found it and held it for the buyer of the desk: disperse the story a little that way.

As long as I sat and schemed, you'd have thought I would have kept at it after I came on the idea of calling Randy. You'd have thought I'd have considered a second possibility: that he had in fact spoken to his uncle, that they were in fact quite close. And despite Randy's regrettable decision about the desk, a stranger in Colorado calling to ask about the family might be worth a confession. But I didn't stay in the window seat long enough for that. My imagination got ahead of me, leaving common sense behind. That would prove an unfortunate mistake.

"Randy? Nyla Wade again, remember? Your mother was good enough to give me your number at school. You happen to tell her about the desk?"

"No. Did you?"

"Certainly not. I've been in money jams myself. I understand those kinds of secrets. How are your studies coming?"

"It's no picnic. You go through the ropes to become a lawyer. But I keep at it."

"The reason I'm calling you, Randy, is that something else has come up about the desk. I thought maybe you could decode it for me."

"I'll try to help."

"The people from the antique store called me last week. Apparently they'd held onto a note that had been wedged into the corner of one of the desk drawers when you sold it to them. They'd almost forgotten about it. The note was faded but it read, 'W. Stone was in town. Call you later. Knew you'd want to visit.' I wonder, was W. Stone one of Spencer's friends? Or a business associate, do you think? It probably isn't important now, but I wasn't sure and since the desk had been in your family, the note really belongs to you. Do you know the name, W. Stone?"

Randy hesitated. I heard him cough. Then he said something in a muffled voice, as if the receiver was covered.

"Excuse me, Miss Wade, my roommate just came in. I wanted to tell . . . uh . . . *him* . . . that I was on long distance."

I didn't say anything in case his explanation was a stall. But Randy seemed forthright.

"I do know the name but only vaguely. I believe W. Stone was Cybil's friend, not Spencer's. I remember Cybil mentioning that name, and my Grandma too."

"Do you know if they were friends from school perhaps?"

"I don't know where Aunt Cybil went to school for sure—maybe Brentwood, a girl's school in Rochester. Most of the Rochester boys go to Dockworth Academy. But Cybil was raised out of state, I think. I could check with my father. Or I could call Uncle William if you think it's that important."

I was very surprised to hear Randy volunteer to involve his family with my questions. The tide of his attitude had definitely turned.

"Oh no, Randy, don't bother to do that. I was only curious about the note and worried it might be something you'd need to know. If you ask, they might think I'm being nosy. Sometimes we collectors get too zealous with business that's not our own."

Randy laughed. "You've been discreet with me. I can be with you. If I find out anything more, I'll give you a call."

When we rang off, I convinced myself things were safe, that calling Randy had been a good decision. He was a college boy with lawyer dreams. He didn't have time to be suspicious of a supercilious antique buyer. I was so sure of that.

I planned to call Brentwood on Monday, supposing the offices were closed on the weekend. I would ask for information about a Cybil Porter who possibly graduated between the years 1919 and 1923. If Cybil had gone there, her records would likely be updated under her married name. Maybe a sister of W. Stone had also gone to Brentwood and could lead me to him. Dockworth seemed a longer shot since I had no idea how close in age W. Stone was to Cybil nor even if they had attended school in the same city. I had the entire weekend to wait through until I had a chance at Randy's clue; the only help to pass the time was my impending dinner with the man from the past—Arthur Quaid.

When I dressed for my evening with the Landrys and Arthur Quaid, I was still distracted from my day's preoccupation with Cybil Porter and W. Stone. But soon I was having a dialogue with myself that didn't make me excited about the evening.

Thank goodness the days of corsets are over. I'd never make it through this evening if I had a prison of fishbone and ruthless rubber to deal with in addition to this dinner with Audrey Louise, Joel, and Arthur.

There are a few sure things I can count on. Audrey Louise will introduce the children and as they leave, she'll tell the joke I've heard her tell at least a hundred times. It is the one thing I can never forgive about her, this joke. Joel will have to be in earshot of it because that's part of their routine.

"Don't count their ages too closely," she'll say to Arthur. "Just trust me. They all came from the same spaniel." Arthur will smile knowingly; Audrey Louise will turn to catch Joel's eye, and he too will smile knowingly and puff on his pipe. Then Audrey Louise will smile too, about her happy spaniel husband and their three happy boys. I will be in the kitchen, I hope, counting to twenty-three, which is how long the joke takes. I am usually putting more scotch into my glass. Scotch, I have found, is the only thing that gets me through this unforgivable joke.

The second thing I can count on is that oldest son Sam will not go to sleep on Audrey Louise's first try at getting the boys settled. He'll sit at the top of the steps and rock back and forth. He'll release some low, creepy, moaning sounds for those moments when everyone is laughing and so you're not really sure you heard anything but you think you did. Middle son Mark likes to scream out at least once: a blood-curdling scream that gurgles at the end. I think that Sam checks with Mark when his moanings fail to raise any response so they work as a team that way. Youngest son Tony is always quiet and what I like about him is that he isn't invested at all in surprises or moanings.

The third thing I can count on is that Joel will try to stir my feminist ire however possible with his especially blatant, sexist remarks. He practices, I'm sure of it, and having Arthur around will only egg him on.

The rest is unknown. For instance, will I take one look at Arthur Quaid and see the sandy-haired poet has taken the worst turn toward maturity? Will he be balding, paunchy, wearing horn-rimmed glasses? No more words streaming from him in rainbowed ribbons. Or will he be beautiful but shallow, his words a success but he himself unversed? How will I act? I'll probably drink too much and start telling stories about my failed marriage to Mike. Or will I drink too much and say too little? With my luck, I'll be unable to drink too much and will have to endure the whole awkward panorama dead sober. But I asked for this so I have to go through with it. Me and my weakness for pleasing Audrey Louise.

What's really wrong is that while I've been getting dressed for the last hour, I've also been getting angry: at my impulse to have Audrey Louise set this ridiculous dinner up in the first place and at myself because I can't decide what to wear. I keep looking for a costume that will dress me up as someone else. The black dress is too slinky; the red one too bold. The skirt and vest look too sedate. My pantsuit would be too polyester. Nothing works! I'm angry at them too. Those three waiting for me to arrive for what should be an innocent dinner but I feel like the main course. Arthur eats me up because we are, after all, both *available,* like two slices no longer attached to the pie. Audrey Louise and Joel eat up our suggested seduction for their own vicarious thrill so that if later I have a spaniel husband and happy boys, they can brag that they introduced us at their kennel! If I go as myself, in soft trousers and a velour shirt with the one button at the neck *buttoned* (Audrey Louise always says I should show more neck), their mouths will go slack the minute I'm in the door. I won't be the dashing divorcée Arthur imagined. Audrey Louise will cluck me to death all evening and Joel will have a heyday with his favorite trouser jokes.

Why do these external matters have to impress them? I don't know but I feel they expect it. The truth is that mostly I don't know what to expect from this evening and I don't know if I'm strong or vulnerable or indifferent. I don't know if I can make Audrey Louise or Joel or Arthur happy, but I don't want to make myself unhappy. I have a closet of my own in the room of my own and once again, I can't get started.

To hell with them: they're getting velour.

Car keys. My bottle of trusty Chivas. It's chilly. Take your coat. Leave on the bathroom light and the lamp in the living room and the one in the bedroom too. I can't stand to come back to this small space and have so much of it in darkness.

I leaned across the bed to reach the lamp and the phone rang with the sudden sting of a small monster, sending the vibration of its bell up my arm. My hand spasmed and the car keys hit the bureau on the other side of the bed.

"Holy shit!"

There was no time to break into a sweat. Through the buzz of long distance the operator said, "This is Rochester 319. Person-to-person for Nyla Wade. William Porter calling."

It was not the mystery woman, but most unexpected attention from Kingston Row! Apparently Randy had made his confession about the desk, turned me over to his uncle. Rotten lousy timing! I was on my bloody way out the door. It was six-thirty Saturday night. Some schedule William Porter kept. He must really want the nosy Denver broad out of his family history but quick.

"This is Nyla Wade."

I wondered if the emerald eyes were watching.

"Your party is on the line, sir. Go ahead."

"Ms. Wade, this is William Porter." There was a poised manner in his tone but certainly not a serene or friendly voice.

"Yes?" I wanted him to take the initiative so I could get a clue as to how much he knew.

"I spoke to my great nephew today. I was somewhat dismayed to learn he sold a valuable family heirloom. It was unfortunate that Randolph felt the need to sell the desk. It has been in our family for quite some time."

"Oh really? How long?"

"Before my older brother Spencer was born. Our mother used the desk."

"I'm not sure of the time frame. When was your brother born?"

"Eighteen ninety-eight. But the desk predates him by quite awhile. Mother used it when she and Father were first married. He bought it for her as a wedding gift."

"It does seem that Randolph's misfortune has become my fortune. Being a writer, the desk is a godsend for me."

I hoped I was sounding light-hearted and conversational as I went on.

"Randy and I had a good conversation about Cybil's desk."

I didn't mean to call the desk Cybil's; it just slipped out. William took immediate issue with the reference, or perhaps my familiar use of Cybil's name.

"The desk, as I said before, was my mother's. She was a social correspondent with many friends and family members. One of her greatest pleasures was to write at that desk. She used to say it was the only thing that kept her organized." William's tone changed. He was warm about Mama, but then he told me, in colder terms, "Cybil used the desk too, much later, when she was married to Spencer. But then, all this you know from Randolph."

I sensed the resentment in his tone that Randy had talked to me so freely about the Porters.

"Well, he told me briefly who was who. As a writer and an antique buff, I feel so much history in that desk and while I don't want to pry, I am interested in its origins and the people who used it."

"We had no literary writers in our family."

Nothing so bohemian as all that. I could glimpse William Porter tugging at his tailored vest.

"Was Cybil a social correspondent too? Like your mother?"

Wing it, Nyla Wade. It's now or never. Keep talking about Cybil. Clearly, William wanted no comparisons made between his mother and Cybil.

"My mother was a Lavernby, born and bred New Yorkers, as are the Porters. Cybil married into the Porter family from out of state. She managed the estate after Spencer died because that was his wish. She used the desk mostly for family business."

He was very formal and used no more warm tones. His voice closed at the end of his sentences when he spoke of Cybil.

"Randy gave me some sense of the importance of your family, Mr. Porter. I don't mean to seem snoopy, only interested. That comes, as I told you, from my enthusiasm for antiques and old letters, that sort of thing."

I felt a rush in my heart: I had absolutely not intended to say anything about letters. William was silent from his distance. I had to keep my calm. Had I blown the secret in this inadvertent mention of letters? I tried to speak reasonably and hoped that he didn't think there was any connection between letters and the desk, between any proof of an affair from that history of his family that he so clearly would protect.

"Of course, Ms. Wade. Pardon my abruptness, but it is difficult for me to dwell upon my family at times. So many of them have gone before me. Tell me, would you be interested in selling the desk back to me? I can make you a handsome and profitable offer."

Thankfully, William Porter did not pursue my comment about letters.

"I don't really think I'd sell the desk, Mr. Porter. It was quite a find. I was surprised, though, when the dealer told me he'd had trouble selling it."

"I wonder why. When I gave the desk to Randolph, it was in perfect condition. I had intended him to keep it for his first law office."

"I know he wishes now that he had done just that. But he didn't notice it either. About the desk, I mean. The flaw."

There was an absolute silence from Rochester, not a breath. Then in a thready voice, William's question: "What flaw?"

"Why, a broken pen point in one corner of the writing area. Jammed into the wood several inches. Must have taken quite a bit of force."

William's silence pervaded and there was just quiet between us, with no clues at all to his unsightable response. In a moment he said, his voice coming as if down a long hollow tunnel, "I don't recall a pen jabbed into the desk. No doubt it was some misuse that occurred later, perhaps in the antique store."

"Well, perhaps. Though the owner was pretty sure the desk came that way. I had hoped maybe you could shed some light on it."

"I'm sorry, Ms. Wade, I can't help you. I can tell you nothing about the pen. But if you change your mind about selling the desk back to me, do contact me again, or my secretary, Peter Gant. I'll leave you to your evening, Ms. Wade." He left his telephone number with me before he hung up.

"Thank you for calling, Mr. Porter."

As I drove over to the Landrys', I lamented that I had been able to get only one date out of William Porter: Spencer's birth year,

1898, the same year that the Lucky Pen was made. This was the pen point embedded in the desk and might be connected to the family by more than circumstance. The desk that was a wedding present to William's mother—perhaps the pen was a gift too, from Cybil to her husband to celebrate his birth year, or from Spencer's father to his mother upon his birth. Randy wasn't kidding when he said William was proper, proper and a tough nut, keeping his family business close to his vest now that he's the last of his generation. If he knew about the letters or connected them in any way to the desk, he was staying mum. And I had thought Mike had the corner on the market for a privacy obsession.

I was back to zero and no further in the search for a sense of Cybil Porter or the whereabouts of W. Stone. William had verified that Cybil married into the family from out of state: that would mean she did not likely attend Brentwood. The web remained tangled. Maybe Audrey Louise would give me some encouragement, as we reached around her pot roast and pretended we were all comfortable adults.

Audrey Louise answered the door in her apron and gave me a hug. I could hear Joel from the living room saying, "Here's our girl now!" as Audrey Louise whispered to me, "Thank god you're on time. Art is so nervous I was afraid he'd be crocked before you got here."

Art? She didn't say a word about my velour and slacks lacking style.

"Come into the living room. We're just toasting old times while I toss the salad." Audrey Louise ushered me into where the men awaited us. Arthur and Joel were both standing and smiling knowingly. Perhaps I'd just been spared the spaniel joke.

"Arty here was just telling me what a peach you were during your college years, Nyla." Joel lifted his glass at Arthur. "You had quite a fan in Arty here and I bet you didn't even know it!"

Arty? Joel hadn't noticed my trousers yet either but he was already trying too hard to get Arthur and me to like each other.

"What're you drinking, Nyla?"

"Joel, she's been a scotch drinker ever since you've known her. Don't be silly. Get some scotch, honey, please." Audrey Louise had the kitchen door open and directed her husband from that vantage point. Joel shrugged and wandered back to the bar as Arthur remained standing quietly. His face was tan and he was still slender and good looking. Not bald or paunchy at all, no horn-rimmed glasses either. He had a few distinctive lines across his forehead and his hair was still thick and sandy colored. He had a knockout smile that went up quick and then back down. I didn't know about his sensitive hands; they were in his pockets.

"Quiet around here," I noticed aloud, wishing Arthur would relax and say hello.

"We got lucky," Joel said from the bar. "Grandma was lonesome tonight so she got three for the price of one."

I knew I would definitely get to miss the spaniel joke and that portended unpredictability. We'd have all the more time to be together. Why didn't Arthur say something? Anything! He just stood, staring at me. Maybe he was dealing with his disappointment that I didn't wear a black slinky dress.

"How're we doing with dinner, Audrey Louise? About ready?" Joel handed me my scotch and called to his wife.

"Just need to pull that roast out of the oven and we're on."

"I'll give you a hand." He patted Arthur's arm on his way to the kitchen, saying, "Loosen up, bud. Tell her hello."

"It's nice to see you, Arthur. But I wish you'd aged a little more."

"We're a match then. You're still . . . how did Joel put it? A peach."

"I rather thought that wasn't your word."

"It's good to see you too, Nyla."

He sat down and so did I. It surprised me though that he stayed quiet until I again pursued some conversation.

"You're guest teaching here, Audrey Louise tells me."

"Yes, two classes. One on sonnets, of course, and the other is on creative integrity."

"Got some decent students? Honors Program, I bet."

Arthur put his drink on the coffee table and leaned toward me to talk. His face began to show more interest as he discussed his teaching.

"Yes, those honors students are quite a crop. But I'm holding my own."

"I'm sure you are. Did you have a book out recently?"

70

"Not for two years. My academic load has been too much. Did you see my last one?"

Shit, I didn't see the first one or any in between. How many had there been?

"I'm sure I did, but the title escapes me."

He didn't notice my lie because he was ahead of my answer, savoring his own comments. "It was titled *Semblance of Love,* a collection of sonnets. My third. I missed the Harvard Poet's Award this time but settled for honorable mention. I was luckier with the first two. Now I'm brewing a novel."

"Good for you. Do you think a novel will be more difficult to write? It seems such a departure from poetry. Especially with the rigid structure of the sonnet."

"Not really. I think you use the rigidity of structure at first to solidify your discipline. Then it becomes such second nature that you can play around with it. That's how you pass from craft to artistry."

I knew I was going to have to pass from craft to artistry in order to make Steve Raymond's graveyard story anything but white-wash unless I told the truth. But that was a planet away from Arthur's sonnets. I hadn't put out three books but I, too, contemplated a novel.

"What are you up to these days, Nyla?" Arthur asked. "Anything exciting?"

I guessed he didn't remember that we had both studied writing in college. He didn't mention it and his question suggested that he expected an answer relating to family rather than work. I must have consumed my scotch too fast; I wanted to say, "I'm writing again and it's the only thing keeping me sane what with visions of giant orchids, anonymous phone calls, visits to graveyards and my thin bedspread." But I didn't really want to tell him that much either. "I'm writing again" was what I wanted to say most of all. Instead, I gave him an inane but telling response. "I've been up to divorce."

Arthur was already informed so he showed no surprise, but raised his distinctive eyebrows and said, "His loss." He allowed his quick-fade smile and one hand came out of a pocket. Maybe he should have been a sculptor instead of a poet. I was sure in that moment that sensitive hands would figure in my novel when I wrote it. And it was bound to be criticized for unrestrained romanticism.

"Food, fun, and frolic!" Joel announced as he and Audrey Louise paraded to the table with the roast and salad. Luckily, Joel and Arthur had the Pittsburgh Steelers in common during dinner, so Audrey Louise and I could trade snatches of some important conversation as we passed and clucked and occasionally interjected something toward the men. But our minds were focused on our own conversation.

"William Porter called me just an hour ago as I was getting into my coat," I told her out of the side of my mouth.

"My goodness, that's a surprise. I guess his nephew decided to fess up, eh?" she asked, her eyes on the mashed potatoes.

"I guess so. Anyway I think he was trying to decide if I'm up to anything."

"Did you get anything out of him?"

"No. Only Spencer's birth date. Same year as the pen."

Joel dropped in on our conversation. "Spencer who? You got a new flame, Nyla? Keeping us in the dark?" He nudged Arthur.

"Hush up, Joel, and eat your pot roast. It's just some guy she works with."

We passed the salad around as diversion. Arthur scooted all the mushrooms in his salad to one side of the bowl.

"So what's next?" Audrey Louise asked.

"I'm not sure. Plus this other thing."

"What? That flower business?"

"No, that hasn't come up again lately. Except in a nightmare. And thank goodness for that."

"More rolls anyone? Nyla?"

Arthur was offering me a roll. I wanted to laugh but no one would have understood.

"No thanks, Arthur." Not you with your tanned forehead or Dino with his unruly hair or anyone else. Not now. Arthur and Joel started talking again; Arthur said something about Mailer and integrity in the same breath. My interest was piqued but Audrey Louise and I were still talking about the Porter phone call.

"But if William Porter won't give you any information about his family, how will you find out anything more?"

I'd been toying with an idea that had come to me in the car as I was driving over. I had thought of it, then rejected it, then it crept back into my brain with a strange persistence.

"Suppose I went there."

"Where? To Rochester? Nyla, that's pretty risky."

"Why? I'd go to the library, check out the newspaper morgue, read the society page. As easy as that. And maybe I'd drop in on William Porter. Don't you think his seeing me in person might throw him off guard enough to give me some information? A little history on the house, a few dates, and while we're chatting, some details on Cybil and Spencer."

"You said he was uncooperative over the phone. I think he might not even let you in the door if you go there in person."

"Yes, but he's got a secretary who might."

"Are you kidding? I bet he's got her trained better than a watch-dog to screen everyone."

"Ah, there's the catch. It's a *him;* Peter Gant's his name. I'll tell him I want to sell the desk back. Or tell him I'm on a story. Or maybe I'll use my feminine wiles."

"That's not like you, Nyla. I didn't think you believed in that sort of thing."

Arthur had finished eating and lit a cigarette; Joel began to clear the table. My time to talk with Audrey Louise was slipping rapidly away.

"What I believe is that you can use the system to get what you want, within limits, of course. If I bat my lashes and Peter Gant will tell me some colorful history about the Porters, will tell me some-thing that will help me find W. Stone, then I will bat to beat the band."

"You're some picture of contrasts, Nyla Wade."

"I know, I know."

Joel quit cleaning the table halfway; he motioned for Arthur to head back to the family room. Audrey Louise finished clearing and I followed her to the kitchen.

"So do you think I should go? I can stay out of trouble. Come on, you know me."

Audrey set the plates down and put her hand on my shoulder. "Maybe. But you'd better remember you'll be on his territory. Rattling his skeletons. I will worry every minute." She shook her head and rinsed the plates.

"I'll call you every two hours." I hugged her shoulder. She didn't acquiesce just yet to my scheme.

"Don't be silly, that would cost you a mint." She kept rinsing. I kept hugging. Then she said, "Call me every four." Over a stack of plates, we laughed at each other and she gave me a hug back that clattered one glass into the sink.

"You will be careful?"

"Of course!"

"Okay. I know I shouldn't be such a mother but I'm very protective of you, especially where strangers are concerned."

It occurred to me then to tell her about the strangers who had been trying to ruin my sleep by tying up my phone line. "I want to tell you this other thing . . . " I was sure if I shared the phone calls with her it wouldn't be so scary going home later. But as I started, Joel yelled at us, "You girls get in here! This isn't a stag party."

Audrey Louise handed me a tray from the refrigerator of bowls filled with melon.

"You take these in. I have to whip up some cream for topping."

As I entered the room, Joel greeted me with, "You two sure were being secretive out there." Arthur followed with a conversational comment that was a bad choice of words. "Perhaps they were plotting the revolution."

"Nyla, maybe, but not my Audrey Louise. She's a happy woman."

Here it came. No doubt the trouser jokes would follow the libber jokes.

"Joel says you're a Women's Libber." Arthur began the probe. Maybe I could josh them around the subject, although it was against my better judgment. I would rather have whacked them both with a rolled-up newspaper for being so predictable and boring.

"Well, Arthur, you can't believe everything Joel tells you. Besides, the appropriate term is feminist." I heard the edge in my voice.

"Pardon my semantics. Or should I say se-*wo*man-tics? Se-*person*-tics?"

Arthur and Joel smiled at each other.

74

"I think a whole new word should be found. One that doesn't have either specific gender in it but includes everyone."

"Do you really think the words are the problem? Or is it the attitudes behind the words?"

They weren't going to be joshed around the subject. They were playing interested, baiting the trap. Ho hum.

"It's both. Language controls people. It's the tool they use to express their attitudes. Therefore the words do the shaping. Change the words, change the attitudes." Simple so far, safe.

"I would think new words would be more distracting than educational. I can't see reading new equalizing terms in Mailer or Cheevers. That would take out all the punch."

"Mailer already has too much punch. But it can work. I've seen it."

"In what? I haven't seen it." Direct challenge from Arthur. What was this? Joel spurred on the fight and then got quiet to watch while Arthur took up the gauntlet. I didn't care about Mailer or Cheevers or punchy style. I had stopped reading male writers anyway and I knew clearly why I hadn't missed them. Or their attitudes.

"Have you heard of Mary Daly? Monique Wittig? And what about Gertrude Stein? She was changing language years ago."

Arthur nodded and blew out smoke from his cigarette. He'd come to a realization. "Oh, I see what you're talking about. Rhetoric, not literature."

The sonnet teacher had dismissed the women's libber. Rhetoric, that's what women wrote. Literature was the male domain. Just then, Audrey Louise arrived with the whipped cream. She sensed the silence was not altogether smooth.

"Let's have some melon and cream. Cleans the palate, settles the meal. How was the roast? Not too dry?"

"It was just right, Audrey Louise," I said. "And I loved the salad. Especially the mushrooms." I kept my eyes on Arthur.

"Oh Nyla, you're easy to please. That has its merits. I'll cook for you anytime."

We chuckled. Joel forgot the discourse on language and went for the melon as if he had not just left a hearty meal. Arthur spooned slowly; I felt a tingle at my neck but it wasn't the flower coming. It was a fight that would waste my energy and I didn't want it. I wanted to go play a quick hand of canasta alone with Audrey Louise or read her the part from W. Stone's letter about those secret places in the grass at the spa. These men wanted a little amusing contest at my expense. Joel wanted to see how Arthur and I sparred because that was exciting to him. They were as closed with their obvious amusement at my beliefs as William Porter was with his family privacy, his clipped and formal tones.

Arthur swallowed and said, "I think fiction is an old-fashioned medium with enough barriers already preventing innovation. Your word-change idea in fiction would just become a gimmick. People stick to what they know." His pronouncement made, he attacked his melon.

"That must be one of the reasons that prejudice has such tenacity, don't you think, Arthur? And ignorance, even in the face of reachable insight. Because people stick to what they know."

Arthur stopped eating. "What about *your* prejudice, Nyla? The idea that changing words is the *right* thing to do?" He had to dab quickly with his napkin to keep from spouting juice. Audrey Louise stopped to look at both of us just before swallowing a sizeable bite of melon. She had just realized there was no joviality in our discussion.

"Arthur, it's my *turn* to be prejudiced. Men have been prejudiced against women long enough."

"Now that doesn't sound like equality to me. That sounds Biblical, the old 'eye for an eye' routine."

"I never said I was interested in equality. I said the language should be changed to include everyone. And I *intend* to be included."

Arthur and I both stopped eating and sat looking at each other, eye to eye.

"You will be, Nyla," Audrey Louise tried to reassure, to disperse the fray. "Let's do play a round of bridge, shall we?"

I hated that awkward moment for her; she didn't get to see the skirmish set up while she whipped cream in the kitchen. I hated what it was in Joel and Arthur that made them need to test me, to provoke me, and then to call it teasing.

"You've made your point, Nyla," Joel tried to placate in his detestable tone, just when the only available next step was to put on boxing gloves. "We didn't mean to get you all riled up."

Like hell: you and Steve Raymond with his "no whitewash." You meant to rile me up but when I push back, you want to pretend it didn't happen.

"I'd like to talk to you some more about this, Nyla. But another time. I'm no primitive man. I think some aspects of changing language are very interesting."

Arthur's face as he said this, his smile, his entire manner told me he was pacifying me with an intellectual come-on. I felt insulted. So there we all were, sitting around, each of us waiting for one of us to lead on to the bridge table or early goodnights or something to ease the ungainly moment. Audrey Louise looked at Joel and Arthur and then at me, her face softening my angry heart. I gave her a smile she understood: not a full smile, just my lips going up, to tell her we were compatriots but I just couldn't make it easy for the men because they never made it easy for me.

Then like some horrible messenger, the hall phone rang. Joel looked toward the door. Arthur finished his melon. But Audrey Louise didn't move because she saw me jump and press a hand to my heart. For one terrifying second, I considered that the woman who had been calling me knew where I went and had followed me there when I thought it was safe.

"You getting that, Audrey Louise?" Joel stared at the door again.

"Yes." But as she moved, she held me with a quizzical, concerned look. I shook my head and waved her on. She returned after a quick conversation to put her hand on my shoulder. Joel asked, "Who was that?"

"Mother. She's had enough. Can't get the boys to settle down." Then she asked me, "You okay? I saw you jump at the phone. Is anything wrong?"

"No, I'm just tired. A little jumpy." I wished she hadn't asked me in front of Joel and Arthur but I couldn't lie to her just because they were there. "Actually, it isn't just that. I've had . . . several . . . phone calls this week. I told you. They call about 4 a.m. and say nothing. Well, they say my name but that's all. As if to let me know they know who I am. And then silence. I guess that's got me a little nervous."

"I didn't know they'd called again. But of course you don't recognize the voice?"

"No."

"You need a good man to protect you, Nyla. Tell that bastard off next time he calls." Joel assumed it was a man calling. Well, that was something: it usually is. Audrey Louise hugged me closer around the shoulders, comforting.

"If it keeps up, you ought to consider getting one of those answering machines. Weirdos usually give up if there's no live body on the line."

"That's a good idea."

"Shall I follow you home, Nyla? Just to check out the apartment, be sure all is in order?" Arthur put on his helpful tone but I was still touchy from our skirmish.

"No, thanks, I live in a security building. I'll be fine."

A part of me wanted him to come along and get any waiting blows in the darkness, but my rational self didn't want to hear his routine for soothing ruffled feathers.

"I do think I ought to call it an evening, though. I've got to get copy to typography on Monday." Still Arthur didn't ask me about *my* writing. In his world, there was only one writer.

At the door, Audrey Louise helped me into my coat and told me, "You call when you get home. Just so I'll sleep okay. I'll wait to go pick up the boys until I hear from you."

"You're a good friend," I said and gave her a kiss. She didn't dodge me.

For once, traffic was a friendly distraction. I took a slightly longer route home through downtown, just to hear the noise and feel the night air. But it wasn't fear I was stalling, fear that I thought might fill up my small apartment. I was considering that Arthur took my elbow as we walked to my car and I never invited him to touch me. My Minneapolis mother would say he was just being polite. But if the attitude behind that word were as it should be, everyone would know touching is by invitation only and not to be assumed. I considered that Audrey Louise and I had talked about feminism and oppression and women's lib twenty different ways: in normal tones, with heated emotion, with an outburst or two. But she had never tried to bait me, box with me, to take jabs at me behind disguised motives. She had never viewed me as an amusement. She never considered my ideas just sport. It was anger I didn't want to wrestle with alone back at my apartment. I decided I'd take the phone off the hook after I called Audrey Louise.

As I unlocked my door, I wished again that Arthur was there just to walk through the rooms first. Let him worry about the distraction of equalizing terms while I worried about the chloroformed towel. Actually, Larry would be the best one to check out the place. Because he would stride right in and turn on the light and suck with his teeth and say, "Nobody here, see. No sweat." Then when I didn't offer him coffee, he'd split without a lot of manufactured politeness. But even before we had begun to argue, Arthur had given himself away to me. By the way he ate his melon: biting hard into that soft tissue, all the way across the slice, too quick, heartlessly leaving a ravaged half moon behind him. He didn't taste the pulp at all. And it was sweet: one perfect day overripe. I dialed Audrey Louise.

"It's me. I'm in okay. Have a light on in every room. I'm unplugging the phone until morning. Thank you for having the dinner, Audrey Louise. I think Arthur and I are too many years too late for each other. But it was interesting. Call you soon."

No anger or fear lurking in the apartment, just weariness. Tomorrow I had to tackle a full draft of the graveyard story. Maybe I could find a happy medium between it and the warehouse story. Does Xanadu lie between craft and artistry? I was thinking I'd rather have one of Arthur's students talk to me about creative integrity than Arthur himself. Punchy style indeed.

The radio said there was a cold front moving in and I believed it. I wanted an extra blanket. The moon was threading silver, crescent-shaped slivers across the carpet. For all its brevity of space, I wouldn't have traded the apartment with its bay window for any place larger or cheaper. I put the blanket across my lap for a moment and sat down in the window. There was one street light halfway down the block; I thought it must be party night because so many cars were gone. Usually you couldn't find a single place to park. At the other end of the block, with no street light, there were two pole lights at the entrance of The Condor, a newly renovated apartment building. The parking lot wasn't quite finished yet and there was a small cement mixer and a bulldozer left on the site. They were ugly: those loud, large machines built strictly to move whatever resisted, be it earth or aspen or grave-stones. Those small, rusty shovels in the graveyard would snap as easy as dry stalks when the Kinter dozers began.

Arthur could probably write twelve sonnets about the Fleming graveyard and still miss its odd beauty, its sad demise. He would never feel the poetry of W. Stone, who wrote from the heart and not from the ego. He would no doubt approach Cybil's desk as merely a desk, not skirts of wood that might birth my prowess with words. I did not envy him his three books, his prize of publica-tion. He was corseted by his own ego in a way that not even the slinky black dress could equal. It seemed fitting that a man who called Stein and Daly rhetoric writers would also have to title his love poems only a "semblance."

The people downstairs were watching Johnny Carson. It was comforting to hear them laugh, to know there was someone else in the building fairly close by. But I'd had enough moon basking. The street was empty; no one about at this hour. And I needed some sleep.

Unfolding the blanket, I threw it around my shoulders and pulled it up close to me. I bid the moon goodnight. But it wasn't the glimmer of moonlight that drew my attention back to the street. It was a brighter flicker of yellow, a lighter to a cigarette. And then the pinpoint of orange, unmoving. Someone was stand-ing in the cold night air smoking, just a vague shadow by the bushes across the street. Someone was standing in that shadow, with a clear view of me at the bay window.

EIGHT

The Watcher

I jolted out of the window seat and immediately got out of sight. By standing very close to the wall and inching back toward the window, I could see the street at an angle and could see that glow of orange move in the shadow of the bushes. This was a slow smoker, no one just stopping to light up and then walk on. I felt hot, pushed the blanket off my shoulders onto the floor. I wanted to wish that was Arthur down there in the street; he'd followed me home and was having a slow smoke to decide if I'd let him in. But I knew it wasn't Arthur, and I also knew that whoever it was was purposely there watching me.

Unexpectedly, the smoker seemed to want me to watch him. He began to move slowly down the sidewalk, the orange dot of the cigarette in the darkness before him. Then he stepped into a small pool of light from the lone street lamp. I saw the profile for a moment and my breath stopped short. Standing there smoking, tall, dressed in jeans and a pea coat with shoulder-length hair: the stranger in the street was watching, both hands in the coat pockets, unmoving in the light. I realized I wasn't breathing. There was no hulking masher down there, ready to move in on me for the kill. Below me on the street, watching me, was a woman. It hit me hard all over again: a woman. I knew it from the phone calls but now I knew it in a totally different way. She looked up toward my

81

window, not just in the general direction, but right at the window where I had been sitting. Then she raised one hand, waved sort of, like a signal.

Car lights down the street went on, then off, with a moment when the whiteness of the light seemed to dissolve in the chilly air. Then the lights came on again. I didn't hear the engine start up but the car pulled away from the curb, gliding slowly up the street, brightening the woman all the way. She flicked her cigarette off into the hedge behind her. As the car slid up even with her and stopped, she looked toward my window again, touched her hand to her forehead in a strange salute, a tip-off to me. I was out of sight but she knew I had sighted her. Knew I didn't miss that lighter on the dark, half-empty street and just stroll off to bed. When the car door opened, she got in quickly. I couldn't see the driver. There was no peel of tires as they left; they just glided slowly down the street, white headlights trading for a red tail that finally blinked out many blocks away.

At least I knew they wouldn't call me. We'd seen each other; whatever game they were playing, their shifty sighting was enough for one night. I felt no malevolence, only a jumpiness that made me pace from room to room.

I made cocoa. I walked up and down the living room just a step out of sight of the window. I knew they wouldn't be back but a part of me felt like the watcher was frozen outside on the sidewalk. What on earth did they want with me? Who were they? When would they get closer? How much closer could they get unless they were inside the apartment with me?

I wondered if I should call the police. Tell them this woman keeps calling me and now I think she's doing her own spooky surveillance. Think of all the questions they'll ask me that will make me feel ridiculous.

"Has she threatened you?"

"Well no, not directly."

"Has she made violent or sexual remarks to you when she calls?"

"No, she hasn't said anything."

"How about violent *and* sexual remarks?"

"I told you, she hasn't said anything."

"Then how do you know it's her?"

"Well, she does say something. She says my name."

"Oh, only your name. Then what makes you think that the woman on the street was the same one who has been calling?"

I realized that I didn't really know if it was the same woman or if she was really tall: it had seemed so from that angle, up above as I was. But I was around the corner and we were both in the dark. I wasn't entirely sure she had dark hair except that for a few seconds in the dim light and the car's headlights, I didn't see blonde hair. I didn't notice the color or shape or length of the car. I stared at the tail lights for minutes but never focused on the license plate. All I could focus on was the bizarre realization that a woman or women were clearly watching me for no imaginable reason and they had let me know it. What would they let me know next?

I should have had better sense, noticed more. That's what this reporting business is all about: observation, careful and concise, asking the right questions, listening to tones that say more than words, knowing who knows whom and what about them that's known. My god, there was just no excuse for my not seeing the license number! Maybe I wasn't cut out to be a reporter, to be any kind of writer with a keen sense of awareness about people and events. Maybe I should have stayed married. No strangers were in that familiar scene, no watchers of my day-to-day wifedom except Mike, and he was at least a familiar stranger. The connections that used to be so clear to me seemed confused.

To hell with the hour; I dialed Audrey Louise, hoping Joel wouldn't answer and be grumpy and uncooperative at midnight.

"Hello?" Joel was groggy but not an awakened warrior.

"Sorry to bug you at this hour. It's Nyla. Let me speak to Audrey Louise for just a sec."

"Oh. Okay." I heard muffled movement across the bed.

"What's up, babe?"

She was my instant hug from across town.

"You know I told you about those phone calls?"

"Yes. Did you get another one?"

"Not a phone call this time. A visitation."

"My god, Nyla, are you all right? Did you call the police? Should I come over there?"

"I'm okay. It wasn't an attack or anything. But there was

someone across the street by the bushes. Watching me."

"Has he left?"

I relived the moment when the watcher stepped into the lamp light, revealing a woman's profile. I couldn't help shuddering.

"That's why I'm so shaken up, Audrey Louise. It's a woman. Two women maybe; someone drove up in a car and picked her up but I didn't see the driver."

"What kind of weirdo women would be doing this? Did you get a good look at her?" I heard her whisper to Joel to hand her her robe. I knew she'd take the phone out on the stairway at the top of the steps, hugging it as if it was me.

"Just for a brief second. I don't know her. But she was across the street and I was scared, it was dark, so maybe . . . "

"Scared or not, you don't have any friends who would do this. Even for a joke. We both know that. It must be weirdos."

It occurred to me that it could be worse; Audrey Louise might not have been home to calm me down and in addition to the voyeur ghosts, I could have had the orchid on my back again.

"You haven't called the police then?"

"To tell them what? That some woman is calling and watching me? I have no proof it's the same woman. I'm not sure what she wants. How do I know it's to harm me?"

"Because she's making you feel unsafe and scaring shit out of both of us. That's harm enough."

"So you think I should call the police?"

"Maybe just so they'll send a patrol car around."

"Watching me isn't a crime. She walked up into the light and let me see her. And the car didn't peel out either. I could have read the tag but I was too upset. So what good would a patrol car do me? That just means more people watching me."

"You know what's wrong with you feminists? You're pathologically fair. Here's some woman harassing you and you want to make exceptions for her."

In spite of everything, I had to laugh at myself.

"I suppose you're right. Harassment is harassment."

"That's better. Sometimes you're too fair to take decent care of yourself."

We stopped talking for a minute; I replayed the whole evening and blamed everything that failed—William Porter's call, Arthur's argumentativeness, my unwelcome watcher—on that black slinky dress which has never been comfortable in my closet.

"Speaking of harassment, did Arthur leave right after I did?"

"Not immediately. He and Joel talked some more. He asked Joel if he'd put a burr under your saddle and Joel said yes. They made me mad."

"Why?"

"Oh, just the way they acted together. Like fraternity boys who got caught in a panty raid."

"Did they say something else? Are you telling me everything?"

She hesitated; now I wanted to give her a hug back.

"I know I don't make things easy, Audrey Louise. But that's just how I am. That's how it is. Both of them wanted some kind of fight too. You weren't in the room when they set it up. Now what else did they say?"

Still she hesitated. It must have been something terrible. Then she snickered.

"Arthur was saying he would never have guessed you'd be the libber type because he knows Mike and that doesn't fit with his impressions. Well hell, what he knows about Mike we could both stuff into a pistachio shell and besides, he isn't interested in anyone but himself anyway. And on top of that, what does Mike's preference in women have to do with how you should be?"

"Go on, go on."

"Well, Joel just sat there for a minute looking at Arthur and then he got very serious and leaned over to him, the perfect picture of commiseration, and said, 'That's the thing, isn't it, Arty? Every peach has a fucking pit.'"

Our laughter sounded good in my apartment.

"I hope to hell they heard me laughing out in the kitchen. I spilled all the rest of the melon on the floor."

I got tears in my eyes from laughing. I could picture Joel and "Arty," both still sure women should be simple.

"But here's the thing," Audrey Louise continued. "It came to me while I was lying in bed just now. I thought to myself, 'Okay, the guy is an asshole, but bearable maybe. He writes sonnets so maybe he isn't a total bore. Then I thought of you two getting married and of course you wouldn't give up your name. So there you would be. Think of it: *Nyla Wade Quaid.* Now I ask you, can you take a Wade-Quaid seriously? Introduce such a person to your other friends without giggling? Wade-Quaid, Wade-Quaid. My god, the more I said it, the worse it sounded. There's just no way, I knew it then!"

I could feel our laughter relaxing me, helping me give up some of my nervousness. We paused again for a moment, holding each other in a safe silence.

"You feeling any better, Nyla?"

"Absolutely. Who would dare mess with a Wade-Quaid?"

"Now will you be able to get some sleep tonight?" Audrey Louise asked me. For a moment I considered driving back to her house.

"My first inclination is to get into my coat this minute. But I can't come running out there every time I get scared."

"Hey, don't berate yourself for wanting some comfort."

I couldn't help it; Mike's face slipped into my consciousness.

"Maybe I took on more of Mike's behavior than I ever realized. Berating the need for comfort was his area of expertise."

"You got him on your mind again? Because of Arthur maybe?"

"Oh partly, I guess. And because I feel like this independent life of mine that I wanted so desperately is out of my control. I'm living alone and I'm on someone's weirdo list. And what do I do? Manufacture visions of a giant orchid that I can see clearly but is invisible to everyone else. Then I stare at a license plate for five minutes and never read a single goddamned number. What the hell would I do if I had an assignment with any real risk involved? Is this what I can expect when I get a little nervous, a little pressured? I guess I'm wondering if I made a big mistake. If I tried hard enough with Mike. Or if the only thing I even moderately succeeded at was being married."

"Listen honey, you're judging yourself way too hard. And it isn't Mike you miss anyway; it's the familiar humdrum. Your life is drastically different now so be patient with yourself. Be as fair to yourself as you want to be with that creepy lady who was watching you on the street tonight."

"Christ, Audrey Louise, I just don't want to end up a failure."

"You won't. Because you're not going to marry again for the wrong reasons or just settle for something familiar and protective. You're done with letting anyone keep you from writing or anything else you want to do, like Mike did."

"I never knew you thought that, Audrey Louise."

"Maybe you never blamed Mike for that, but I do. You worked hard at that marriage. It failed because you were working by yourself. You've finally got yourself back again and you're writing. It can only get better."

Suddenly I was sure again. I knew I wasn't a failure or a lousy reporter or a writer wearing blinders. I was a woman slightly out of practice at living alone and making my living as a journalist.

"Thank you, Audrey Louise. I am delivered once again from the abyss by your wisdom. Even at midnight."

"Sleep well, my friend. If you wake up nervous, give me a call. I'm here for you. And think about giving the police a call. Just to make your old friend happy."

Even though Audrey Louise was able to restore my sanity, I still couldn't sleep. And I didn't want to deal with the police. So I sat up writing the graveyard story. Be constructive, I told myself, don't concentrate on noises in the building, creaks in the apartment, or shifting in the darkness. What I actually wrote were two stories: one purely editorial, my feelings about the graveyard and the planned warehouse construction. The other one was more objective, though it played up the graveyard more than the prefab metal building that would displace it. I planned to take them both to Steve Raymond with a note that said, "While I'm not sure what you put into your paint, I know I can't get any closer to whitewash than this." I finally fell asleep about 5 a.m.

When I awakened about eleven, I reread my stories, but I didn't see the words I was reading. A decision was forming for me. There was another graveyard I must visit, that of Cybil Porter. For no tangible reason, I felt a trip to Rochester would reveal to me if there was indeed a third grave, the one that would end my troubled connection with the hidden letters, would finish for me any need to provide delivery to W. Stone of his lover's letter to him. Someone in Rochester must give me a clue to W. Stone. I spent a quiet Sunday making my plan for the start of the week: I would take care of business. Get the copy that was due out to Kinter, pick up a few groceries, and then get a ticket East. Audrey Louise told me the trip was risky business, but a few days away from the apartment would do me good. At least in Rochester I wouldn't worry about the watcher.

Monday I missed any direct observation of Steve Raymond's reaction to my copy; he was not in his office when I delivered the stories. I expected he would call me later. I wondered how his attempt to soothe ruffled feathers would compare to Arthur's. I was glad to avoid both for the moment. I wished I could avoid grocery shopping, never my favorite errand. Bread and garbage bags, apples and chicken: I only needed four items but they were worlds apart within the store so I had to chart my way down every crowded aisle. I wasn't in the mood to stand in line, except in the ticket line at the airport. I was ready to take a trip.

Then I remembered a revelation of one of the couples in a counseling group Mike and I had attended. He wanted to prove to me that counseling groups were ridiculous and the revelation of this particular couple satisfied his scorn. Ted and Kaye were their names and they had admitted to the group that they found the grocery store to be an extremely erotic place, full of colors and shapes to be seen in a new way. The produce department was their favorite section. They would imagine fondling each other as they fondled the cantaloupes and eggplants.

I couldn't help touching a cantaloupe after I got my apples. I could see the attraction: the smooth shape contrasted to the slightly rough texture. I tried to imagine groping a cantaloupe in one hand and some part of a lover with the other. No doubt it would be hard for me because it took both my hands to hold the cantaloupe. I got a vision of Ted and Kaye, each holding a cantaloupe with one of their hands and using the other for groping. Or maybe they alternately fondled the fruit and then each other. As I was envisioning them draped across the entire stand of cantaloupes, their legs and arms entwined around each other and various invited melons, someone bumped my cart. When I turned to look, the figure I saw rounding the corner sent a shiver up my spine: jeans and a pea coat, shoulder-length dark hair.

Don't be so jumpy, Wade. The description fits half the women in this city.

Leaving behind the erotic promise of the produce, I made an extra stop for some chamomile tea to calm my nerves in case my watcher was at her post again before I left for Rochester. I wasn't aware of anyone else in the aisle until a voice behind me said, "Nyla Wade, keep reading the labels and don't turn around."

I riveted my eyes on the chamomile tea.

"We had to check you out last night. And with the calls. To see if you had a man."

It was my female watcher. She had her back to me and was staring at cans of vegetables.

"Can't have a man in the way right now. We want to make a deal with you."

"We? Who the hell . . . " I half turned away from the tea; she scooted her basket on up the aisle, keeping her back to me.

Keep cool, Wade, and read the labels. Let her do the talking if you're going to find out what she wants.

I slowly pushed my basket back toward where she was now standing. I turned so that we were again back to back.

"Sorry. But while you and your partner were checking me out, you scared hell out of me."

"You'll meet her later. You want to hear the deal? Or do you scare too easily?"

She wasn't testing; she was letting me know we weren't talking low-risk assignments here.

"What does it cost me to listen? A blood pact? A secret society? Eternal silence?"

"Shit!"

She slammed down a can of peas and pushed her cart resolutely away from me toward the milk and cheese.

Too flip, Wade. She dislikes your style.

"Wait!"

I realized I couldn't run after her pushing my cart ahead of me: that would be too obvious. I went the opposite way down my aisle, hoping I could head her off near the exit. Glancing rapidly down the next aisle where I expected to see her, she seemed to have disappeared. She was not near the door. Or the cottage cheese. Not in pork chops or cereal.

I doubled back, passing chamomile tea again. At the top end of the store, I could see over all the frozen foods to both ends of the building. She was nowhere in sight. I stared hard, hoping she'd turn into view where the limas and ice cream were frosting together.

Okay Wade, now what? You and your uppity comebacks. They're one up on you but you had to get cute. She's split without you getting to hear the deal.

I pushed my cart toward the prescription counter. I was about to give it a heave right into a stack of hemorroid tubes when I spotted her again, standing at the greeting cards, one corner of her mouth down as she read a "Happy Birthday to My Favorite Nephew" card. I tried to glide up to her, hoping slower movement would calm both of us.

"Sorry, but I'm not used to any of this. Cut me some slack."

She didn't answer but moved down the section of cards to anniversary messages. I wanted to look over at her, even for a second; her profile this close would show me more than last night's brief exchange. But I didn't dare. I'd almost blown it already.

"It won't cost you anything to listen. But we don't have a whole lot of time."

"Fine. I want to hear the deal."

"Okay, you'll hear from me soon." She headed for the express lane check-out as my lowered voice slipped into the blank envelopes behind the cards.

"But when? I'm going out of town . . . " My last sight of her was her back again.

The watcher didn't reappear in the parking lot. She said I'd hear from her soon. But when? I headed for the airport. I also wanted to be on a train part of the journey to ruminate, to absorb some of Cybil Porter's landscape. Maybe I could set that up for the return.

The problem with working free-lance is that you're on your own time and you forget other people's time schedules. When I got to the airport, I was facing a lunch-hour line at the airline ticket desk. I guessed it would be forty minutes before I could get up to that desk; there were at least twenty people ahead of me. I should have taken a book to read. I couldn't decide when to go. Tomorrow? Could I get ready that fast? Maybe the best thing to do was not worry, just throw a shirt or two into a bag. Spend the flight time considering how to get into the Porter home to talk to William or better, to have a try with his secretary. Call Brentwood School just in case the long shot panned out. Yes, I would go tomorrow: give myself the morning at the Rochester library and then the afternoon to attempt the assault on the estate. Go to the cemetery Wednesday. Pursue promising leads.

Ticket finally in hand, my excitement growing, I nearly forgot the clandestine conversation amidst the groceries. I got lost in scheming my way over the Porterfield threshold. But when I reached the car, clipped under the windshield wiper was a business card that read: "Bevo's Lounge." Above the address had been penciled the words: "Wednesday. 7 p.m. Come alone." The last words were underlined with three short pencil marks. A warning. If they could find my car here at the airport, then they could find out about the trip. I knew then for sure that I was up against a woman who was not fooling around with me. Women: she had identified her partner as female. They could get where I was and know what I was doing with relative ease. I wished then that I had the gleam of precision in the emerald eye that had made its sighting into my life out of Cybil Porter's, so I could check the front and guard the rear and cover the sights of me these women had. The watcher said they were checking me out to see if I had a man around. Can't have a man in the way, she said. So I'm to go alone Wednesday night to Bevo's Lounge. Definitely with no man. None of the ones I know would believe any of this, but then, I wouldn't tell them anyway. I could just get back from Rochester in time to meet them. Step carefully, Wade. Someone definitely has your number.

"Do you think you can bring one over this afternoon? I'll be out of town a few days and I want to be sure I don't miss any calls."

"Yes, Miss. That will be no problem. AnswerBack Phone Machines Company always tries for same-day installation. I can have an installer there before two."

"Send a woman, will you?"

"Yes, Miss, I'll try to do that."

I was amazed in these days of incredibly bad service to find an efficient, cooperative person who could do what I needed to have done almost immediately. I was to get my automatic phone answering machine by the afternoon. Just in case the tall stranger and her partner got lonesome and wanted to give me a call. Or if Steve Raymond had a cryptic response to my graveyard-warehouse stories.

I gave Audrey Louise a quick call. She was on the way out the door to go to school. But she took time to give me her special benediction and agreed to take me to the airport. The afternoon went well; I couldn't remember as good a day in years. Adventure in the morning, but now I wasn't afraid. I was unsure of what the woman and her partner wanted or what it would entail but I was no longer terrified of some unexpected and violent invasion.

The AnswerBack installer arrived around two. She was cute, puttering quietly around the phone, her belt of equipment slung around one hip at a jaunty, confident angle. She could have been a high school cheerleader: a real blonde, with an upturned nose, but holding her own in the real world, walking around in worker's boots that didn't hide her small, competent feet. She came and went in a matter of minutes but left me with some additional sureness, a subtle convincing that I was going to take care of my own business right on the button.

As I was lifting up my feet to rest them on the coffee table and settling my back against a cushion, ready to savor a sip of scotch, the phone rang. The automatic recorder switched on; I felt a certain instant power in knowing I could choose to answer or not but the caller would never know if I was home. I heard Steve Raymond's voice crackling through the recorded message so I hurried to pick up the receiver.

"Hi, Steve. Like my new machine?"

"Does this mean you've got so much business that you need to screen your calls?"

"Absolutely." Let him see Nyla Wade, Industrious and Successful.

"Not going to cut our *Brush Stroke* loose, are you? Once you get too big you know there's no reversing the trend. We need you; our directors are quite pleased with your work."

"Well that's good to hear, Steve. Don't worry; I'll keep you on awhile longer."

"That's good." We traded good-natured chuckles over the phone. Get to it, Steve, I thought to myself. I can't wait to hear your approach to my stories.

"Say Nyla, I appreciate your taking the time to write up two versions of the warehouse story. Gives me options, you know."

"Yes, it does."

No patronizing tones so far. He was amazingly civil.

"I hadn't realized what a unique cemetery they had out there in Fleming."

I'll bet. Nor what a shiny gloss you get with whitewash.

"Anyway, can we get together for a few minutes to discuss a way to combine the best parts of each story?"

Well, well, he wants a compromise. So do I. I want the warehouse built on the meadow if we can't ship it to Toledo as Dino suggested.

"I can't do that until later this week, Steve. I've got ... I've got such a sore throat that I'm staying in." Mainly from trying to swallow this whole warehouse situation ...

"Okay, you take care of that. Think you can give me a call Thursday or Friday?"

"Will do. Goodbye."

Only a small lie; it went down easy with the scotch. A small lie for a good cause; some things were getting easier.

NINE

After the Morgue, a Willing Secretary

I started off my New York adventure with a harangue from Audrey Louise as she drove me to the airport. I was to call her at least twice during my two days with full details of all my findings. She slipped me a fifty dollar bill as I was trying to hug her goodbye.

"This is an advance for your long distance phone calls," she said. When I protested, she closed her hand around my fingers holding the money. "What the hell, babe. Between you and me, there's no owing."

For the next three hours in the air, I went over the phone calls I'd made just before Audrey Louise came to pick me up. I had committed a breach of good breeding by actually requesting information from two private Eastern schools about a person who not only was not me, but to whom I was not even related. The people I spoke to at Brentwood School and Dockworth Academy were both trained by the same tyrannical snippet. They were totally averse to giving out information about students, even past students by twenty years, except to members of their families. When I explained I was researching a gothic romance novel about a Rochester family, they were completely unimpressed. Though my story line didn't budge the snippets, I considered it might be a good one to continue with Peter Gant if I was able to get into Porterfield.

I could hardly pretend to be a member of Cybil's family when I didn't know her maiden name, but I knew if she had by some chance graduated from Brentwood, there should be some records updated to show her married name. But Brentwood's administrator supplied me with nothing. Dockworth was worse; supposedly sniffing out a society-chaser, they hung up on me. A very stand-offish sniff it was.

I considered I might locate Cybil's maiden name in the newspaper morgue or extract it from Peter Gant. He might be safely approachable in regard to W. Stone as well, but I'd have to play that by ear. After all, if Gant was William's personal agent as well as his secretary, and if William knew of the affair, Gant might know also. Any hint that someone else outside the family knew might alarm them both. The result of that alarm I could not yet gauge.

My imagination fell short on the Porter family: a fully fledged Rochester first family, they made news before the turn of the century. I worried that my dig into the Rochester library newspaper morgue would prove difficult. But at the card catalog, I found a file number for the Porters and the file was burgeoning with news of their doings: clippings back to Spencer's parents and some mention of Porters even previous to that. All the chronology was there, in yellowed and slightly tattered columns of the Rochester *Register*. Cybil was born Cybil Walling in 1902; Spencer in 1898. Cybil's death was announced in 1970; she was sixty-eight. Spencer preceeded her at the age of forty-four in 1942, of a heart attack. Lawrence's birth announcement appeared in the *Register* issue dated September 16, 1938. His obituary was dated November 12, 1969. That was only a year before Cybil's passing: he was a tender thirty-one.

The articles told that Spencer fell ill in the midst of a dinner party at the home of Leonard Rush. He died later that same night of an apparent heart attack. The details of Lawrence's death were brief. While hunting in upstate New York with his uncle and a party of four others, the young man tripped and fell, his own gun discharging into his chest. He died before he could be carried back to the car. Audrey Louise would call that handy, no doubt, and begin to wonder immediately how William and his Gang of Four carried out poor Larry's demise.

Two striking facts were revealed by the numbers and the articles. For one, Cybil Porter was thirty-six years old when her son was born. She had a child at an age even modern doctors consider risky; she must indeed have been a maternity maverick of grand proportion those nearly fifty years ago. Second and more important, while there were lengthy funeral stories for both Spencer and Lawrence, Cybil was only accorded a short notice of a memorial ceremony: closed casket and no wake. A further, unexpected fact was learning that she died of hepatitis, contracted on a holiday in England. She did not die in this country nor was it mentioned that she was attended by any relatives or friends at her death. I wondered immediately if Cybil had gone to England possibly for a meeting with W. Stone.

There were a few pictures with the articles but they were so muddied by the aging newsprint as to be nearly indistinguishable. Ironically, in some a clear detail remained, but of unavailing objects rather than faces: a hat, a pair of spectacles, a lady's shoe boot with very handsome clasps. Those were worn by Spencer's mother and their lasting detail convinced me they were definitely made for walking. Walking around sizeable Rochester territory as the articles also revealed, a region registered in proud Porter history. These were rich and powerful people with investments reaching out of the state as well: to farms in Virginia, to Pennsylvania steel, to a major Eastern brewery, and to Catskill real estate where some very exclusive Holsteins herded over some very exclusive topsoil. There was mention of Spencer's father, Bernard, but something unnameable in the clippings, in the murky pictures, convinced me that much of the present Porter money came into the family with Maye Della Lavernby Porter, the mother of Spencer, Dorie, and William. The press clippings showed me a woman much more vital than William's description of a "social correspondent with many friends." Here was a woman who dedicated banks and schools, launched ships in a splatter of champagne, spoke at the Rochester Ladies of Distinction in Education banquet, a woman not easily imaginable as a simple social correspondent. Bernard had his moments in the news: with a new thoroughbred at the race track, taking a near spin-out at a vintage car rally, and handing out checks to charity. His press was there all right, but it was dim stuff. There was a matriarch shining in Maye Della, one that may well have set the style for Cybil Porter to follow. I wondered if William had railed as much at the same cast of strength in his mother as he did in his sister-in-law.

When I pushed back the file of clippings, it wasn't jet lag or the hunger of lunch time gnawing at me. It was that twinge again, that same twinge of regret I had felt when Randy first told me that Cybil was buried at Crestlawn. The Porter men had what you might expect men in their position to have; they showed up and were written up at all the right social events of the city. But the Porter women, though they came into the family with other names, seemed to live out of their copy, larger than the words used to describe them. Even Dorie, the only female Porter by blood, was not just another Rochester debutante, not just the equestrian talent of the family. She learned to fly and for her college graduation, proudly flew her brother Spencer to Rio de Janeiro. She not only owned but managed the farms in Virginia until her death.

I thought again of W. Stone's letters, how they made me feel when I first read them. He wrote about his love for Cybil, for the woman in Cybil that he knew, the woman who came out of his words, outside the simple size and meaning of their written communication.

> "You were never much for telling the whole truth, darling, or for emptying out your most obvious feelings. I wonder how your face looks when I write to you that we are lovers. Lovers, and married in our own way despite obvious circumstance. You are so much to me and always have been. A giver in many layers, beyond even the obvious feelings you'd like to avoid and the obvious circumstance we can neither of us ignore."

This was one of the letters from Atlanta, in the earlier years of their correspondence. As I thought of that letter, I couldn't ignore that I wished there was no grave in Rochester for Cybil. Wished that somewhere she and W. Stone still remembered together over tea the time they danced nude on a terrace, making their own music in the moonlight. How had it happened that hepatitis had taken Cybil so quickly, in a matter of days, when there was no press to show her as other than a hearty fixture among Rochester's rich? She had been a woman with a firm and healthy hold for thirty years over farms, cattle, kegs, and steel. Maybe the tragic accident that took Lawrence's life had something to do with it. Maybe she tired of the feud with William. But what nagged me most was that maybe she lost W. Stone too, perhaps soon after Lawrence. And I might never be able to verify that, especially if Stone met his demise in England. I certainly couldn't hop a plane over a sea and a past that vast with any hope of unraveling those last events in 1970.

My answers were not in the file of past history in ten-point type. But I photocopied the funeral stories to take back with me anyway and the articles with the picture of a determined Maye Porter in her boots.

If there was any trace of Dorothy Thompson in me, I prayed for it as I left the Rochester library and headed for Porterfield. I barely noticed any detail of Rochester as I drove over to the estate, ending up in my rented car within sight of the estate gates. What grand parades of cars must have rounded this bend and filled the driveway for those galas which Cybil told W. Stone were such a part of Spencer's life and such a drain on her own. I wondered if I would be able to beg my way across William Porter's threshold for a chance to look into Cybil's helmsroom. It occurred to me that there were so few grand women in my own field, so few who scratched their mark clear through the barrier posts. I wanted some spirit of all those who did make it to be with me before I tried to approach the estate. I was not on the front line of the Italian revolution as was Margaret Fuller, but I was on a front line of my own, about to make a crossing that was of the utmost importance to me and possibly to another fleeting spirit who might still be among us: W. Stone.

I was sure a rational approach would only net me a closed door in my face. So I decided I was willing to play dingbat, hussy, or eccentric, if I must, to get into that house. I would prattle or ramble or insult or bombard. I would so surprise old William that he wouldn't know what to do but answer my non-stop questions if he thought that would get me back out the door. I'd be half crazy with him, able to find out everything I wanted to know, because even a man too proper for his own good is unnerved by a woman hinting hysteria.

Taking a deep breath, I tried to ignore a great black blot behind my own eyes that was the mass of my personal and professional ethics. Those which were about to be entirely abandoned if necessary. Keep the end result in mind, I told myself. I had suffered probes into darkness for this moment: the darkness of The Gravy Boat hiding the shroud-covered desk; the darkness of the desk itself, holding its secret; the darkness of the past which revealed Cybil and W. Stone to me. I had suffered the visitation of an apparition not my own, that great pulsating orchid. If I had now to entertain a ruse or play a role to finally disperse that darkness and that turbid dream, then so be it. Whatever they might think of me, beyond those doors of Porterfield for the short time I would be there, I alone knew I was not the woman they might see. But then neither had Cybil Porter been. This whole letter business was one monkey I wanted off my back. Another awaited me in Denver at Bevo's Lounge.

As I started my car to enter the drive, the sound of another engine interrupted it. Slowly, edging first its wide black nose through the gate and then following with sleek sides that seemed of enormous length, a limousine appeared. Black and polished, an efficient monster, the long car rolled toward me with a purring engine. A small slung spear of gravel from the limo's wheel took a nasty pinch out of the paint in my car door. For a moment, I glimpsed the chauffeur, dressed entirely in black, his profile formal and resolute. And then my window and the rear passenger window were parallel so I could see a small grey man. He seemed as perfectly polished as the car. He had a thin grey moustache and wore a black hat. Raiments of restraint, this absolute and inviolate black and white: the car, the chauffeur's uniform, and the passenger's clothing. All were a surrounding of reality with colors that were not colors at all but the cast of control. The man turned his face, not to look at me but at something in the seat beside him. On his face was the bleakest expression I have ever seen. Not one holding sorrow or depression for its bleakness, but rather apprehension and suspicion, not uninteresting but entirely joyless. The limousine slid past me; I felt more than knew who I had just sighted—William Porter, in person.

In the next instant I realized my luck: Porter had left the estate. Perhaps a persuasive appeal to Peter Gant could get me into the inner sanctum of Porterfield. I seized my opportunity.

The road from the gate to the house could not be seen from the street so its shortness surprised me. It was really just a half-bend of wide gravel with well-planted trees to give the illusion that the house was set farther back off the street. There was a half acre of courtyard on the left, shielded by linden trees. On the right was a covered portico, no doubt an old carriage entry, connected to a smaller dwelling of the same brick as the main house, probably for tack and the driver's quarters. Back behind this was an ample garage. All the parts flowed from the two story, central house, the line of brick scarcely seeming to break at the angles of the archi- tecture. There were four towers with turrets, somewhat medieval, as if signaling that the dwelling could be guarded. Without climb- ing a single stair, I guessed that much of Rochester could be over- seen from those tower windows.

At least there were no collapsing pits or vicious dogs to ensnare me as I approached the front door. There was a large brass knock- er on the door. When I lifted it, it did not fall back loose; a ten- sequence set of bells began. The door knocker moved in stages with the bells sounding back to its place of origin. Such festive welcome from such a joyless-looking William Porter. No doubt the bells were put in by someone in the family who was more jovial than he—probably Maye Della.

I had not considered a butler but there he was answering the door. He was as polished as the limousine, dressed also in im- peccable black and white. He was another efficient monster; I stifled a giggle when he spoke. I'm sure I expected a sepulchral bass voice to come out of him.

"May I help you?" he asked softly.

"Yes. I have an appointment with Peter Gant." Bluff Number One: Margaret Fuller stay with me in trench-jumper spirit.

"He's in the front work study. Whom shall I announce?"

"Nyla Wade. I am a friend of Randolph Porter's."

An evanescent twinge at the corners of the butler's mouth suf- ficed for a smile. "Wait here, please."

His back may well have been pressed with the coat he wore; he walked with no natural curve of any kind, a straight up-and-down man. I wondered at that inflexible back, at that instantly disappear- ing smile. Was it of approval or amusement?

As I waited, I noticed no sounds from any other part of the

house, but I could see there was a great deal of light for every room that was visible off the hallway. At least William put no garnishment on sunshine.

"Ms. Wade?"

With the butler this time was a slightly built man in his mid-forties, dressed in a pale blue suit. I was surprised that the color of his suit did not follow the black and white motif. The man held a file on one hand. From behind his glasses, I could see a small wrinkle of puzzlement as he said my name again. The butler didn't lurk behind pillars in the hall to eavesdrop. He flowed away from us unobtrusively.

I extended my hand immediately and walked across the tiled anteroom. An unusually assertive approach was part of Bluff Number Two.

"Hello, Mr. Gant. I'm Nyla Wade from Denver. I purchased Cybil Porter's desk from Randolph recently. Surely William mentioned it to you?"

His wrinkle deepened; we stood in the hallway, holding our handshake: my hand in his, my bluff challenging his puzzlement.

"Cybil's desk? I don't recall anything about a desk that was hers."

"Actually the desk belonged to Maye Della Porter but apparently Cybil used it exclusively during her lifetime here at Porterfield. I spoke to William only briefly on the phone, explaining I might stop in while I was here visiting my aunt. Is he around?"

"Who?"

"William."

There must have been a dearth of souls who called William Porter by his first name. Lucky bravado from me; it unsettled Mr. Gant. He had a small head and fine black hair, blinking black eyelashes, smooth cheeks. No wedding ring and very soft hands.

"Oh, no. He's left for a brief appointment. I expect him back in an hour or so."

He stopped, a cue for me to ask to wait, to suggest tea until William returned, to tell him more about why I was there with no warning of my visit.

"I'm a writer, you see, Mr. Gant. In fact, I'm working on a novel right now. I can't tell you what a luxury it is to be working at Cybil's masterful desk."

I began to wander a few steps toward the study where the butler had fetched the secretary. Peter made a quick step in front of me, agitated but anxious to appear polite and poised.

"Ms. Wade, did you have a specific request from Mr. Porter?"

"You mean William?"

Peter's eyelashes fluttered. He adjusted his glasses. "Yes."

"Only to see a small portion of the estate. But especially where Cybil's desk was located, where she used to work. Oh and any pictures there are of her."

"Pictures? Of Cybil?" He was genuinely dismayed.

"Why yes, wouldn't there be pictures? Of Spencer, Cybil, Lawrence, of everyone?" Play it, innocent and nonplussed, but familiar with the family.

"Well yes, there are a few still in the left wing, I suppose."

Try some entreaty with charm. Peter's eyes met mine. "I'd really like to see them."

"Ms. Wade, I think perhaps I should offer you tea until Mr. Porter returns. You should no doubt see him personally since you spoke with him on the phone."

I couldn't let myself be stalled now; time was awasting and there was no question that the face before me would reveal a million secrets before the one I'd seen in the limousine would reveal a one.

"But Mr. Gant . . . " I oozed charm tinged with beseeching. I put my hand on his arm. "Mr. Porter told me on the phone that I could contact you if he was not available. And my aunt is expecting me back soon. She's not well, so she must be watched closely. I only have a few minutes."

"Yes, but Mr. Porter is quite strict about visitors and he's the one who knows all the details of the family history."

I dug my fingers into his arm ever so slightly.

"I won't disturb a thing. The truth is, Peter . . . " His black eyes swept from his arm and my hand upon it up to my eyes where he searched for escape. He swallowed, fearful and yet entranced.

"The truth is that the desk figures prominently in this new plot of mine. It's a romance novel . . . " I was breathy now. "Set right here in Rochester. And the Porters are . . . well . . . sort of a model for my characters. Only a model but . . . " Gant was absolutely petrified I would move in closer to him. "I've been writing for many years now and I'm finally on the brink of a success. There is an atmosphere here that only a writer's eye could detect. I knew it when I bought the desk and even more so after I talked with Randolph. But the clincher was when I walked up the magnificent lane that is the gateway to this estate. I only need a few minutes of your time. Just a look at the main floor. I'm not after gossip, Mr. Gant. *Peter . . .* " I clamped my own intense look upon him. "I am only after a few minutes of genuine atmosphere in Cybil's home."

I increased the pressure of my fingers. He jerked slightly. "It would mean ever so much to me, Peter. If you could just take me through a few of the rooms."

"I don't know, Ms. Wade . . . "

He moved away; I moved with him, symbiotic, my hand with his arm. He took a deep breath, looked back down the hall to the door as if the butler was still with us, as if William might return unexpectedly and demand an explanation for this stranger in the house.

"Oh, I guess it would be all right."

"Thank you! Thank you, I knew you wouldn't fail me."

Ebullient, I gave his shoulder a squeeze and he moved immediately out of my reach, his hair glistening, politely moist at the temples. I was convinced a lively dialogue with Peter would elicit some involuntary responses from him, information that would not seem important or revealing to him. He didn't strike me as the cool, collected type I had expected. A sensitive heart lurked beneath that pale blue coat. I could reach him through that heart.

"You know, from my talks with Randolph, I've almost come to know the Porter family as if they were my own. They're such an interesting bunch, don't you think? Well probably not, since you work for them. But Randolph told me some very amusing and colorful stories."

"They're a colorful family, all right."

"His grandmother in Virginia was a horsewoman, wasn't she? And an aviator?" I thought rapidly back to all the articles I had consumed at the library. "No doubt she got her hand in on the selection for those fine Virginia thoroughbreds. I see that 'Lucky Dancer' made the family proud again last year at Belmont."

"Yes." Peter and I walked slowly toward the study. When I stepped into the room, I was immediately quiet. Peter probably thought this was my way of awaiting his remarks as tour guide. But in fact, here I was, easier than I ever imagined, standing in the very room where Cybil Porter worked at our special desk. Despite the blurred news photos of her, I didn't need any clearer pictures of what went on here. I could imagine it all: Cybil at the desk, writing to W. Stone and keeping one arm slightly curved over the top of the page; Cybil standing at the fireplace conferring with Spencer; Cybil making mock chase of Lawrence around the ottoman, greeting guests and making grand entrances. There was a sense in the room of a woman I never knew except as she was reported and observed by others. Yet I did know her, perhaps better than some of her own family, for I had been privy to her innermost thoughts for W. Stone and their secret liaison. I wanted now more than ever to understand more about her and what I could do with her single, crucial letter.

Peter was busily and hurriedly covering what he had been working on at a large corner desk.

"You wanted to see some of the main rooms. I expect this was where Cybil worked. This room has always been a working study, though Spencer had a separate office at the back of the house just off the carriage way."

"So he could come and go for his appointments?"

"I expect so."

"My, my, these big windows let in so much light. And look at the courtyard. Oh yes, this *must* have been Cybil's study because I'll bet that yard is in full bloom in spring, isn't it?"

He took a step toward me but looked beyond me toward the yard.

"Yes, it's beautiful. We even have a private greenhouse out there. Some of the flowers are hybrids developed here on the estate."

He was slightly less tense as he pointed out the small structure near the back of the carriage house.

"It must be so special to have flowers all year round. What with the greenhouse, I mean." I made my sigh tell untold stories of a life without springtime. Peter stared at me, not moving away. Then he smiled.

"Yes, yes, it is."

I headed for the fireplace, examining the inlaid tile in the mantel and the sweep.

"Did she have fires often? I do imagine her working in front of a fire."

"I'm sure they did. But I didn't ever know Cybil, you see. Or Spencer. Or even Lawrence."

"Certainly not Spencer, since he died in . . . when was that? Oh yes, '42. Heart attack, wasn't it?"

"I understand that it was."

"Too bad. I'm sure the family had the best of specialists for him. Did he have a history of that trouble? Randolph portrayed him quite differently. A swimmer, a racer, very robust."

"Yes, he was that."

When Gant hesitated after his statement, it was apparent that there was more to the story. But I was still a relative stranger. I took a step toward him and lowered my voice.

"It doesn't quite fit, you see. His death by heart attack."

Peter's face flushed. "Why, what do you mean?"

"In my romance novel. How would it look? Here's this hearty socializer, frequent to the races, sails off the Cape every summer, brisk swim every morning and all. Can't have him dropping dead in his tracks at a dinner party. No, no. The family would have to have some knowledge of heart trouble, don't you think? Wouldn't that play better?"

"I see what you mean. In your story, I mean. Well, death in fiction is certainly more calculable than it is in life. But when you model characters on real people, don't forget that some are too proud to admit to physical problems. That might play quite well, actually."

"Oh, I know what you mean. Stubborn pride can run in a family, can't it? Take Spencer and William: not at all the same on the surface, but that underlying pride is there."

"Oh, absolutely," Peter nodded his small head resolutely. My bluff was working, my pretense of knowledge of the Porters.

"You've not been with the family long, then?"

Peter didn't answer but frowned again.

"I mean, Cybil died in 1970 and you say you didn't know her."

"I've been here since 1972 and that seems quite awhile to me in terms of my own job history. But no, not in terms of service to the Porters. I came here when the estate was finally being settled after Cybil's death. In fact, one of my first duties was the dispensing of much of her property. Some family heirlooms which she used exclusively were given away. I don't remember a thing about a desk, though. William must have done that on his own."

"Randolph said he only sold the desk two years ago. Was the desk that's in this room always the one here since you came to work?"

"Yes. Perhaps William had the other one in storage."

"Perhaps."

It was all that I could do not to blurt out, "What heirlooms did you dispense? Why did William give them away? Were any given to W. Stone?" But I had to maintain some strategy. I stopped just short of batting my eyelashes at Peter; it was so obvious that he was enjoying our conversation.

Ethics, Wade. Politics, Wade. But what about getting the story, Wade? My conflicted emotions were having a heyday Peter Gant would never have guessed.

"Did William have a secretary before you? Surely there is so much to do in his business."

"Yes, my uncle, Simon Gant, was with William for more than thirty years. When he retired in 1972, I was recommended to succeed him. Our family has been connected with the Porters for many years."

"Born and bred New Yorkers, no doubt."

"We are indeed."

"Like the Lavernbys?" I was testing.

"We're a step or ten down from their bank account but not their breeding," he smiled.

"And what about Cybil? I know Walling was her family name." Her wedding announcement from the newspaper morgue had told me that. "I'm trying to get a picture of the major families in Rochester. All part of the background for the novel, you know." And hopefully, Stone is one of the names I'll hear among this list.

"Cybil's family originated in Michigan, I believe. But Rochester became the family home and she was very much of Spencer's ilk here."

"She was a Brentwood girl, no doubt?"

"It's possible; that's certainly the school you'd expect she'd have attended. But I don't really know that for sure."

I noticed a door out onto the terrace. Indicating it, I asked, "May I?"

"Of course." Gant swung open the door for me; I saw to it that he caught my smile full face when I passed him. Easy pigeon. This boy hasn't had attention in a long time.

"It's chilly out here. But what a view. Almost as good as the towers, I bet."

Peter was silent, surveying the courtyard through frosty breath.

"Can you see much of the city from those windows?" I leaned out over the terrace railing and strained to see part of the turret's edge, persisting about the towers. Gant put a tentative hand on my shoulder.

"Careful of that railing, Ms. Wade. I'm sure . . . "

"Can't you just see a tortured lover poised in that tower window, about to throw herself into the abyss?"

Gant mumbled, "Or *himself.*" I went on. "All for lost love. Or love unrequited. Or love gone amiss. I can see her up there, yes, clearly at the edge."

I turned quickly around almost into the dumbfounded secretary's embrace.

"*Love,* Mr. Gant, is the very essence of life!"

I stared deeply into his eyes; he was speechless.

"Not to mention the absolute fertile fodder for gothic plot and romance. It's cold out here. Shall we go in?"

He stood immobile staring first at me, then at the tower's edge above us. I felt like a boxer shifting steps to keep an opponent off-balance.

"You have several other rooms to show me? Peter?"

Slowly, ever so slowly, his eyes traveled down the facade of the house, out across the courtyard, and back to me. Had he been counting the bricks and the blooms that would come in the spring? He was hooked, and I could reel him in, find those pictures of Cybil and possibly of W. Stone.

We moved on to a sitting room, empty of everything except a piano, fireplace, and chairs in front of the piano.

"This was used as a small ballroom when Spencer entertained here. No one plays now, of course."

"That's sad. No music in William?"

"No."

"What about you, Peter? I bet you could pick out a tune."

"Well no, I have no formal training . . . " Gant looked longingly at the piano.

"Come on," I coaxed. "If this room had ears, they'd be full of lonely dust. No one's around. Play something. Please, for me."

Gant looked at me and then at the piano. I nodded my head toward it and so he walked a little stiffly over and sat down at the bench. I noticed how little noise he made when he slid the bench forward; this was not the first time. Effortlessly, he began a sweet concerto, lilting music. When he stopped and quietly closed the lid over the keys, he was blushing.

"Bravo, oh bravo, Peter!" I did a few grand dance steps around in front of him at the piano; when I stopped, I held the position a moment and said to him: "Think of it. The heroine, in her older years, alone in this small ballroom, only her memories to keep her company. And she thinks of the young lover who played Brahms for her." I let my gesture follow back toward Peter at the piano, and he blushed again.

"This way, Ms. Wade, to the dining room."

We passed a breakfast nook warm from sunlight and then went into the formal dining room, with its predictable long table and handsome set of heavy chairs.

"That is all there is on the main floor, Ms. Wade, except the kitchen."

"Well, I do appreciate your showing me around, Peter. You did mention some pictures in the left wing. Could I see those?"

His black eyes closed quickly again but opened with more than general hesitance behind them. He checked his watch. I could feel the minutes ticking away.

"Oh, please, just a quick look."

I knew the pictures could be crucial to me, to get a final sense of Cybil and of course, to ask Peter about W. Stone. He seemed to be flagging and so did my own strategy for flirtation. Then he surprised me.

"Very well. But I warn you, it's cold. That wing of the house has been sealed off for winter so all the heat is off."

Through a maze of doors and hallways, we found our way to the wing in question. Peter was telling the truth: a wave of cold air bit right through my coat as we entered the hall running the length of the wing. It was even more quiet in this space than in the other part of the house. Curtains had been drawn so most of the rooms were quite dark.

"The pictures are in the den at the very back."

Our footsteps echoed against the walls. Perhaps this was really a time tunnel or that crucial window that would show me more clearly Cybil's life. When we reached the den, Peter pulled one curtain back and as a lance of light came into the room, a familiar and frightening tingling rippled up my spine, settling at the base of my neck. I stepped immediately back out into the hall up against the wall outside the door. I felt faint for a moment, pushed on my diaphragm again, and tried to breathe deeply. Swimming behind my eyes was black murkiness and beating its way through that blackness was the orchid, the pulsating, persistent, purple orchid. Damn it, I'm no fainting woman! When will that flower behave!

The feeling passed just as Peter appeared with his questioning wrinkle formed above his eyes.

"You all right, Ms. Wade?"

"Absolutely. I just thought I heard someone call from the door."

He leaned around me to look.

"Isabelle, maybe. Nosy cook. Never liked her a bit."

He winked. Had a less constrained man passed with me into this sealed space?

"Smells a bit musty back here. Well, there are the pictures. On the mantel."

Peter urged me gently back into the room. I was sure he wondered why I suddenly seemed to drag my feet but I didn't want to look toward the mantel and see a crimson jungle of thrashing blossoms that were invisible to him. I went to the window instead of the mantel, grabbing a handful of curtain, squaring myself in sunlight as if it were my exorcist or my sacred cross for protection from the orchid. With my back to Peter, I asked, "Why is this wing closed off? Heating, did you say?"

I could tell Peter was still bewildered by my avoidance of the pictures I had come to see. He was watching me, perhaps deciding this tour was a mistake after all.

"Is it really so expensive to heat?" I asked again, turning back to him. But I found that he was not watching me at all; he had picked up a racket of some sort and was swinging it back and forth.

"What?" He looked up. "Oh, I am sorry. I really enjoy tennis . . ."

He held up the racket and it was my turn to offer a quizzical glance.

"This was Larry's, no doubt . . . that is, Lawrence." He motioned to other objects in the room. "Quite a lot of this was his."

"Larry's death was a major tragedy for the family, I'm sure." As I wandered toward a couch, I thought about the article describing the accident. There were some pictures on an end table by the couch. Mostly of William and a younger man. "Is this Lawrence?"

Gant brought his racket with him to check out the pictures.

"Yes. They used to hunt together. Even went for big game once. Or so my Uncle Simon tells me. He arranged all that sort of thing."

In all three of the pictures, William was sober but Lawrence was smiling; in one picture, he had his arm around his uncle's shoulders.

"Does your uncle talk much to you about the Porters? Lawrence, for instance: he lost his father very young. I suppose William was then a sort of father-figure to him."

"Oh yes. Lawrence's memory is one of the few things that livens Mr. Porter. Having never married, Lawrence was the son he never himself had."

"Why do you suppose he didn't marry?"

I had my back to the mantel; feeling slightly more confident, I turned and headed toward it. The tingle of warning didn't reoccur. The room grew less dim. Peter grew more talkative there in the cold and closed-up left wing.

"He's a very serious sort. I think the family business was always his passion. And of course, he didn't have the physique or good looks like Spencer did. Spencer loved being out in the fray of people and their problems. Sometimes I really think my uncle and I should have reversed lifetimes. He was fond of William but found Spencer much too enthusiastic. Said he let people take advantage of him. Said he was too casual with money. And of course, Uncle Simon felt that Spencer should have taken a more firm hand with Cybil. But I think it was Spencer's plan to let her run things. So he could just enjoy."

"Perhaps he was a tennis player too?"

"I'm sure of it. And I'll bet he had a killer serve."

Peter took a swat or two with the racket, as if he was imagining

Spencer's deadly serve spinning toward him.

"Cybil didn't join him in the games then?"

"No, I don't think so. Well, maybe for awhile. Simon told me she had some arthritis and went yearly to a spa for treatment."

Peter's mention of the spa caught my interest. W. Stone had mentioned the spa in the special letter about the hidden places by the lake. I swallowed hard, trying to appear casual.

"Another luxury of the well-to-do, spas. Wish I could go when my bones ache. Was it close by?"

Gant was still swinging the racket, making small noises. "Pow, pow!" In his imagining, Spencer was not racking up aces.

"What's that? Was what close by?"

"The spa."

"No . . . in Florida, I think. But I don't know the name."

There it was, a crucial connection. W. Stone's letters from Jacksonville and the spa in Florida. It was all I could do not to blurt out my excitement. But Peter didn't seem to notice.

"Ms. Wade, I don't know any of this about the Porters for a fact; I've only just gathered most of it from the few remarks my uncle has made. And also from what Uncle Simon and Mr. Porter *don't* say. Their silence is often very telling."

"Oh, how's that?"

I began picking up objects, giving Gant my back. He followed me now with his story, trying to command my interest with his gossip.

"I have noticed on a number of occasions that Mr. Porter will speak about the funerals. Spencer's and especially Lawrence's. But he never mentions Cybil's funeral. That is one funeral he simply will not discuss."

When I turned, we nearly bumped into one another. Peter retreated slightly and I followed him, speaking confidentially.

"You know, Peter, when I talked to Randolph, he intimated that . . . well, not in so many words . . . just hinting, that William and Cybil had a long-standing sort of feud going on between them. Is there any truth to that?"

Peter didn't confirm this immediately. He paced around the couch and the stuffed chairs, rolling the racket in his hands. Then he stopped in the doorway, surveyed the hall and then turned back to me.

"I don't have the trust with William that Uncle Simon did. I get to do my job but there's something missing. I'm not a *trusted* man, you know? He doesn't hide anything exactly, I don't mean that. But we don't have a rapport past business. Not like he had with Simon. I think he was William's confidant. I think . . . " He paused, narrowing his eyes, checking the hallway again and then speaking more softly. "I think that neither Mr. Porter nor Uncle Simon cared much for Cybil. I think my uncle watched her ever so carefully. He may even have done some tasks for William that were, well, above and beyond the normal call of duty."

I nearly whispered my response. "You mean . . . like . . . spying on Cybil?"

Gant took a deep breath. "Possibly. He just kept an extra sharp eye on Cybil's business. It chapped him that she handled the estate rather than William after Spencer died."

"Chapped them both, I'm sure."

"Uncle Simon likes to talk about the Porters in one way: their power, their grander scale of life. But as to details, he is a rock of silence. Nothing rolls out of him about his life here that he hasn't carefully considered before he says it."

"Then working here with William, him being a sober sort, must make you somewhat lonely at times, Peter. A man of your . . . obvious good nature and special temperament."

Peter let his eyes meet mine again to give his answer. For all that I wanted him to tell me, this was not a moment I could misuse. I changed the subject to avoid his vulnerability.

"So . . . to the pictures on the mantel. And then I'll leave you to your work again, Peter."

And to William soon too, I thought, if I don't get moving. But I still hadn't brought up W. Stone. That was the name I hoped to find a history for here, a living history.

There were about eight photographs in frames on the mantel, groups of men and women: friends and family, candid together staring back at me from their own time. There she was, with an uncommon face: not a beautiful woman but one who had an admirable look about her. Cybil Porter was neither horsey nor lovely. She had a slightly wide face, but there was strong bearing to it. She was a woman who could say no and not give up any of her generosity with that action. As I looked at the pictures, I wondered if that look could be cultivated. Wondered if it could in these times, when it is still hard for women to say no to men and yes to each other. I was sure the man in one of the pictures with Cybil was Spencer; he held a ruggedness under the polish. He wore a long coat with broad shoulders, had slick black hair and a black mustache. He had a square jaw and an open smile. No doubt he had a twinkle in his eye and he could toss his hat from the door so that it landed right on the rack.

In two of the photographs, William appeared, and in another two unidentified women and a man. I took a deep breath. Could this be W. Stone? Dare I ask?

"Peter, who are these people with Spencer and Cybil? Friends or family?"

He was preoccupied with a nautical sextant but came over and gave the pictures a glance.

"That's Spencer's sister Dorothy and her husband."

No luck for me in this mirage. No W. Stone in the photographs. My hopes were dashed. I almost forgot about the other woman in the picture but Peter absolutely livened as he identified her.

"This woman with Dorie and Red is Sheila Rush, Cybil's best friend. She still lives here in Rochester. She's of the Whitmore-Rush people. William never liked her but she was great friends with Spencer. I know that because she's told me so. I love any party where Sheila appears. She speaks her mind but she's never left off a guest list in this town. She's still the toast of some circles."

"She's nearly in her eighties though, isn't she?"

"Indeed. With eighty years of interesting stories to tell."

"Rush, Rush . . . wasn't that the home where Spencer fell ill?"

"I believe you're right. The two families were nearly inseparable according to Uncle Simon's accounts."

Peter Gant had handed me treasure in the photograph even if he hadn't handed me W. Stone. If Sheila Rush would see me, I might be on to something. She might not balk at the mention of W. Stone. She sounded as if she was a woman after Cybil's own heart.

"Well, this is all there is to show you, Ms. Wade."

"Do call me Nyla."

Gant blushed again. "Yes, well . . . I hope this very brief tour of the house will help with your . . . atmosphere for the novel. And I wish you the best of success with it . . . Nyla."

He dropped his eyes from mine and took a step toward the door.

"I do thank you, Peter, very much for . . . "

My words to signal departure were interrupted by the sound of a car coming up the drive. The slightly opened curtain revealed that wide black nose again of the limousine. William Porter had returned. My god, I wanted to get out without seeing him! But Peter didn't seem disturbed at all by his return.

"Ah, Mr. Porter is home. I'm sure he'll want to speak to you. Let's get out of this wing anyway. It's freezing."

I had only a second to get out; with nothing to lose, I put my question to Peter.

"Tell me, Peter, you remember you said you dispensed some of Cybil's property when you first came to work here. Did she bequeath anything to a friend named W. Stone?"

He did not color or startle or show any recognition of the name.

"She did not bequeath anything because, despite the fact that she and Spencer had a will, many of her personal possessions were not bestowed specifically to anyone. And many of the possessions she used were not in fact hers. They were family heirlooms. You see, she died rather suddenly so I understand."

"So you don't recognize that name? I thought perhaps it was another of her close friends."

I didn't say where I got the name. Suppose he mentions this to William? Suppose William finds this out before I get out of this house? Then he'll know I've been snooping about. I can't pin it on Randy either because that would check out amiss also.

"Peter . . . " I stepped up close to him again; he didn't retreat but took my confidence readily. "You have been so considerate in showing me Cybil's study and these pictures. I assure you my plot is based only loosely on the Porters, so any details you've given me will be kept in confidence. But I would like to credit you in the novel, if that's all right with you." I didn't lie; he would get credit if I ever wrote the thing. "But Peter, I have a confession to make."

Some psychological wizard once wrote that dependence in women encourages even the weakest male ego. I hoped the wizard was right.

"When I spoke to William recently, he was not at all thrilled about my being a writer. I think he wondered why I wasn't making a home and babies. I recognize in you a truly contemporary man without such outmoded values. And now I need your help for one more favor."

Gant began to flush slightly red at the neck.

"You can guess I'm not just a busybody. The most you can say for my invasion into Porter privacy is that you told me the courtyard is in full bloom in springtime. Now that's a scene I can't wait to write. The heroine amidst those flowers . . . " I paused, holding my breath of hope that Gant was on my side. He was getting squirmy and redder by the moment. "I've appreciated your taking me seriously, Peter, and now I would like this conversation and my visit kept personal between us."

The puzzled gathering in Peter's forehead appeared fleetingly as the flush in his neck dissipated. Then he smiled, and squeezed one of my hands. Not a smile that said he thought he'd been taken and had just figured it out. This was the smile of a believer. He bought the bait; he was going to help me out. Moving with new confidence to take my arm, he told me with a twinkle of adventure in his dark eyes, "I understand. We can go out past the greenhouse right from this wing. When I return by the front, they'll just think I was out for a walk. The butler will stay mum, I'll see to that too. I'll walk you to your car, Nyla."

As my escape was inevitable, I told him with relief, "William doesn't know what he's missing, Peter. You are indeed a trusted man." As we dropped the curtain back over the window and headed out of the sealed wing, as we passed through the doorway no more than two short steps toward the greenhouse, I caught a moment's strong scent of orchids.

TEN

Two Monkeys on One Back

Having eluded William Porter twice on his own doorstep and gained access to Porterfield and the malleable Peter Gant, I still had little of substance to show for my trip. Back at my hotel, I sat for almost two hours making notes, rereading the articles, reviewing dates: shifting the information I had like puzzle pieces and coming up with too many blanks. I made two phone calls: one to Brentwood School, to be told that Cybil Walling did not attend that illustrious bastion of Eastern education any time during the years 1920-25. Luckily the snippet I had previously wrangled with was off-duty so I talked with a very cooperative apprentice records keeper. My other phone call was to an anxious Audrey Louise. I gave her a briefing about my visit with Gant, though she interrupted me constantly.

"Did Gant know about the Party of Four present at Lawrence's accident? What was the color scheme in the breakfast nook? Did William Porter look like a man who could harm his nephew? Did the butler say 'You rang?' And what was the *real* reason the towers were locked?"

She was as disappointed as I to learn that Gant had no knowledge of W. Stone. I told her I planned to have an early supper and a long sleep, then would try to visit Sheila Rush the next day as well as Cybil's grave before I headed home. I gave up the idea of a train ride into New York City and a flight out of there after a quick glance at my checkbook. I had to relinquish Audrey Louise's fifty to the hotel and then some. I would have to finish my pondering swiftly, among the clouds. Besides, a train ride would have made it impossible for me to make my date at Bevo's Lounge.

Before we rang off, I asked Audrey Louise to call the phone company and order me a Jacksonville, Florida, phone book. She agreed enthusiastically to the errand and wondered if there was anything else she could do.

"Joel's brother is a banker, you know. I bet we could get him to check the Porter accounts. Just for fun. Nothing amiss, I'm sure. But you know, I'll tell him it's for a friend."

"How can a Colorado banker get access to account information in New York, Audrey Louise?"

"They have those handy computers," she said and I knew she was smiling. "Interstate link-up and other marvels of technology. Wouldn't hurt to ask, Nyla Wade."

"Ask away, sweetie, ask away."

The hotel I had distractedly chosen was a small, old establishment but one permeated with the gentle charm of unpretentious decor and faultless service. My room was not impersonal and full of the stale ghosts of previous guests. Instead the linen was crisp and fresh, the light in the room precisely between cheer and gloom, and the "bellboy" a delight: a round-faced brunette no more than a girlish fifteen, who was happy to bring me not just tea but chamomile and orange-spice brewed together.

"I snuck you a side of cream," she winked at me. "Just the way the English do." She had her pockets all stuffed and bulging, and she whistled down the hall when she left me. She even wore an old-fashioned square bellboy's hat, the kind I was sure had gone completely out of use.

I found the dining room in the hotel followed suit with my other accommodations. I was served with exquisite attention by not one but two waiters. I was seated and given a menu by an older man with very broad shoulders and a crinkly but quiet smile. He spoke so softly that I had to ask him twice about the soup of the day. Vichyssoise, of course. When I settled on beef bourguignon for my main course, I was invited to the "salad sampler" by a tall swarthy boy. I could tell by his voice that he was at least in his early twenties although he looked younger. Slender, with black eyes and oiled black hair, when he slipped my chair back, he did not touch me to indicate the salad sampler, but placed his hand very near my arm and bowed slightly toward a cart across the room. Here was someone who understood rather than assumed the meaning of politeness.

For all my preoccupation with the Porters and W. Stone, I enjoyed my meal and my dinner attendants so completely that I forgot about the missing pieces to the puzzle. I basked in contentment and once back in my room, pulled up the comforter and almost drifted off to sleep without so much as putting on my pj's. I awoke to the alarm of one of those instinctive clocks within each of us, realizing I intended to give Sheila Rush a call and set up a meeting with her. It was nine p.m.

The phone number was listed under Leonard's name and rang six times before anyone answered. I was about to give up when a woman's voice informed me that Sheila Rush would be to the phone shortly. Again I waited, this time for more than several minutes, until a voice greeted me: "Sheila Rush here. Though by no means true to my name this evening. Pardon the wait. Do I know you, Ms. Wade?"

My trepidacious heart lurched and then loosened at the sound of her voice; here was an instant friend, a well-wisher even to a stranger over the phone.

"We have not met but we share a mutual friend: Cybil Porter."

"My heart's delight, Cybil. Gone from us before anyone was ready to give her up. Are you a relative? She had so many adoring cousins."

"No, I'm not a relative. I'm not even from this state. My connection with Cybil will take a few minutes to explain."

"Now that I've made it to the phone, I have the time. Do go on."

"I'd like to arrange to see you for a few minutes tomorrow, Mrs. Rush. Then I can tell you the whole story."

"Do persist for now, my dear. We can arrange the meeting later. I'm most intrigued."

I took a deep breath, prayed for clarity and brevity, and began. I explained simply about the desk, my conversations with Randy Porter, and my avid interest as a writer in romance novels, antiques, and old letters. Sheila listened without interruption until I finished. I had not played my aces, however: mention either of the real letters, the construed note left in the desk, or the name W. Stone.

"What is it that I can do for you then, Ms. Wade? Give you more background information for your novel, based only *vaguely* on the Porters, of course. Is that what you wish from me?"

"Yes, Mrs. Rush, and also to fill in some details about Cybil. Just, I suppose, because the desk she used has become so important in my life. Somehow I feel her presence when I am writing there."

"I don't wonder," she responded, her voice fading. She paused a moment; despite the fact that I did feel Cybil's presence at the desk and that was no lie, I wondered if Sheila Rush would be as suspicious as William Porter or as hesitant as Peter Gant as she considered a meeting with me. But she proved instead to be as forthright as Randy had been.

"I would be happy to talk to you tomorrow. Shall we say brunch about 11:30? Perhaps we'll have a warmer day and we can eat under huge quilts out on the terrace. I love that variety. The pool is completely frozen over and I'm afraid my people think such things are quite crazy of me, but I like to do it anyway. We'll hope for that."

For that and for so much more, I'll be hoping, I thought to myself as I hung up the phone. My entry into Porterfield and now my appointment with Sheila Rush so far had gone well. Yet I had only a flimsy story, glimpses of connection in conversations, faded newsprint, and my own ever-changing theory. I hoped I was on the verge of a telling conversation with Sheila Rush. I heard no hesitance in her voice. Eighty years of interesting stories to tell, Peter had said, and probably there was no fear left in her for anyone, either, after eighty years of independent living in the closed community of the Rochester rich.

Yawning, I stretched and got into my pj's; I stepped into the bathroom to brush my teeth. With my back to the door, I washed my face and inspected for premature wrinkles in the mirror. As I was leaning up close to the mirror, I heard a sound like something brushing against my door. I thought it must be the bellboy again rushing down the hall. I went on with my inspection, ever wary for the first sign of crow's feet, especially near my left eye. Left, the sinister side of my face that always started to frown first. Whether with worry or wisdom didn't matter; it was wrinkles all the same.

Again I heard the brushing noise. When I turned and looked down at the bottom of the door, the light coming underneath it from the hall was blocked in the middle, as if someone was standing there.

"Hello?" I called out, fairly loudly. No sound or movement. "Hello? Is that you, Stanley? For petessakes, it took you long enough to get the ice. Here, I'll open the door for you."

I hoped the ruse would discourage anyone who was standing at the door. Somewhat nervously, I went to the door and rattled the handle and the chain as if I was about to open it. When I stepped back to look again at the bottom of the door, immediately the blocked light disappeared and I heard footsteps receding softly.

There was no question in my mind that none of the hotel people would have any interest in eavesdropping on me. I doubted that my Denver watchers had any use for following me to New York. All of Audrey Louise's comments began to worm their way into my thoughts as I went over to my balcony window and looked through the filmy curtain out into the hotel parking lot.

"You may think you're sifting through ash and find one live fire ... too many accidents in that family if you ask me ... you'll be on *his* territory ... you're rattling a closet full of someone else's skeletons ... "

If it hadn't had a polish that glistened even in moonlight, the long black car might well have passed out of the lot innocently into traffic. I watched it, knowing even before it slid into the night that it was out there. But why did William have me followed? What had most disturbed him about my appearance in his town?

The Rush home was several miles north of Porterfield; I had to ring an intercom when I reached the gate. As I drove underneath the stone archway announcing Whitmore-Rush Estate in carved letters, I felt so much more relaxed than I had yesterday rounding the short drive to William Porter's home. I drove another quarter mile in from the gate down a tree-lined road and still could not see the house until a sharp left bend. There it sat in an unexpected hollow. Though the trees were bare now, I imagined that the ones along the road and those around the house in full leaf would clearly rival the blooming Porter courtyard in springtime.

I took a great breath of winter air, felt the chill of the wind through my coat and the crunch of my shoes on the stones as I went to the front door. The house looked high and narrow from the outside: brownstone with a lighter stone set in around the windows and vine fully covering one part of the front facade. I would remember that detail for Audrey Louise. I awaited a butler who might open the door and say, "You rang?"

The smile I had as I thought about Audrey Louise matched the one on the face of a small Spanish woman who opened the door for me. She was dressed casually in a skirt and sweater, with glasses on a chain resting on her bosom.

"Ms. Wade?" I nodded.

"Come in. We've been expecting you."

I was escorted down a carpeted hall with walls lined by portraits of men and women from various centuries. The gilded frames reminded me of a movie set—I hadn't imagined anyone had this many illustrious relatives or enough money to frame all these affected faces. When I looked up, we were approaching the end of the hall. From the wide doorway, colored light flowed out over us through an immense stained glass window, set nearly to the ceiling of the end room. The design in the window was of a Madonna and Child. The rich blue, green, and yellow light fell over my shoes and the bottom of my skirt like invisible paint. Sandwiched between the sensory exposure of the histrionic portraits and the vivid stained glass, I stood for a moment before I noticed Sheila Rush waiting in the doorway.

"Gaudy as hell, don't you think?"

I heard her voice and recognized in it again companionable warmth. Sheila Rush swept a long arm toward the hallway.

"All those silly portraits, I mean. But . . . that's Leonard for you. Getting every blasted member of the family into a frame was his project."

I must have seemed entranced, for she came toward me and took my arm.

"Come in, come in."

As I walked with her through the curtain of prismed light, again she drew her arm across her chest in that sweeping gesture toward the window.

121

"I love this house, you know. And this window is one of my favorite features. Though our parents had great respect for religion, they had no guess at the irony of this window. Madonna and Child, you see. Leonard and I were never destined to be parents. But if one is going to have a woman looking over her shoulder, the Madonna does quite well."

She looked up at the window and at the Madonna.

"We're old and dear friends after all these years."

With her face in the light, I took a good look at her. Sheila Rush at nearly eighty was a woman who did not get smaller as she aged. She was thin and she had an enviably slender waist. She wore a mauve dress with a deep purple overgown that resembled an open kimono. Her white hair still held its own full wave. She was tall and graceful in her movements.

As I was about to ask, "Perhaps I'll meet Leonard also?", Sheila put her hand to her face and said, still pondering the Madonna: "Maybe that's what I'll put on my tombstone. 'Woman with a Madonna Over Her Shoulder.' That ought to give the lot of them a laugh!"

She laughed and headed for one of the great armchairs in front of a hearty midday fire. I followed her, wondering how she could joke about death and appear so full of life. When I sat down, she read my perplexity.

"Never mind me, dear. I have a group of friends rare and rowdy for this city and they love a bizarre joke. However, as things have gone, I'll be reading their tombstones before they read mine. Have you seen the one for Cybil?"

"No. I was planning to go to Crestlawn on my way out of town."

"Well," she said, putting one white hand upon my arm, "that sneak William saw to it that her stone is smaller than Spencer's or Larry's. It sits there like an oversight. And she did so much to benefit him."

The Spanish woman who had answered the door arrived soundlessly with tea for both of us.

"Thank you, Yolanda," Sheila told her.

"I'm going to see Arthur Lester this afternoon, Sheila. Do you want to go with me?" Yolanda asked.

"Oh, splendid!" Sheila clapped her hands. "I can beat him at backgammon and he makes the most marvelous daiquiris! Absolutely, dear. What time shall we go?"

"Say, two o'clock? I'll bet we can coax him into cornish game hens if we stay too long."

"You are a devil, Yolanda!"

"I had the best of teachers."

They laughed together and Sheila Rush put out both hands to Yolanda. She took them in her own and leaned down to give Sheila a kiss on the cheek.

"Warm enough?"

"Don't fuss over me." Sheila's tone was playful.

"Enjoy your talk." Yolanda smiled at me and then left us.

"She's been with me for years," Sheila said as Yolanda left us. "She's a godsend." She sipped her tea. I backtracked to our interrupted conversation.

"I'm not too surprised about the gravestone. Randy Porter intimated to me that William and Cybil never got along very well. When I spoke to William, he was rather crisp in his mention of her."

"William is a stuffy snob who would cross the street to avoid a decent soul. He's an empty spirit, you know. Did you meet him?"

"Not exactly, but I saw him."

"Grey looking, isn't he? Empty, I tell you. A feud with Cybil was simply one among many. I'm feuding with him myself."

"Why's that?"

Sheila shifted in her chair so that she turned fully to face me. She set her teacup down deliberately and picked her words in the same way.

"William was very . . . selfish . . . about the funeral for Cybil."

"Yes, I understand it was quite hurried. Closed casket, no wake. Why didn't he have the funeral back here in the states, among her friends and the family?"

"Why indeed. To deprive us all of any public show of sympathy, of course. When it comes to selfishness, that man is an expert. Do you know he held the so-called 'memorial service' without letting anyone know? Most of us read about it in the paper. Oh well, that was in keeping with his behavior for years. No generosity in those bones. William has spent his whole life being jealous of Spencer, hateful to Cybil, and strict with poor Lawrence, who, in spite of William's obvious lack of humanity, loved him dearly."

"Lawrence's accident must have been quite a blow."

Sheila pushed her teacup away in disgust.

"A blow for everyone. The final blow for Cybil to be sure. As for William, that was the only time I ever saw him show any feeling for anyone. You know, they had no business out hunting anyway. Lawrence never liked to hunt; he only went because that was one of William's favorite games. The peculiar entertainment of exploding small creatures with too much firepower."

Sheila put her hand to her face and then frowned.

"William is too much like Bernard, you see. Bernard, his father, had a jealous heart too."

"Who was he jealous of?"

"Maye Della, of course . . . his wife."

Sheila rose slowly, leaning heavily on the arm of the chair. When she was upright, she took several steps closer to the fire and leaned one arm up on the mantel.

"You know," she chuckled, "I distinctly remember one of their fights. Cybil and I were probably . . . oh, sixteen or so. We'd all gone out to the country club for some charity thing. And they were having a skeet shoot with prizes being money awarded to the charity. Biggest skeet score, biggest donation. Now Maye Della loved to shoot skeet. She wanted to enter the little contest and win some money for the orphans of Guam or some such thing. Maye Della was steel on bone, no question, but she was also one of those rare souls who couldn't resist a sorry looking, lost creature of any kind. So anyway, Bernard was furious. He had already entered the contest and refused to let Maye Della enter. When she persisted, we heard them arguing in the lounge. 'Let me shoot a little skeet, for chrissakes, Bernie,' she said. 'Why do you always have to do this to me in front of people?' we heard him whine. I'll say this of William: at least he doesn't whine. 'Oh, buck up your pride,' Maye Della scolded Bernard. 'I'll miss a few.' 'Don't pity me, Maye Della,' he warned. 'All right then, it's to be *no* pity and *some* skeet, you stubborn man.' She thought it was settled but he said, 'It's *no* skeet at all. Not today or any day. I won't have my wife outshoot me!' With that, Bernard stomped out of the lounge. We all thought she'd stomp after him, take up her gun and fire a perfect score salvo. But she didn't."

"She gave in to him?" I set my teacup down in amazement, remembering those boots from the newspaper picture, and all those dedications, speeches, obvious activities of Maye Della's accomplishment. Surely she wouldn't back down about shooting skeet!

"Oh, no. She got a hold of Giffy Larkspur, one of Bernard's long-standing rivals, and bet him a thousand dollars to beat the pants off Bernard. For an easy thou, Giffy did just that."

We both laughed.

"That was something Cybil eventually learned from Maye Della. There are many ways to win what you want. She proved that right up to the last."

"But did she? You called Lawrence's death the final blow for Cybil and she herself followed him in death only a year later. After those many strong years fighting back all the Porter history and William's obvious disapproval of her involvement in the business, what could that last year have been like for Cybil? She must have changed drastically."

"Yes, she did that all right." There was a gathering movement in Sheila, as she stood at the mantel looking into the fire and remembering her old friend. Then she stood up straight and turned all sight of her expression away from me.

"When Lawrence was gone, I think Cybil felt her duty . . . with the family . . . was finally completed."

"With the Porter family, you mean? With William?"

"Yes, but on a more personal level as well. Her duty as a mother and wife, you see." She waited. The fire clicked and snapped before both of us.

"Yes, I think I do see. She spent most of her life as many women do, serving others with whatever talents they possess." I was glad in that moment for my own choices, my determination not to give my talent away but to serve it. Sheila's face was fervent and fire-glow warm when she turned around again, reading my mood as she spoke.

"You're exactly right, Ms. Wade. She served Spencer and Lawrence well, making a safe nest for them, preserving their comfort. But she was never an ordinary woman in that way, destined only to fulfill herself in domesticity. Destined only to live out the conventions of one era. Even before Larry died, Cybil was beginning to change the nest and make her own comfort more important. She started to paint again. That was something she'd done when we were growing up together; painting gave her great pleasure.

125

She messed up the whole of a Porterfield wing with canvas and the trappings. Made William mad as hell, of course. He still keeps that wing locked up, I understand. Lawrence was surprised but pleasantly so when Cybil was painting again. He indulged her just as Spencer had because they both sensed they could trust her completely, whatever her directions were or if they understood them."

Sheila was far away from me for a moment. Maybe she was picturing Cybil at an easel, working in a pattern of ochre and azure. I thought about that maze of dark rooms in the cold left wing of Porterfield. If I had only looked into one of them, I might have seen some of Cybil's paintings.

"Still, she succumbed so quickly after her son died, just at a point when her life was on an upswing." What I didn't surmise out loud was just at a point when she could have joined W. Stone, if he was still alive.

"Succumbed?"

The word I chose drew an intense frown across Sheila Rush's wise face.

"Cybil never *succumbed* to anyone or anything. Her son's death, William's insistent harangue, and the changes in her own life poured rapidly in on her that last year, that's true. But succumb? Never."

"I only meant the quickness of Lawrence's . . . "

"I prefer to think that Cybil was finally allowed her own desires. She went on to circumstances she deserved after years of duty well spent."

There was finality in Sheila's tone. It interested me that she used the word *circumstance;* that had been W. Stone's word as well, "the difficult circumstances" that separated him from Cybil. I had never imagined Cybil as a painter. But it fit in its own way. Perhaps that was how she expressed those innermost feelings Stone had said she was hesitant to empty out of herself.

Sheila Rush had left religion to her parents and yet she had a somewhat cosmic bent in her perspective of Cybil Porter as a soul finally released into death. I knew there was a bondage in domesticity even in Cybil's case, even with so much obvious comfort. I saw in Sheila Rush an intense understanding and sympathy for this form of constraint, but I did not sense that she herself had fallen victim to it—an enviable avoidance in her eighty years.

"Tell me, Mrs. Rush, how did you and Cybil meet? *Your* family name is part of Rochester's historic legacy. But she hailed from Michigan and did not attend Brentwood. Did you meet after she was married to Spencer?"

"My dear Ms. Wade . . . what *is* your first name?"

"Oh, I'm sorry. It's Nyla."

"Now Nyla, not everyone in the money in Rochester considers Brentwood School the ultimate in education. Most do, that's true, but my father was a curious mixture of conservative and non-conformist. He decided early on that I needed a taste of worldly experience and so he sent me to public school for my high school years. There I met Cybil Walling. I think Father thought that I would become less headstrong in competitive, mainstream schooling. Unfortunately for him, Cybil and I made a perfect team and our major goal in school was to coddle, cultivate, and carry out completely our total, headstrong personalities."

I got an immediate picture of two ornery girls arm in arm for adventures upon unsuspecting school teachers.

"When did Cybil meet Spencer?"

Sheila came back to the armchair, rubbing her arms as if she might be cold.

"I remember that day well. We were all having a picnic here. Lots of boys were here: Leonard's fancy friends, posing and bragging out on the lawn. Spencer, a little less so because he was always a gorgeous figure of a man. Anyway, they got up a game of badminton. Most of the girls were just sitting on the lawn watching. Cybil and I had sneaked up to my room because I used to pilfer my father's small mild cigars and we shared them. At one point while we were smoking, she pulled back the curtain at the window, the cigar hanging from her lips, very tough, and looked down at the boys in the game. 'That Spencer Porter isn't bad,' she told me. 'He serves almost as well as I do.' She was no dewy-eyed romantic, not Cybil."

I thought of the letters; truly W. Stone was the romantic, but Cybil's letter had a passionate tone to it, especially when she wrote, "I want to say another meeting *must* be possible." Perhaps she let more of her passion out in her paintings.

Sheila Rush went on with her story.

"Later that day, Cybil caught Spencer's eye. He tried to flirt with her but to his surprise, she would have none of it. As it was not often that he was rebuffed, he was intrigued to say the least. It wasn't until he invited her to play badminton that she would even talk to him. I think what she did was challenge him on his serve. From then on, their own private game began. And they both won certain things when they married."

"But was his world of so much affluence comfortable to her?"

"Not entirely, although her parents were well off. It was more a getting used to the whirlwind of intense and strong egos within the Porter family that took her energy. Maye Della, Spencer, and in their own way, Bernard and William. Luckily, Cybil was a quick study and was able to learn some strategy, to learn many of the customs Spencer took for granted. She admired what he could do, you see. And because he took his own position and talent for granted, he quickly passed on to her the opportunity to do many of the things she admired. In that way, they had a perfect interplay; Cybil gained gradually more and more control of her life and the Porter business, while Spencer gained more leisure time. He loved to gamble, play tennis, drive fast cars and be a very dressed-up clown. Spencer had no lack of intellect. He just wanted to use it almost entirely for play."

"Meanwhile, Cybil became a very competent business woman and hostess for Spencer's friends."

"Exactly. Maye Della and Bernard could have enjoyed the same exchange but Bernard was too resentful. But before she died, Maye Della gave Cybil a great deal of support. There was still a great cost to Cybil's energy. Spencer was kind and she respected him. They played together a lot too and enjoyed life, until Cybil's arthritis meant she had to curtail some of that. They were both quite surprised by her pregnancy. Their life changed radically when Lawrence was born."

Was it Lawrence that changed their lives or that fateful visit to the spa? When Cybil and W. Stone became lovers and possibly conceived the son Spencer called his own? Yolanda returned as I was forming these silent questions. She had a quilt folded over her arm.

"You read my mind," Sheila said and allowed the quilt to be tucked in around her.

"You aren't going to persist about brunch out by the pool, are you, Sheila?" There was a guiding concern in Yolanda's question.

"What's the temperature?"

"Too cold."

"I mean the exact degrees."

"Too cold."

"It says that right on the thermometer?"

"Yes. The little mercury drop shiveringly held up a sign reading 'Too Cold.'"

They were playing their own game.

"Speak of persistence to me no more, Yolanda."

They smiled at each other.

"I'll get Bernice to bring you a serving cart in here with brunch. All right?"

"Did she make home-fried potatoes? I won't look at anything less."

Yolanda patted Sheila's shoulder.

"Would you *ever* look at anything less?"

Sheila winked at me.

"Of course not. But won't you join us, Yolanda?"

"No, thank you. I'm catching up on our holiday mail. I want to get that done before we go to Arthur's."

"And the daiquiris!"

Yolanda left again, laughing. "And the cornish game hens!"

"Nyla, go over to that desk over there in the corner. Bottom drawer, left hand side. I have a photo album. Pictures of Cybil and me."

I retrieved the album and we pored over the pictures for the next hour. The album contained pictures that gave me a unique perspective of Cybil. From her days as a teenager, young bride, and then some reflecting her early twenties and the middle years. During this time, the housekeeper, Bernice, served us a scrumptious brunch that nearly surpassed my hotel's tasty offerings.

When Sheila finished her home-fried potatoes, she easily reminisced again about Cybil.

"When Cybil reached forty, Leonard started insisting that she get portraits done every tenth year. I have several here at the back of the album. Yes, here's when she turned sixty."

When Sheila turned to the picture, it blurred on my first sight then came slowly into focus as I fought back the tingling on my neck; I was not breathing. There stood in the portrait an elegant, indomitable Cybil Porter, her hand gracefully resting upon the piano in the small ballroom at Porterfield, that room where Peter Gant had played a little Brahms for me. Her square face had softened with maturity but her eyes still held their unquestionable

command. But I couldn't concentrate on Cybil; I could barely concentrate on the album, or on Sheila Rush. The tingling was about to engulf me as I saw in the portrait Cybil Porter surrounded by innumerable vases with large bouquets of scarlet orchids.

"Takes your breath away, doesn't she?" Sheila stared at the portrait.

I couldn't answer. I was terrified that my own orchid might rise out of that picture and send me into an unexplainable panic.

"Nyla, you're quite pale. Are you all right?" Sheila Rush patted my hand. "Nyla?" The tingling began to recede. Sheila continued to pat, her face concerned and puzzled.

"It's the flowers . . . I . . . do forgive me. They remind me so . . . "

Before I could finish, Sheila interrupted. "Cybil adored orchids. She got Spencer to build her a greenhouse so she could have them all year 'round. She even considered trying to make her own perfume from the scent. William hated the flowers. He said their smell reminded him of funerals."

My sigh as the tingling disappeared seemed to quiet Sheila. I knew now that it was my turn to do some talking. There was no question in my mind that Sheila Rush could be trusted. And she was my last hope in Rochester for a lead on W. Stone.

It took me only twenty minutes to tell her the entire story about the desk, the pen, the hidden letters, and the orchid's bizarre visitation. But by the time I'd finished, I felt as if I'd been pulling an unmovable burden for many days and suddenly I could let go of it. I also detailed my attempts to trace W. Stone and asked Sheila Rush if she could help. Unnameable moods seemed to cross in her face while she listened. Bernice came to remove the dishes; Sheila waited quietly, watching the flame in the fireplace. When the room was silent again with just the two of us, she responded to what I had told her.

"I don't know anything about the pen in Cybil's desk. That is indeed a mystery to me. W. Stone was a friend of mine. We met through other mutual friends and shared a sense of humor that I knew Cybil too would appreciate. When they met, they discovered they were both afflicted with arthritis and Stone told Cybil about a certain spa and their effective treatment. From then on, Cybil went every year to that spa."

I knew about the spa, of course, from the letters and from Peter Gant.

"When did Stone and Cybil meet?"

"I'm not exactly sure. Nineteen forty-two perhaps? I don't remember."

I knew exactly. The first letters from W. Stone began in 1937. So they had met at the spa not just once but many times over the thirty-two years of their relationship.

"What does the 'W' stand for? William, perhaps? Or Walter? Wayne?"

Sheila Rush now was the one who looked quite pale. She reached for a small bell on the table next to her and rang it.

"A little sherry, don't you think?"

Bernice came quickly and then went for the liquor as Sheila requested.

"I can't recall what it stands for. I'm not sure I ever knew; everyone just used the letter *W*. Perhaps it stood for something unpronounceable. Or something embarrassing like Waringford or Wenglemeier. Warhorse, maybe."

Sheila's laugh was more like a cough.

"Where is that sherry!"

Bernice appeared with the bottle and glasses. "Thank you, thank you," Sheila said distractedly, pouring immediately. She shook her head, thinking to herself as if I was not in the same room with her.

"Do you know if W. Stone is still alive? And where I might find him? I want very much to deliver Cybil's letter to him if he can be reached."

To my great surprise, Sheila quaffed off the first drink of sherry and then poured herself another. It was some minutes before she answered me. She stared into the fire again and turned the sherry glass slowly in her hands. Her voice and her manner were then again convivial as they had been when I first arrived.

"Much to my regret, Stone was a good friend whose circumstances caused us to lose track of each other. Stone did a lot of traveling. Postcards came and went for awhile with all manner of addresses. Eventually I only heard at Christmas and then not at all."

"Do you remember the last address you received?"

As I sat forward in my chair, Sheila seemed to push back away into hers. She didn't answer immediately but ran her eyes over my face, not meeting my eyes but reading my expression. Then she said, "No, I don't. I'm sorry but it has been too long."

"Do you think Stone could be in England? I wonder if Cybil didn't go there that last year to be with him."

"Perhaps you're right. And Cybil went on holiday quite a lot, though I don't think their paths crossed all that often."

Sheila's remark said one thing and then another, but in total only, "*Maybe* you're right. Maybe this search leaves you at the end of one continent and the trail picks up on another. Maybe it doesn't. Maybe their paths *didn't* cross in England." Maybes—as if she wanted to tell no truths and no lies in the same wish.

I felt as if all the air in the room suddenly was sucked out, and out of me too. The promise of locating W. Stone through Sheila Rush was just another brick wall, a tunnel into time sealed off. Sheila was quiet, still scanning my face.

"One last question, Mrs. Rush. Do you know the name of the spa where W. Stone and Cybil Porter went for arthritis treatments?"

Sheila could scarcely miss the disappointment in my voice. But as I looked at her, again the color in her face waned. She looked away from me, at her hands. The room seemed to buzz with her silence and my waiting. She took a deep breath and just as I thought she would answer, she didn't. She smoothed the top of the quilt, running her hand in a long stroke across the material.

"Sorry to interrupt," Yolanda called from the door. "But it's one-thirty, Sheila. I think we should start out for Arthur's soon."

Without looking up, Sheila answered, "Yes, I'll be right there."

I wasn't sure if I should ask her again, drop it, or make the motions of leaving. The hesitance in Sheila Rush's manner kept me rooted to my chair. I was most puzzled by this reticence.

"I believe the name of the spa was Greenwood. Yes, Greenwood Spa."

"In Jacksonville, yes?"

"Yes; that's right. How did you know?"

Her face told me that she was surprised by my information.

"Peter Gant knew the location but not the name."

"I see. Good fellow, Peter. A gentle heart, that one."

We both sat still even as both of us knew we should be leaving soon. We didn't speak but there was something still on Sheila's mind. I felt myself frowning as I wondered how I could let her know it was safe to ask me now before I went away and we lost our chance to talk further. When I caught Sheila's eye, she was frowning too. Again she touched my arm and said, "Nyla, what will you do with the letters if you can't find W. Stone?"

"I've thought about nothing else since I found them. That is the reason I want to find Stone. The letters should go to him since he wrote them and especially since there is one that Cybil wrote that was never delivered. I still can't figure that out. I feel they should be turned over to someone if I can't find Stone. They aren't mine to keep."

"But certainly not to William Porter." There was clear warning in her tone.

"No, of course not. I never considered that. I don't even know if he knows about the letters."

Yolanda came to the doorway, holding a coat for Sheila. I saw her out of the corner of my eye as I said to Sheila, "But I have a feeling . . . "

"Yes?" We were speaking almost in whispers, as people do sometimes when they are telling secrets.

"I have a feeling if William does know about the letters, he will do a lot to get them."

"You must be very careful of him, Nyla. He's . . . "

"Sheila, the car's waiting."

Sheila rubbed her arms again, looked into the fire. She didn't move to leave despite Yolanda's prodding.

"Mrs. Rush, thank you for seeing me and for telling me about Cybil and the Porters. She is so much closer to me now that I have seen her through your eyes."

Sheila raised her eyes and repeated, "So much closer?"

Now it was not warning but some unnameable intense concern in her voice.

"Yes, I mean her presence. I feel I know about her now in a way that I never would have before. Through your stories about her mother, and of course by the photographs. And perhaps now that I know the orchids are a symbol for her and she had departed in peace, I won't be affected by them in the curious way that I have before."

Sheila smiled up at me but we were both still trying to say something.

"As for W. Stone, I will continue to search. The pen point may not be connected to any of this. It may well just have been an unexplainable accident."

"Yes, yes, perhaps."

"I can't thank you enough, Mrs. Rush. For all your time and company."

"My pleasure. Good luck with your book. I know your thoughts of Cybil when you work at her desk are a kind she would respond to favorably. No doubt she's good luck for you too in your endeavors."

Sheila put her hands out to me as she had done to Yolanda, and I took them in my own. She stood up and as she did so, the photo album dropped from her lap to the floor. I bent to pick it up, noticing as I did that a newspaper photo had slipped out of the back of the book. The picture was a profile of several women. One had on sunglasses and another a hat. The third, next to Cybil, was bareheaded, with a thin face but a sturdy chin and the kind of smile that makes photographers grateful. The lead read "Summerfest for Seniors." Cybil Porter's face, even in profile, was clear.

"I'm always stuffing clippings into everything," Sheila said, reaching for the book emphatically and for the clipping before I could look at it more closely. "I keep finding letters I meant to answer in the middle of cookbooks."

"Me too. Filing isn't my forte either. What's the date on this newspaper shot of Cybil?"

"Well, let's see if there's a date on it." Sheila turned the piece of newspaper around in her hands. "No. Only the picture. No date."

I got my coat and said to her, "Thank you again. I can find my way out."

"You'll have to run the gauntlet again past those portraits." She smiled and stepped back into the light from her colorful window. I left her as she wanted to be left, with a Madonna on her shoulder.

"I'm sorry I didn't get to meet your husband, Mrs. Rush. The portrait keeper, so to speak."

I smiled back at her. Standing before the majestic window, she said, "Dispense with the 'Mrs.' Leonard isn't my husband. He's my brother."

As I passed the portraits again, they weren't the only faces in the house with secrets and surprises behind them. Sheila Rush was an eighty year old maiden: my surprise. The back of the newspaper photo of Cybil had advertised a shoe store in Jacksonville, Florida: my secret.

Yolanda had drawn me a map to the cemetery before I left the Whitmore Rush estate. The day had not greyed as they so often do in winter and for that, I was grateful. Lots of sun at Crestlawn would keep me from imagining any ghosts, gargoyles, or greenery on the prowl. With any luck, not one single soul remembering a lost loved one would decorate the grave with orchids today.

Approaching the grave was a lot like approaching the pictures of Cybil that were on the mantel in the left wing at Porterfield. I was awash with sensations of body and mind as I wound my way around the mounds of earth, spotted green and brown for winter. I felt prickles, tingling, a shiver of my shoulders as if someone I didn't notice had brushed against me. A rush of blood to my heart started with a sting, spread into a quick pain, and then subsided so fast that I felt foolish at my own alarm. I stopped several feet away from the Porter plot. I stood and looked toward the place where Cybil remained, giving myself a chance to catch my breath before I looked at what is considered the complete truth in this life: the end and burial of individual history. I remembered again that wide but competent face, so unpretty and so uncommon. There are no details to report out of the pictures, not the details I have been trained to look for. In Cybil it was not the shape of her chin, the height of her cheekbones, the color of her eyes, or the style of her hair that told how she looked. The strength of mind and will that showed in her face made every expression an identity in itself. No wonder she feuded with William. I thought about the letters and the desk, the room where she wrote those letters, her traded and written sentiments with W. Stone. Parts of them rushed past me like shouts that were only echoes now. They fell on my ears like the quick pain to my heart.

"Parted by circumstance we cannot ignore . . . your ardent mouth . . . myself so willing to receive you . . . emptying out the most obvious feeling . . . our innocence and discovery, our pleasure in the taste of freedom . . . those private places in the grass, moist and torrid as new lovers, made for us as new lovers . . . I am alive and will be for the rest of my life because of you . . . we are a secret I intend to keep . . . "

Then I took the last few steps. After I read her name and the dates once, I had to look at the other stones, to keep my eyes off her grave, to calm my feeling of helplessness. She seemed so alive to me, even as I stood at her grave.

Lawrence and Spencer had matching markers of the same height and color, elaborate and almost sparkly quartz, with tile painstakingly inlaid around their names. No such ceremony for Cybil; her marker was quite plain granite, her first and maiden name on one line, "Porter" chiseled underneath them, as if she was never really connected to that name. She lived longer than both of them, raised one and managed the other so he could just enjoy his life. Yet her stone was smaller. At least the ground was smooth over all three graves. There was no avoiding the effect of sinking earth in the cemetery upon my living spirit. There were no rusted shovels here, no aspen four-posters. But what was the same was my feeling of loss for a stranger, this woman who was entirely beyond reach and yet pervasive in my life because of one letter, a property of hers that could not be bestowed as yet to its rightful owner.

I ran my hand over the granite arch, the top of Cybil's grave-stone. Then I spoke to the stone, as if it was Cybil herself.

"I have your letters, if that's any comfort. They're in the hands of an ally. I'm sure Sheila Rush would vouch for me. But what should I do with them? To whom do they really belong? Especially if I can't find W. Stone? Do I keep them, Cybil, as a strange legacy I will someday understand? Do I give them to Sheila? She loved you more than any of the Porters."

137

I patted the top of the stone again and turned around, to put my back to this painful site and to look at the cemetery cloaked for the season. But what I saw was not an unbroken panorama of peaceful, quiet, and somber trees. I saw the long black limousine parked on the opposite drive into the graveyard. The chauffeur was standing on the far side of the car and, dwarfed by his huge machines, stood the man Sheila had called "empty and grey looking." He was nattily bundled up against the cold in a grey coat and muffler, his head down to the eyebrows covered by a black hat. He was clearly waiting for me. William Porter: I could slip around him in his own house but not out here among the floating souls.

Consider your options, Wade. You could just stroll off in the opposite direction and then once you're downhill from them, sprint like hell to the street. Or double around through the trees to the rental car. You could walk right up to him and then pass him by. You're not obligated to talk to him just because he shows up with muscle. Muscle who likes to shadow walk down hotel hallways. Something tells me if I go any closer, the muscle could get hold of me and things could get very sticky. Something also tells me the muscle may be more fleet of foot than I. I wonder if they're packing heat. Not Porter, but maybe the muscle. No, they don't mean to do any more than threaten me. Tell the nosy out-of-stater to steer clear. If that's the worst of it, I'll survive. No one ever got to the bottom of a story by running away from it.

I mustered all my primeval energy, envisioned myself as a fire-breathing chimera as I took resolute steps toward William Porter. Another part of me tried to materialize a suit of armor or at least a bullet-proof vest. When I was within several feet of him, he twitched his moustache to one side of his mouth. His hands were clasped and at rest when I stopped in front of him.

"Not a very tall grave stone for Cybil Porter," I said, dripping sarcasm.

"It suffices," he answered, unruffled.

"Suffice, meaning adequate? But not always *enough*."

"Enough is a relative state."

Word games. Intellect check. But so far the muscle wasn't moving toward me.

"If adequate had been enough for you, William, you certainly wouldn't be where you are today."

138

"On the contrary. I was born into more than enough, that's true. But unlike most wealthy people, I worked for pleasure, not out of necessity."

"You worked? When was that? After Cybil wasn't around to do it anymore?"

His moustache twitched again. His words were meant to bite as deep as the wind that whipped up leaves in a mad whirl at our feet when he responded.

"Ms. Wade, you are a virtual stranger to this state and to my family. You know only about Cybil and the Porters by hearsay."

"Was Randy's information hearsay?"

William sighed. He squared his small shoulders in his tailored coat.

"My great-nephew is an enthusiastic and sometimes impetuous young man. He was also only a child during Cybil's lifetime."

"But he is a Porter. He cannot be taken at his word?"

William's grey eyes blinked and he reached among the stones for patience. There was no color in his eyes except grey, grey as granite, when he said to me, "Your best interests will be suited if you go home *now,* Ms. Wade, and stop snooping into the business of my family."

"I thought you didn't claim Cybil in your family."

"She was family by marriage. Out of respect for Spencer, I . . . "

"Ah yes, Spencer, another enthusiastic, impetuous young man. Unlike you." The chimera burned in my breast. I feared neither the small, rich man nor his black and white chauffeur monster. I was my own fearless monster. The tone of William's answer was in a voice suited to the site, a voice nearly of the dead, as he leveled his empty eyes on me and said, "Yes."

"Why did you hold Cybil's funeral in England? Why didn't you let her friends know about the memorial ceremony?"

William stared silently at me. I shook my head and started to walk away from him.

"It must get very tight walking around in a soul that small," I flung at him over my shoulder. Two sets of steps crunched on the road as the chauffeur moved up in front of me to block my way.

"Garson."

Porter didn't bark the name with alarm. He simply said it and the monster behaved.

"This must be the slight-of-step watchdog. Are you in the habit of sending your chauffeur around to eavesdrop on people?"

Porter walked up to me. He was half a foot shorter than I.

"Are you in the habit of charming unsuspecting and vulnerable secretaries?"

His emphasis on the word *vulnerable* gave me a twinge of regret. But only a small twinge.

"I charmed no one. I walked in in the light of day. That's more than I can say for your messenger of the shadows here." I gave Garson a look of disgust.

"Garson is on his own time in the evenings. He goes where he wishes with neither my approval nor my bidding. Really, Ms. Wade, you are too much a part of your own plots." I saw in Porter where his butler had learned that peculiar elusive non-smile. "You should be very careful that no harm comes to you as a result of that."

Now his smile was a real one and something glimmered behind his eyes. The comment and that flicker of feeling gave me prickles of warning on my neck.

"But I will answer the question you've asked about Cybil's funeral. So that you know I have nothing to hide and am only interested in the privacy my family rightfully deserves. I held the funeral in a manner entirely in accordance with Cybil's wishes. I spoke to her just three days before her death when I was summoned to England by her doctor there. Cybil was fully aware of her condition. She had jaundiced terribly and told me in no uncertain terms that she wished a closed casket funeral with no wake. This was witnessed by the doctor and his nurse. I, of course, carried out those wishes to the letter."

He didn't comment on the quick memorial ceremony and he was nondescript as he told me about the funeral. It sounded too plausible to be fishy. Something wasn't quite right but I couldn't finger it immediately. I looked at the wheels on the limo, and then at William Porter's grey shoes as I tried to sort the facts. He said to me in that leaden tone of his, "Cybil was very vain, you know. Even at the end."

He could speak cruelly with his hands folded so calmly. I wanted to hit him right under his twitchy little moustache.

"I suppose that doctor could be reached to verify this?"

The grey eyes widened just perceptibly.

"If it was necessary."

Porter glanced over at the chauffeur, who stood up to his full height and assumed a position of readiness that did not sit well in my heart.

"But I hope that won't be necessary. I hope you won't pursue this 'investigation' of yours any further, Ms. Wade. After all, it is pointless. Whatever you hoped to really ascertain behind this story of yours about writing the romance novel, the truth of the matter is you're trying to find W. Stone. And W. Stone is dead."

Peter Gant had talked to William Porter and now he had me in a ringer with those four leaden words, in the voice of the dead, calling my search to a halt. Final, the answer I was looking for but not expecting to hear: Stone was dead.

"I suspect that fact was what you really wanted to know, although I'm not sure why. Or sure how you learned about Stone. But now you know what you came here to find out and I don't want to hear from you again. Don't bother my nephew again either. Good day, Ms. Wade."

The chauffeur moved around me, his bulk threateningly near, as he opened the door for William Porter. I surprised both of them by throwing myself full force in between them and slamming the door shut.

"Why should I believe you? What makes you think I didn't find out about W. Stone for myself?"

As the chauffeur grabbed me powerfully by the shoulder, Porter put his hand on the other man's huge black glove. "Easy, Garson." I shook at his grasp; he held me just tight enough to make me wince.

"If he didn't keep in touch with his good friends like Sheila Rush, why would Stone keep you informed? I know you're aware I went to see her; your boy here would have told you that from his listening escapades last night."

William Porter frowned at me. "*His good friends?*"

"That's right. Rush knew him extremely well and she hadn't heard from him in many years."

"One need not be a friend to someone to know about their life, Ms. Wade. Even you are not so naive."

With a nod to Garson, Porter got the brute to let go of me.

"And if you knew Stone was alive, you would not have grilled Peter. I have been playing this game much longer than you have."

We both knew he was right about that. But I still smelled fish. He wanted me off Stone's trail. And he was in a position to know. But even if Stone was dead, his letters to Cybil spoke in a voice that could reach the living. With a blind lust for revenge against the grey empty man and his disrespect for the joy that Cybil and W. Stone embodied, I made a foolish mistake in judgment.

"Even if W. Stone is dead, there's a part of him that's still alive."

The expression that crossed William Porter's face was one I had seen before. That same expression had been on the face of the man in my nightmare at the greenhouse. The man with the watch fob who had been demanding the emerald. He had a terrible face, with nothing behind it but a menacing anger. There I was, sandwiched in between them, up against the car, and I didn't have better sense. The minute the words left me, I knew I was in trouble. Porter leaned up next to me, standing nearly on tiptoe to speak into my face.

"What do you mean, Ms. Wade? Have you something tangible from W. Stone? Something in writing perhaps?"

He didn't guess at other possibilities. He must know about the letters. A spear of fear ran up from my toes like an electric shock. They could have me in the car and whisked back to the fortress towers for interrogation in a flash. He'd probably been searching for those letters for years. I could wait or scoot, bluff or belly-up. I scooted.

The chauffeur wasn't expecting it and what they taught me in self-defense worked. I had two things in my favor: surprise and the miracle of adrenalin. I came down on the chauffeur's instep with a stomp that crunched into his boot. Outweighing Porter by at least twenty pounds, I hit him in the chest with my shoulder. Mean Joe Greene had nothing on me as I left Porter on his butt in the gravel. I went flying down the road, two hundred yards in record time. I fishtailed the rented Mercury out of the graveyard and hit the expressway in four minutes flat. Along that short way, a garbage truck slid sideways into a curb to accommodate me.

Though the limo could easily have overtaken me, that would not have been Porter's style. Chasing me would have been a common, if high speed, display. I figured I was safe, not only when they didn't come after me from the graveyard, but when I got on the airplane without a hitch. After all, I would soon be out of the sphere of Porter's influence.

I'm sure it wasn't until the pilot invited us to see Chicago in lights that I let go of the seat and allowed my confidence to return. I could have reached outside my window and hooked onto one of those sable night clouds, tugged it along with me like a scarf. But I couldn't touch it even as it seemed so real. I, like the plane, hung in mid-air, with only hope that I could stay aloft. I hung in between William Porter and W. Stone, with no proof that Stone was dead or alive and only hope to keep me from burning the letters when I got home, to keep me from putting one monkey off my back forever. I tried to ignore a nagging voice that sang in my ears and brewed up a terrific headache: "Ignorance is bliss . . . " I rolled in the seat of the plane, positioned and re-positioned myself, trying to drown out the voice, trying to make myself sleepy. But I knew I couldn't relax or forget or just fall asleep. I couldn't ignore anything. I couldn't ignore the letters of those lovers, the broken pen point, the emerald eye, the hope of delivery. Audrey Louise would put it to me in a lecture: "It's sorta like feminist rhetoric, you see. Once you read it, you can't go backwards. You can't ignore it. You can't pretend you don't know."

I did know something. I knew a few hard facts. I had the name of the spa. I had the parts of the story that had been missing, filled in by Sheila Rush: how W. Stone and Cybil met, how the Wallings had mixed with the Porters in Rochester, how Cybil took no part in common flirtation. I knew dates and chronology. I'd been in the room where the main parties lived. But those places and facts were still not a complete answer. Its shadow flirted elsewhere. I knew too that the people in Rochester had a peculiar reaction whenever I mentioned W. Stone.

I remembered the moment when Sheila Rush lost her color. The woman with the Madonna on her shoulder had paled before me when I asked what the "W." in Stone's name stood for. Her hesitance to help me trace this elusive lover was not in keeping with the rest of our conversation. And William—even that cold, calculating, empty man had shown a quicksilver reaction when I brought up Stone and his friends. More than any tangible evidence, I knew that the letters meant something to William Porter.

He knew I had them. If W. Stone was dead, I had to find a safe place for those letters or destroy them. Could I burn those tender sentiments, those documents of passion? I winced again as if the chauffeur had me in his meathooks. I knew I would light a match to every page of the letters rather than give them up to William Porter.

As I ran from the airline gate to the baggage area, I knew Audrey Louise would gripe at me for not letting her meet my flight. But I had another date that was as urgent as locating W. Stone. Bevo's Lounge. It was a quarter to seven. I skidded up to a yellow cab and banged the door with my suitcase. The driver sat up with a growl; his rumpled hair told me he'd just rolled out of the sack.

"You gotta problem, lady?"

Any other time he would have been a polite, half-handsome college kid.

"Yea. I got a twenty says you can get me to 68th and Wadsworth in fifteen minutes."

"Shit lady, get back on the jet."

He started to roll up his window.

"Thirty-five, chump, and step on it. Take me right up to the front door."

The kid blinked against temptation.

"What's at 68th and Wads?"

"Bevo's Lounge."

He cocked his head at me.

"You sure that's where you wanna go?"

"Yea, I'm sure. You gotta problem with that?"

As he swung his legs off the seat and reached for my bag, he said, "Nah. You just don't look the type."

"Come on, we're wasting time."

As he slammed the door and fired up the engine, he said, "It's just you don't look the type, that's all. Bevo's is a hooker hangout."

Only a few people turned to look at me when I stepped into the bar. The college kid cabbie had done all right by me. I was in the door of Bevo's by 7:02 and he got my last dime. The place was crowded and loud, poorly lighted, and thick with cigarette smoke. There was a pool table at the back with a yellow light over it that reminded me of Mike's old dust burner. The clang of a pinball machine careened off thin walls to my right. Someone stepped out of the bathroom door and nearly pinned me to the wall. As the door closed, I saw a tall woman standing in front of the pool table. She was holding a cue, leaning on one hip and staring at me from behind mirrored dark glasses. I couldn't imagine why anyone would need to wear shades in a place like this. Get wise, Wade: for *image,* of course.

I stared back at the woman, unsure if she was my watcher, since I had only seen her previously in profile. I was unable now to get a clear look at her through the obtuse light and smoke. She moved, held the cue out away from her body. Appearing out of the smoke, another woman took the cue. Their heads tipped together momentarily as they spoke to each other. Then they both looked at me. The one with the cue nodded, then disappeared again into the smoke.

The other people in the bar faded into fuzzy backdrop as the tall woman came toward me. She rolled her shoulders as she walked, as if uncoiling all her body energy from the center and pushing it forward. As she got closer to me, I saw she was wearing a bibbed, black satin jumpsuit and high black boots. Her shoulders were bare; she was long from elbow to hand but well-muscled. When she stopped in front of me, she stood with her legs apart, hands on hips. She was easily six foot or more, with olive skin, and thick black hair cut in the popular shag. It framed her face and touched her shoulders. She had a black satin cap sitting back on her hair and a silver glitter star decorating her left cheek. I figured her for about twenty-five.

We stood about three feet apart, squared off from one another. The glasses showed me only a dull reflection, a curtain of some further distance between us. Unexpectedly, she pushed them up into her hair. The features of her face were delicate, despite her size. She was not a child, but something in the softness at the line of her lips had stopped just at the crossover into maturity. This softness surprised me; it seemed not to fit the rest of the way she framed herself, the image toughened around her. As I took her in from top to bottom, the expression on her face let me know I had entered her territory and she was in charge. She took another three steps toward me until we were close enough to touch noses.

I could feel her breath upon my cheeks when she said, "Have a nice trip, Wade? How was New York?"

A white flame seemed to flash in her eyes, but she didn't smile. I felt as if the last two days were whirling away from me, becoming smoke and layering out in the air around us. My heart was pounding. I thought the woman before me, her black eyes a maelstrom of mystery, was the most beautiful I had ever seen.

"Cat got your tongue, Wade?"

Her kneecap pressed against my own.

"New York was . . ."

I wasn't sure why but I couldn't grasp a single clear image of Rochester. The bar, the swirling smoke, the woman's closeness, all stifled my memory. All I could say was "New York was interesting." She shook her head as if she understood my empty answer. I was memorizing her face with thunder in my ears. And I had thought the orchid was bad enough.

"We've never had a formal introduction. I'm Sara. I was the one in the grocery store."

I nodded.

"Chamomile tea, remember?" She inched her face closer to mine. I nodded. "Anniversary cards, remember?" Her black eyes were a tunnel drawing me in.

"Yes."

She bored into me with those eyes and I could smell lilac in the satin.

"Anniversary cards," I mumbled. If she got any closer, I would fall over backwards. The air was turning to mud around me. I felt Sara's fingers close around my arm; she stepped to my left and said into my ear, "Come and meet my partner." She rammed one lean thumb toward a booth near the back of the bar. I looked toward the booth; the woman who was waiting there was short, wide-hipped, and with pink skin that absorbed the rouge she wore. She was blonde and buxom, full-lipped, with none of Sara's hardness.

I expected her to put out her hand to me; this she did as we approached the booth. Sara didn't let go of my arm as we walked. I could feel her fingers digging into my skin.

"Glad you could make it. I'm Nikki."

She smiled, nervously at first but when I smiled back, she

147

relaxed and we both sat down. "I really am glad you could make it," she said again.

Sara remained standing until we were both settled. Then she turned and grabbed a chair, straddling it, the black satin straining its mold across her thighs. As she rested her arms on the chair back, she settled her eyes upon me again, in a manner far from restful.

The noise in the bar surrounded us. I looked into Sara's intent expression. She was waiting, still sizing me up on her own ground. If what the cabbie told me was true, Sara was a hooker with a specialty for anticipation. When I shifted my eyes to Nikki, she looked down at her drink, then to Sara's face. She was waiting too, but not for any direction from me. She was waiting for Sara to reel out their story, the one that I could be part of, the one requiring that I have no man in my life.

Sara moved one bare shoulder forward. I stared at the round muscle and smooth skin of her shoulder for a moment but she drew my eyes up to her own and riveted them there.

"You ready to hear the deal, Wade?"

I wasn't breathing at all when I said, "I'm ready."

ELEVEN

Eight Years Stale

The smoke got thicker. It socked us in like fog around an island. Nikki chewed her plastic stir stick. Sara did the talking.

"We want something written up. You sift all the details and make it simple. A one-pager. You may work with us on the printing too. The distribution is strictly our end. No questions asked."

She and Nikki exchanged a glance as the smoke circled us, keeping our lowered voices close within the space of the booth. My heart was still thudding against my breastbone as Sara lit a lean brown cigar. It smelled of woodruff and I watched her hands, close to her face, close to mine. They slid on and off objects and surfaces: the cigar, the satin, the pool cue, with a measured laziness. I had no doubt she could snatch and scratch with those hands if the occasion arose, but as I looked at her hands and felt my heart protest, I wanted to reach out and take hold of them. The very thought made me catch my breath. Sara tipped forward on the two legs of her chair and said, "You still with us, Wade?"

Keep your mind on business, I told myself, hoping to get my haywire physiology in check. "So, what is this one-pager that you want me to compose? I gather from your stake-out of me it's a big secret and you want it pronto. How did you find me anyway?"

Sara slipped her hand inside the bib of the satin jumpsuit and flicked a card at me. It was one of the three-by-fives I'd given

Audrey Louise to put up on campus. "You advertised," she said.

"Okay." I picked up the card. "Let's have the scoop."

Nikki brightened, sitting up straight in the booth, turning toward Sara. Her eyes widened when Sara spoke.

"You're right. This job is top secret and we need it within the week. More like two days," Sara said around her cigar. "Like Friday."

"I still don't know what it is I'm supposed to deliver in two days."

Sara scooted the chair up so that it touched the edge of the booth. We were eye to eye but I had to push somewhere in my heart to harden myself; otherwise I'd barely hear what she was saying. These feelings were so new to me I had to concentrate with every waning ounce of my energy. I had to listen close.

"Nikki and I . . . saw a crime committed. We've been running from it but we can't anymore. Other people might get hurt unless somehow we tell what we know. We were working D.C. eight years ago for a guy who'd been around: Chicago, Detroit, Philly. He was no ordinary pimp; the guy could hustle connections of the best kind. The Saint, everyone called him. Very high class. He didn't deal in streetware: strictly selective, set-ups for congressmen, that sort of thing. But he was careful. No traces, this guy. Like he could walk in sand and leave no footprints."

"Really. He was like that, really," Nikki chimed in. "Three-piece suits, a limo, everything. I'd never seen anything like him in the business before."

"We were doing okay. Nikki had just turned out; she was only sixteen. I had been floating most of the time. The Saint was some charmer; he could make you feel like you'd found a home. But even so, Nikki and I were thinking about working for ourselves. We had this dream we'd have our own house. No more splits with anyone. We'd be our own best protection. The Saint, he smelled it: disloyalty. We never said a word to him. He just knew and it started to work on him. Then one night . . . well, he wasn't so careful."

"Wait, Sara." Nikki put her hand on Sara's arm. "Don't tell it. Give me a sec." She had tears in her eyes. Sara slipped her hand into Nikki's, her fingers flexing strong and the muscle all the way up her arm standing out.

"Easy, babe. I know it still seems like yesterday to you. But we gotta keep the plan rolling. We finally have a chance to do something about what happened."

My heart was roaring, at their tender consolation, at the foreboding I felt in the pit of my stomach. Sara went on.

"We had a friend working with us in D.C. Her name was Carlie. She was from Nikki's hometown."

Wiping her eyes with the back of her hand, Nikki said, "Indianapolis. We were in school together. Carlie was real sweet. She really was. Usually you can't afford to get tight with anyone, you know? It's bad for the work. But the three of us, especially Carlie and me . . . we . . . we helped each other, you know? We'd go out for drinks and give each other a back rub now and then, talk about home, talk about getting our own place. She was the only other one Sara and I ever told about that dream. The Saint, he put up with it. Until he thought we were gonna split from him." Nikki sobbed then, just a quiet little cry, and turned her head away from me. Sara rubbed her neck with one hand.

"We came in after a heavy night. Convention time or something. We wanted to get Carlie and go for a drink. The house was dead quiet. When I snapped on a light, one of the other girls screamed at the sight of us. She was just sitting in the dark. She told us to get out quick. She said the Saint had killed Carlie, as a lesson to us. He told her, told all the girls who were in the house, he'd kill them and us if we tried to quit him. We started to leave but then I asked if he was in the house. The girl told us he was out looking for us. I asked where Carlie was. She said the Saint had taken her upstairs."

Sara stubbed out her cigar. Stubbed it and stubbed it until it was nearly a flat square in the bottom of the ashtray. She kept rubbing Nikki's neck. The bar now seemed empty or soundproofed from any other noise. All I could hear was my heart clamoring and Sara telling the story, the nightmare that came true.

"I made Nikki wait downstairs. I went up to the office. The light in it was off. But the light in the bathroom was on. It looked okay. Like nothing was wrong. Maybe he'd just been trying to scare everyone. I just walked over to the bathroom door like I thought the room would be empty and I'd shut off the light. Like it was all just a stupid story. But there she was. In the tub. In pieces."

Nikki sobbed again. Sara slid the chair back behind her and put her arms around the other woman.

"Come on, baby. Let's take a walk. Easy now. Come on." They moved away from me slowly, fading into the fog, leaving me behind with their horrible story. I couldn't breathe, couldn't move. I couldn't doubt them. I might be naive and they might be street-wise, but they weren't acting. Little cries were going off inside me too. Why hadn't they gone to the police? How had they kept out of the reach of the Saint? And what could I possibly do to help them?

I needed a drink badly. I felt like I had fire in all of my body, painful flames. Of course they couldn't go to the police. They were hookers; I didn't need any great education to figure law enforcement's response to the killing. One less to haul in on Friday night. If any of them testified, their own lives might be endangered. Who was likely to be able to buy an alibi? The hookers or the pimp? I wanted to think times had changed and the cops had more of a heart and justice was for all. But I came up empty convincing myself of that.

In a few minutes, Sara came back to the booth alone. She slid in beside me and put a scotch down in front of me. I gulped it down, lavishing in the instant fire that ran down my throat. It seemed to extinguish the other fire running inside me.

"Did you even *try* to go to the police?"

"We got the hell out. We split up for awhile and made seven or eight stops. So if he could tail us, we'd spin him off the trail. We met back in Albuquerque, stayed there a couple of months. No one was sniffing around after us. We heard the Saint's D.C. operations broke up. The other girls left him too. He went out of sight. We came here.

"He wasn't ordinary, see. We knew that. He had connections. We didn't see a chance in hell that he'd ever go to trial, that anyone would believe us. And he could have bought himself out of it anyway. Then he'd have come after us. It isn't hard to find someone who stays in the life."

I didn't know beans about hookers or police or murder, even one eight years stale. Maybe I should have been a hard-ass and worried about libel and proving their story and possible danger to myself. But even before Sara offered proof, I was ready to run with them, headlong, ignoring the angels who might have stepped back. Whether she guessed my decision or not, Sara went on.

"Even though I was the one who went up to that bathroom, Nikki took it harder. She was so young and Carlie was her friend. We've tried to forget it. We got a good business here. We're first rate. No hypes. And no johns ever get cleaned at our place. Everyone stays safe. But every day for the last eight years, there comes an hour, a minute, a moment when we look at each other and we're right back in D.C. again, that same night. Here, read this."

She unfolded something out of the bib. It was a newspaper clipping. News item about a woman identified as Carlie Sampler found brutally murdered in Washington's red light district. Alleged prostitute. Assailant unknown. Motive unknown. I knew when I got to the end of the article they might as well have written "Case Closed."

"So what happened that you want to tell your story now? What's ended the eight years of trying to forget?"

"We got word last week that the Saint is back in business in the U.S. He's been in South America but now he's in Boston. I guess he figures by now that no one will remember Carlie. But we do. And one thing we wouldn't forget is if it happened again."

"But isn't there some other way? Can't you go to the police here? Get some protection? Get a lawyer?"

"With what proof? Who would testify? This guy didn't just blow away a hooker, see? Shoot her or strangle her. He cut her up as if she was dogmeat, *for a lesson.* His version of a *principle.* We can't wait around for due process."

"So what do you intend to do? And how can I help?"

Maybe Sara was more used to straightforward money transactions than I, and she had certainly been in that bathroom in D.C. and I had not. But the quaver at her mouth, the mouth formed before her hardness, told me she also knew what she was asking of me and that I had answered.

"Like I said, Wade, something on one page. Telling what we know about the murder. Nikki is gonna draw a picture of the Saint to go with it. Our source tells us he hasn't even grown a beard or nothin'. He doesn't think he needs any kind of disguise. No hookers are gonna fool with him. Well, he's in for a surprise. Any other hooker who sees this piece of paper will know him and will pass the word. Pretty soon he won't be able to hustle any business. Not here, not anywhere. No girls and no johns. He'll be untouchable. He'll have to disappear. Or . . . "

"What? You think the police might . . . "

"Wade, you gotta get the police out of your mind. They come in handy for a very few things. You can get to know a few and they might fail to notice you somewhere when you're working. Or they'll just give you a nice friendly lecture in the squad car and then you can split. You might trade some business. Some vice can be bought though they're a slightly different breed. But we're talking *murder* here. So they're useless to us. If the word gets out on the Saint and other pimps see what happens, if the stink we raise is big enough, well, it's kinda like a pack of dogs. You know, they can turn on each other."

"But Sara, how do you keep them from knowing it was you and Nikki? And how will you get the word out?"

A sort of smile curved on her lips, not a hard one this time but one that was meant for me.

"Let's just review a couple of things here, Wade. What's the Saint's real name?"

"You didn't tell me."

"And do you know any specific dates or places he's ever worked? Do you know the date of the crime or the exact location? Or any complete names of anyone involved? Except Carlie's and that's public knowledge."

I wasn't sure what Sara was driving at. First she wants me to write up details on a murder, then she grills me to convince me there are no details.

"No, Sara, I don't know any of that. Just general information. All public record."

"Look around this bar, Wade. Who in here saw you with Nikki and me tonight? And how would you find either of us again?"

I looked around the bar. Heads here and there were visible through the smoke; the low buzz of conversations hummed in the air. Other hookers were playing pool and laughing over beer. This place, their place, was the only real protection any of them had.

"Now Wade, after all the pains we've taken to get your help, do you really think we'd endanger you or ourselves or our plan by telling you how we're gonna burn this bastard? It's not personal. But it is. The less you know about our end of the deal, if anything should go wrong, the less danger you'll be in."

"All I know is that a guy nicknamed the Saint butchered a hooker in D.C. eight years ago. And you want a one-page piece of paper that tells what the Saint did. A piece of paper that no one can trace."

"Right. A piece of paper with a clear meaning and a clear warning. One page that might save someone's life."

I knew I couldn't ask where or how that piece of paper would get to the hookers. No questions asked—that was their end of the deal. We had no more words to trade. The moment was already overloaded. With a motion to the bartender, Sara got two more drinks brought to the table.

"Are you serious about two days? Doesn't give me much time." I wanted to talk deadlines like I wanted to be alone thinking about Carlie.

"We can't give the grapevine a lot of time. News travels both ways."

"What else do I need to do besides write this up?"

"We've got to find a printer who can be bought. Paid to turn over a press to someone else for a couple of hours. I can run an offset. Scout that, if you can."

"Okay. How will I get in touch with you?"

Sara's smile flirted again on her lips. If she could have, she might well have lifted the veil of smoke to look at me and say, "Come on, Wade, wise up. Weren't you listening to me before?" I saved her the effort. "Sorry. *You'll* find *me,* right?"

Her smile held me, her eyes held me; there was such a strange and drawing intensity in her face that I knew I would do whatever she asked of me.

"Right. We'll be in touch."

I didn't move, though, as I was expected to. I wanted to get away from the three of us and what we knew but I didn't want to leave Sara. I wanted to be in touch, to stay in touch, to touch her. But I knew we'd closed our deal and there wasn't anything more personal to be said.

"Will Nikki be all right?" She still hadn't come back to the booth. Sara's eyes didn't flicker; her hands were quiet on the table, fingers spread.

"She'll be all right. She's with me."

I knew that was enough. I left her without looking back or making small talk. But when I got to the door of the bar, I was afraid for them. Afraid it wouldn't be enough much longer.

The cab ride to my apartment from Bevo's seemed interminable. I kept thinking, "I'm in the back seat of this cab holding the secret of a murder. I'm in a perfectly normal situation knowing an incredible, awful truth." I never set out to write up the announcement of a murder. Weddings maybe. Term papers even. But murder? And not some abstract story you get from a crime report. I'd had the eyewitnesses' account. They had known eight years of grief with the secret. They wanted me to help, but I had to keep my questions to myself for my own safety. I had to do my part and only wonder about theirs.

My apartment was as far from Bevo's Lounge as Denver was from Rochester. We were in two separate realities, in the same world. They existed in a place where women who sold sex could be murdered and the killer could escape any retribution. I wandered around my small space, emptying my suitcase aimlessly. How important I thought my trip to New York had been, and my search for W. Stone. My need to deliver the letters. W. Stone suddenly seemed insignificant compared to the gravity of Carlie's death. A woman was murdered.

My apartment was cold. I turned up the heat. I had no answers. Drinking cocoa with a blanket around my shoulders, I listened to the phone answering machine. I'd had some calls. One from a male voice that sounded like Barry Beefeater asking could I please write a paper for him on Marat-de Sade by Friday for twenty-five bucks. A female caller from the Sorority Association excitedly announced the new inter-sorority newsletter and would I edit it? "We can't wait until the first issue hits," she giggled. "We're calling it *The Sob Sister*." Steve Raymond asked me to check in with him, hoping my sore throat was better. The last caller surprised me. It was Mike. All he said was, "I hope by now we've both had enough time to make a civilized luncheon date possible."

Sorority newsletters, term papers, the damned warehouse being built where a grove of trees would have to be torn down instead of using a meadow already leveled by nature, and Mike wants to have lunch with me. None of it made any sense to me because all I could think about was that Carlie was dead and no one had paid for taking her life. Well, I could sit up all night visualizing the grisly sight Sara had seen in the bathroom or I could give in to getting some sleep. I knew as I headed for my thin but familiar bedspread that I wasn't entirely ready yet to trust my dreams.

I'd had a long two days. Being alone in the apartment and approaching midnight was getting to me. William Porter's face floated above my desk lamp with that driven, manic expression he'd had when he asked me, "Something in *writing*, perhaps?" I hadn't thought about my safety in regard to the letters, not until that tense moment between Porter and his chauffeur in the graveyard. Now, after personal safety had become such an issue tonight at Bevo's, I thought of it again. Was it possible Porter might try to get the letters from me? The hour and the telling of a murder were making me paranoid and nervous. What if he did try? I ought to get those letters into safekeeping. Who could I give them to? Not the one person I trusted more than anyone else, though. Not Audrey Louise because she was too easy to trace in the most casual shake-down. What about a locker at the airport? Then where would I hide the key? Maybe I could bundle them in with some old sweaters and send them to Milwaukee, ask Mother to store them for me. I knew even though it was late and I was tired, the idea was a sound one. I must get those letters out of this apartment and soon.

Audrey Louise—I wanted desperately to call her, confide everything to her. But if *I* wasn't safe, she might not be either. We were talking murder now and someone else's letters. She lived in suburbia with a good heart and hope for the American dream. If she could help me with any of this, I would have to disguise all of it. For once, she couldn't save me and I couldn't involve her.

There was no more stalling; even if nightmares awaited me, I couldn't keep my eyes open another minute. But as I pulled back the bedspread, what livened in my thoughts was not W. Stone or Carlie Sampler. My pulse began racing as it had the moment I had seen Sara through the smoke in the bar. What was this confusion in the midst of everything else? That desire to grab hold of her hands. What I couldn't reconcile was that I wasn't bone weary earlier in the evening when I'd felt that surge in myself, when I was unable to take my eyes from hers or to notice anything except the feelings that rose up in me whenever she talked or moved or looked at me.

The cocoa had been too mild for me. I padded back to the kitchen in my slippers and had myself two quick bolts of scotch. I wanted to go to sleep and here I was breathing as if I'd been sprinting around the building. What I wanted to ignore most was that this was a physical reaction. I'd managed to keep my body off-limits to myself for quite a while.

"Hell, Wade, you're falling apart again."

Padding back toward the bed with another scotch, I considered a book to fall asleep by and ruled out any murder mysteries. It occurred to me that I hadn't checked my mail. As I went to the mail slot in the living room, I thought at least I had one less worry now. I knew I wouldn't be getting any more strange phone calls.

I had a few envelopes so I went over to the desk and sat down to open them. I had rolled down the desk top before I left. Now I remembered the little sign that had been on it when we found it at The Gravy Boat. "Don't roll. Works fine." With a gentle push, I rolled back the top, lifted those sacred skirts I'd come to know as sanctuary. I looked at the spot where the pen point had been and remembered digging it out to find the emerald eye. Such a small crime, someone stabbing the desk with the pen. Nothing compared to the Saint's crime. William Porter said W. Stone was dead. If he wasn't, it would suit Porter to have me think so and bury the letters and the history of that affair forever. I didn't want to believe there was no one to deliver Cybil's letter to. I didn't want so much death in my life. "Don't roll." That's what the message from Rochester was. Let it lay. Give it up. Stop the search. But life was too precious for that. Too precious when someone could just snuff you out for a perverse principle. I never knew Carlie Sampler, but her life taken so casually made the one that might be left in W. Stone all the more necessary to prove.

Once again the desk seemed to hold a clue for me, even too late on a long night. I ran my hand over the wood, appreciating, feeling Cybil's presence and a calming that had not come before. I glanced at my letters; one caught my attention on stationery from Northwestern Colorado University. Dr. Walter Peistermeister was writing to me. I wondered if he'd heard that I was back in the jungle of journalistic endeavor, perhaps when Steve Raymond checked my references.

His letter was newsy with activities of some other alumni who had been my classmates. I didn't remember most of them. He didn't get to the point until the last paragraph.

"You probably remember our department's esteemed Dr. Julia Ramsey. No senior worth his or her mettle was degreed without passing Dr. Ramsey's Advanced Reporting class. She has since moved on to New York University but sends me special job notices every now and then. I thought the one enclosed might interest you, in case you're considering relocating and want to start with a small town newspaper to get your feet wet again. I'll certainly give you a recommendation. I'm glad to hear you're writing. I always enjoyed your contributions."

He signed himself "Sincerely"; I wondered if he'd ever handled any murder cases during his pre-instructor stint as a reporter. Maybe he could tell me how to reconcile the lurid details. How to get past dwelling on the victim. Enclosed with Dr. Peistermeister's letter was Dr. Ramsey's New York address and phone number, as well as the job description for the reporter's job he had mentioned. The contact was editor "Gruff" Hamilton, with the *Burnton Beckoner,* in Burnton, Oregon.

Apparently ole Walter had heard more than that I was writing again. His suggestion that I might be "considering relocating" was probably a sensitive way of acknowledging my divorce. Maybe he was still as wise as I'd thought when I was just an impressionable, fledgling student of journalism. As I stood in my apartment at past midnight, considering all that had befallen me since my divorce, nothing made more sense than the distance and anonymity of Oregon.

TWELVE

A Million Bucks

Sunlight in the living room inched over the rug and reached me with its brightness, the way water covers a beach and wets your feet no matter how far back in the sand you sit. My sleep was a restless miasma of half dreams and ghost faces. Again and again I saw myself standing in Sara's place in that darkened office, about to walk to the bathroom door, "like nothing was wrong." When I awakened, my neck was stiff and my shoulders ached. One hip felt like it was wrenched out of the socket. My own arthritis twinging, I guess, in some cosmic act of sympathy for Cybil and W. Stone. The spa: today I might be able to contact Greenwood Spa or at least find out how Audrey Louise had fared with the Jacksonville phone book. Seeing Audrey Louise was just what I needed. I wanted to give her a hug, feel her warmth, drive myself out of the inner city too ready to remind me of violence. Over coffee, she would give me that total attention she was capable of, give me her humor and her hopeful face. Over the years, moments with her had been like a time warp outside of everything else: clear and safe and loving.

Loving: that was something I didn't want to think about, nor remember the last brief part of a dream I had right before I awakened. It was still sitting in my mind, not dispelled by the sunlight, making me irritable with its persistence. I'd had too much stimulus in the last few days. I needed rest with no one's secrets to involve me. I ought to pack now for Oregon and forget the murder and the letters and the divorce. Cover school board meetings, arguments about mundane things like a shortage of paper for the stencil machine or the length of hair for male students. But it was Thursday and I had one page of great importance to write by tomorrow. I couldn't get away from the secrets just yet. I'd been entrusted. Thinking about that was thinking about loving again, because of Sara.

My heart leapt like a restless engine turning over for a race, though I got no hint that the flag had dropped. Maybe I'm ill. Symptoms of exhaustion, that's what. Simple arrhythmia. Racing across the country, lurking in the chilly wings of Porterfield and graveyards in winter: no wonder my heart is uneasy.

Flat on my back with an uncontrollable pulse, I shivered under my covers, then shook them back, sat up, jerking my stiff self with irritability. Who's kidding whom here? I didn't say it out loud but I might as well have. My own unspoken words followed me into the bathroom, stood behind me while I splashed my face with water, looked over my shoulder when I looked into the mirror. I wasn't inspecting for wrinkles. I was looking at myself and seeing someone not entirely familiar. I was looking at my face but what I saw was that squib of a dream, that nagging little mind picture that had danced by just as the sunlight made me open my eyes. Dancing—we were dancing in that scrap of a dream. Like Cybil and W. Stone on their sequestered terrace at the spa. Our faces were radiant, as if the moon had vacated the night sky and we passed it between us. We held each other so tight, every part of us touching in those small turns on that terrace above the silent street, our signal kneecaps pressing lightly against each other. We were lovers in the dream, deep in our own quixotic romance. My partner's hands held me in my dream so that I knew I could never drop away or fall back into uncertainty. My partner had been Sara.

It was Sara dancing with me, her lips just above my cheekbone with a quiet breath upon my ear. Then the terrace melted away and I was walking alone in a grove of trees. I heard someone coming for me. I turned and reached out my hand and Sara was with me again, taking my hand, running electricity through me

161

with her touch. I felt so alive. I was smiling; we were smiling. We were walking among the infants left in Fleming's aspen grove.

I felt no alarm and some elation. So Sara turns me on and it's high time someone did. For once, I wanted to let myself feel without holding back, without guarding that one scared spot that had always been with me. I wanted to dare to express myself in that strong, sure way that came straight from my deepest self. With Mike, I had always felt a door was closed to me. I had never felt free to love in the way Cybil described, "I am alive and will be for the rest of my life because of you." I wasn't positive about the relationship of Sara and Nikki, but it was clear that they cared deeply for each other. Seeing them together, their open concern and affection, released in me a flood of exhilaration that I knew was right. It was not just a crush I felt for Sara, though that was part of it, but a recognition of the kind of feeling that two women could share. That was what I wanted, that syncopation of body and mind. I had no past experience to clinch it easily for me, but something clearly felt like square peg finally in square slot. My feelings were catching up to my reason.

The face before me was tired at the eyes. But there was something like a smile rising above the chin, on the horizon of the mouth. Does this mean I'm a Lesbian? I didn't ask out loud but I heard the question clearly, saw the word in my own friendly neon sign vision. I liked the colors of that light. I liked what it announced. I could be dancing again and happy and no stranger to myself or a lover. I could be a little less scared. There just wasn't a lot of baggage to open and sort through when I answered my own question, as I was on my way to dress for the business of the day. Yes, I'm probably a Lesbian.

"Nyla Wade, get yourself right in here and sit down. You have a lot of catching up to do for me."

Audrey Louise had me by my arm as we headed for the kitchen. She had Sam by his arm too; he was squirming to get into his coat.

"You watch out for Mark and Tony. And don't go over to that vacant lot, you hear me?"

He was sing-songing at her, "Yea, yea, yea," over and over.

"Stop that!"

He did. He looked up at her, very sober-faced.

"Tony is too little to be messing around in those abandoned cars."

Sam worked his lips back and forth. I thought of Sara's lips and felt a rush of nerves prickle in my stomach.

"Help me out on this, bud. You're the oldest. I need to be able to count on you."

Sam cocked his head to one side. Then he zipped his coat resolutely and said, "Okay, Mom." He was out the door like a shot. Audrey Louise sighed with relief and went for cups of coffee.

"I know you just love these days when they aren't in school."

"I think teachers' meetings are just a way of testing parents. Today I doubt if I'd make a very good grade."

"Nonsense, Audrey Louise, you've always been an A-plus mother."

She came back with coffee and a delighted twinkle in her eye.

"What's up?" I asked.

"I have a surprise for you." She had a Cheshire cat smile. "Two, actually."

"Tell me!"

"Not until you give me a blow-by-blow of Rochester and an apology for not telling me when you were coming in last night."

There's no more intent listener than Audrey Louise. She barely took her eyes off me as I described Porterfield, the culpable Mr. Gant, my cozy hotel, and the Grand Lady with the Madonna on her shoulder. "Oh, Nyla, no!" she nearly shouted when I told her about my splashy exit from Crestlawn and the threatening grasp of William Porter's chauffeur, the ominous Garson. It was hard to have a murder on my mind in the cheery clutter of Audrey Louise's home. It was hard not to tell her about last night. But it was hardest to have no words for this morning and what I saw in the mirror. Not to be able yet to share this strange joy I felt in the midst of so much, this finding out of myself. For the first time, I couldn't tell her everything, and it was a little painful.

"You've earned your rewards," she said, rummaging in a lower cupboard and then plunking two pounds of phone book on the counter before me.

"But I thought you were just going to copy . . ."

"Copy schmopy, I committed petty theft. It would have taken

weeks to get one from the phone company and I wasn't exactly sure what you'd be looking for. What the heck; the university library can live without their copy of the Jacksonville phone book."

We both giggled. I toasted her with my coffee. It always tasted rich and hot when we were scheming together.

"But now for the coup de grace. A juicy morsel from my brother-in-law, the banker. I think he, too, committed some infractions to get this for me."

"What, what?"

"Well, I didn't really know what to ask him to look for. And if you hadn't called me to tell me what you were up to in Rochester, we wouldn't have noticed it."

"Noticed what?"

"The wonders of microfiche—checks, checks, and more checks. But in this case, *not* a check."

She was teasing me. I was going crazy. "What then, for godssakes!"

"A transfer of funds, tucked away on an account statement and not so obvious as a check."

"To whom? For how much?"

"To the tune of a million smackers."

"For what? Some property deal? Geez, does William Porter own Greenwood Spa or something bizarre like that? Tell me!"

"No indeed." Audrey Louise just kept stringing me from moment to moment.

"Give me the scoop, Audrey Louise, or I'll explode!"

We stared at each other wide-eyed. Sam came bursting in the back door just as Audrey Louise said, "The funds were transferred to . . . " He was followed hot on his heels by Mark, both of them screaming. Tony limped in last, his hands over his face and blood streaming through his fingers.

"My god!" I stood up and knocked over my cup of coffee. The beagle started barking in the garage.

"Don't worry, it's only a nose bleed. He gets one every day."

With the other two boys jumping and whooping around her, Audrey Louise plucked Tony up in her arms and sat him down by the sink. With a quick swipe, she turned cold water over a hand towel and leaned her son's head back. The crisis was over in less than a minute. She kissed Tony and smoothed his hair. He smiled.

Sam and Mark never let up on their racket, first as soldiers and then as Indians in riotous combat. The tribe was back out the door as quickly as they had come in. "Faster than a white tornado," she said, tidying the counter and replacing my spilled coffee.

"For petessakes, Audrey Louise, the transfer!"

Her words made my heart stop.

"It was made a week before Cybil's funeral. For a million dollars. To Sheila Rush."

"Cybil transferred a million dollars of Porter money to Sheila Rush? But why?"

"That's the weird part, Nyla. Cybil didn't make the transfer. William did. *He's* the one who gave the money to Sheila Rush."

Both of us were speechless. But we were also both thinking on the same wavelength. "Some kind of payoff, do you think?"

Audrey Louise shook her head. "Maybe. But what could she know that was worth a million bucks?"

We both pondered the new twist of information. William Porter had shown himself at Crestlawn to make me think W. Stone was dead. Sheila Rush, close friend with Stone for years, claimed she'd lost track of him. Those things just happen. And I had trusted her story. My coffee was cold but the trail was getting hot.

"I think there's only one thing she could know."

"Yes, only one thing."

"The whereabouts of W. Stone."

The transfer made me all the more sure that everyone was covering up in Rochester. And that the one thing they wanted me to believe was a lie. I knew W. Stone was alive. We had a clear direction for finding Stone right in front of us, in the Jacksonville phone book. Neither of us expected that Stone would be boldly listed in the white pages. And he was not. But even more surprising was that there was no listing for Greenwood Spa.

"It *has* to be here! Cybil and Stone met there every year for more than twenty years. Places like that just don't disappear overnight."

I called Jacksonville Information. They had no listing for the spa. They referred me to the Chamber of Commerce. My hand was shaking when I dialed that number. The Director wasn't in. I settled for the Assistant Director. I would have settled for the Assistant's Assistant.

165

"This is Mrs. Montrose. Can I help you?"

I explained I was trying to get the number for Greenwood Spa. I had heard it highly recommended as quite a landmark in Jacksonville and yet there was no listing for it, even from Information.

"That's quite true. Greenwood Spa closed its doors some four or five years ago after a fire destroyed a major portion of it. Because we have quite a community of retired people down here, most of the patients were able to get treatment from some of the newer spas that have opened here in the last decade."

"Do any of them specialize in arthritis treatments, like Greenwood?"

"Not really. As I said, with the migration of retired folks to Florida, geriatrics specialization and treatment of arthritis and other diseases are common in most of the spas here now."

"And how many do you have in the area?"

"Probably fifteen or twenty. It's a booming business."

She was too cheerful as I considered fifteen or twenty phone calls and the unlikelihood of cooperative record clerks or worse yet, the likelihood that W. Stone's records burned at Greenwood Spa.

"A fatal fire," I said as I hung up the phone.

"What do you mean?"

I told Audrey Louise Mrs. Montrose's unhappy news. "That fire was fatal to my hopes unless I go to Jacksonville and every spa and insist they confirm records on W. Stone."

"We both knew you were going anyway. From the start."

"We did?"

She smiled and gave me a spontaneous hug. "Yes, we did." Audrey Louise went to the window to check on her Indians and be sure they weren't camped in amongst the forbidden abandoned cars.

"But not today," I considered out loud, realizing time was flying by and I had yet to sit down to my most difficult task as a writer: a one-page depiction of the Saint's crime against Carlie Sampler. "I have another job to take care of. I better be on my way."

"Anything I can help you with?"

Her concern tempted me sorely. Desire tugged at me to empty my heart to her about Sara and Nikki and Carlie. But I didn't know exactly what they were up to and if they were traceable. What if the Saint came after them? What if we were all traceable? I could only take that chance for myself, not for this A-plus mother of three.

"You have been of immeasurable help already. Petty theft was sufficient. Not to mention helping bankroll my research in Rochester. Hey, can I send your brother-in-law some cigars? For his wizardry with inter-state microfiche?"

"Sure. Here, I'll write out his address for you."

I wasn't eager to leave Audrey Louise. The way the sun shone into her living room, the sounds outside her house of children and dogs running in and out: it was real, but in a secure way, with no room for an unpunished murder, a million-dollar payoff, the need to be untraceable.

"Can't even persuade you to stay for lunch, I bet." She didn't want me to leave her either. She sensed I had more on my mind than W. Stone and Cybil. But she had always had the good sense to know when not to ask me questions. As we walked to the door, Audrey Louise linked her arm through mine.

"You're limping. You okay?"

"Yes, it's just a return of my arthritis. A cranky sign to me of premature ageing."

"If it's any comfort, you used to limp every now and then in college. So you're not ageing at all. You're still the girl who loves unicorns and got sore muscles from field hockey."

Sam's basketball thudded against the side of the house.

"But we aren't girls anymore, Audrey Louise."

I kissed her and she hugged me again.

"Nope. We grew up and got better."

I never did get lunch. I went directly back to the apartment from Audrey Louise's, sat down at the desk, and didn't look up again until I had two different drafts of a one-page announcement of murder and a wastebasket full of attempts. DO YOU KNOW THIS MAN? read across both drafts. I couldn't imagine the face of the kind of man who could dismember a woman, who could kill in cold blood and continue his life as though he had not taken someone else's. I thought about Nikki drawing the picture to go with my writing; I knew why she would never forget his face.

It was past seven when I finally gave up, couldn't choose which

167

draft to use. I decided I'd spent enough time with the crime and the victim. I needed air. A short trip. I thought of Sivu's Sundae Shoppe and knew that would do the trick.

My phone answering machine clicked on as I was collecting my coat and gloves. Steve Raymond was calling so I picked up the receiver.

"Sure like your real voice better than that recording, Nyla. How's the sore throat?"

"Much better. How's our issue on the warehouse looking?"

"That's why I'm calling. Before we go to press, why don't you come back out here and we'll talk over the story in detail."

Go to press. Suddenly Raymond's words weren't just ordinary shop talk. Kinter had an in-house press plant. And I needed a press for Sara.

"Sure. Is tomorrow okay? By the way, Steve, I've never seen your printing department. Think you'd have time to give me a tour? Never hurts to know as much as you can about the whole operation."

He sounded enthused. "Plan to meet me for lunch out here. I'll bring our press foreman along."

I was snapping the deadbolt and anticipating mocha majesty when I thought of the letters. I remembered I'd wanted to put them somewhere for safekeeping. Maybe I'd get a locker out at the airport after all and just jam the key in a flowerpot. I went back in, unlocked the desk, and took out the manilla folder where I'd put the letter bundles together. It fit entirely out of sight in my purse. I closed a folder around the two drafts and locked my desk again.

Maybe spring was on the way. The night air had lost a little of its usual winter chill. I rolled the car window down enough to get some of the air as I drove. Traffic was light. I was heavy on the accelerator. When I checked the rearview mirror at my turn onto Downing, I had a red light flashing behind me. Just my luck; I was going thirty-five in a thirty zone and this cop couldn't resist me.

I dug in my purse for my license after I pulled over and what I was saying beneath my breath was no flattery for the cop. I didn't look up when someone leaned against the car and peered in my window.

"Trusting soul, aren't you, Wade? Just any ole red light and you pull over."

To my shock, Sara was smiling at me. She walked back to her car and pulled the red flashing light off her hood.

"Magnetic," she called to me, pointing to the bottom of the light. "Very handy!" When she'd shut the light off, she came back and slid into the passenger seat of my car.

"You should keep these doors locked at all times."

"Yes, because who knows what kind of person might be able to just slide right in next to me." Sara smiled at me when I said this, very contented with her police car impression.

"I told you I'd be in touch. Where were you headed?"

"Sivu's Sundae Shoppe."

"Ice cream. I love it. Let's go!"

Ensconced behind the biggest sundae Sivu made, Sara didn't seem to have a care in the world. Certainly she didn't seem to be carrying the secret of murder with her. I sipped a shake and stared at her. But only partly because she seemed so calm. The other reason was because it was hard to keep my eyes off her, especially her mouth and her hands. She looked up at me around a huge bite of whipped cream and nuts. "What?" She could tell my wheels were turning.

"Nothing."

She wasn't convinced. "Come on. You look tired."

"Well, deep and dreamy sleep after what you told me last night would have been a little impossible."

She wiped her lips with a napkin. No lipstick. She wasn't working tonight.

"Carlie's been dead for eight years. It's not like it happened yesterday to me and I'm still there. Back off from it, Wade. Don't let it get in the way. We need your part. Is it done?"

"Mostly."

"What about a press?"

"I'll know by tomorrow after lunch."

"Can we get it on short notice?"

"How short?"

"Tomorrow night."

"I knew you needed to move fast but I don't know if I can get keys and everything checked out that soon. What's the big rush?"

"We don't need keys. I can get us past locks. We need a press without a pressman around. The rush is, as I told you, news travels both ways. We gotta act before the Saint does something."

"I think I can get you access to the press. I'll work as fast as I can."

"Good."

She finished her sundae and I kept on looking at her. She didn't seem bothered by that. We sat in silence. Then out of the blue she asked, "You find out what you wanted to know in Rochester?"

I didn't need to ask her how much she knew. I was aware from her stake-out on me that she could find out whatever she wanted to know. And she was perceptive enough to be making a good guess.

"Not exactly."

"Is it going to get in the way of our deal?"

"No. But I'll have to make another trip soon. In a few days."

"We'll be all done tomorrow night if you can get us to the press."

"Don't worry. I want to be done as much as you do."

"Hey Wade, how come you never talk about money?"

"What do you mean?"

"You never asked what we were going to pay you for this."

"I never thought about the money. My version of a principle, I guess."

"Well, your part is crucial. So you'll be well-paid. Five hundred bucks. That ought to get you at least part of the way on your next trip."

"Yes. I'm going to Jacksonville."

For some reason, I was surprised when Sara mentioned money. I hadn't considered I was doing a job. A woman had been killed and I could contribute something to letting the world know. But I knew Sara didn't mean anything by her question. It was probably just her business, cash and carry, being sure she was paid.

"So what's in Jacksonville?"

Maybe because I felt so thoroughly trusting of Sara, or maybe because I was still too tired to edit my story, I spilled the entire W. Stone saga to her. Eventually I was just rambling, worn out with too many feelings and too much uncertainty everywhere I turned.

"So you're going to try and find this W. Stone? And then what?"

"Deliver a package."

170

I patted my purse and the letters within it. Then it occurred to me. Who would they be safer with than Sara? She was trusting me and I could trust her—I sensed that. William Porter would never find the letters if they were with her. Since I didn't know how to find her, I couldn't tip my hand even if I wanted to.

"Would you do me a favor?"

Sara smiled disarmingly and answered, "People are always asking me that."

"I mean it. Keep these letters for me. Just until your plan is finished. I have a feeling . . . nothing. Just stash them in your car for a couple of days, okay?"

"Sure. And you can do me a favor too."

I hoped she didn't notice how willing I was when I asked, "What?"

She pulled the black satin cap she'd been wearing at Bevo's out of her pocket.

"Keep this on your head tomorrow night. If we get the press, some friends will be helping me out. You don't know all of them, so to spot you, I told them you'd have on my cap."

I guess I looked a little dubious.

"It will bring you good luck to wear part of a hooker's outfit." She was enjoying teasing me. "Trust me."

"Why do you do it?" My own question came out of the blue as I took the cap from Sara.

"Do what?"

"Sell sex."

"Money. Adventure. Variety. Kicks. I'm good at it and I don't have to work too hard. If you have a reform lecture ready, stow it."

I smiled and that caught her off guard. But she smiled back, her eyes sparkling. I wanted desperately to kiss her, right there over the plastic sundae dishes and Sivu's surprised expression. But for the moment, I was just satisfied to keep her talking and with me a little longer.

"I promise. No reform lecture."

Sara shook her head, reassured. I giggled. "Now what?"

"So tell me, Sara . . . uh . . . do you have any, uh, *hobbies?*"

She giggled too.

"Let me see. Hobbies, huh? Dancing, I really like to dance. No, I *love* to dance. If johns could get off dancing, I'd already be a millionaire."

"Disco? Rock and roll? Jazz? What's your favorite music?"

She leaned forward to answer me and pressed closer; I felt my leg touch hers underneath the booth at Sivu's.

"I like it all. But I like the fifties' stuff the best. I can still do all those old steps: the camelwalk, continental, hitchhiker."

"The watusi?"

"You bet! Limbo, twist, everything. Wade, I won awards in school. I was a damned dancing queen!"

The way Sara grinned at me as she remembered her awards was like hide and seek, her comments a quick peek into her past, a moment when she dropped her facade. But just as we were able to share a comfortable moment together, she pulled her protective curtain between us again and became all business.

"The plan for tomorrow is you meet me here about seven to give me the information on the press. And wear the cap."

"All right. Anything else?"

"Be careful, Wade."

I gave her the packet of letters and she sauntered out to her car, stretching before she got in. The light from Sivu's sign reflected off her red velvet slacks. She had on black boots with a gold chain around the back of each one. She didn't look at me before she drove off.

I couldn't believe Sheila Rush took hush money. All the way back to the apartment, wearing Sara's cap cocked to one side of my head, I puzzled why she had done such a thing. I felt foolish and nervous because if she and William were not the enemies she portrayed them to be, then he knew clearly that I had the letters. And he might come after them. How could I have misread her so completely? All that business about them feuding and his selfishness. Just an act to send me off W. Stone's trail, to get my confidence. William was more right than I wanted to admit when he said he'd been playing the game longer than I had. I hadn't even seen the game when I had been right in the midst of it.

My mind was on the draft locked in my desk when I got out of the car, and on my own hip which was making itself known with a dull ache. I hardly noticed another car pulling away from the opposite side of the street. It jerked and squealed tires and still I didn't look up. "Noisy college kids," I said.

172

I had never been able to break the habit of dropping my keys into the bottom of my purse even when I intended to use them momentarily. So as usual, I was groping around for them when I got to my door. As I turned more toward the hallway light and brushed the door with my shoulder, it gave way and opened slightly. Frozen for a second with my hand in the purse, I ran my eyes down to the lock. No amateur break-in with jimmy marks. They had used a pick set. And even in that crack of the door, I could see strange shapes in the darkness: my few pieces of furniture overturned.

THIRTEEN

Pick Lock, Kiss for Good Luck

They had come and gone and left nothing in my small living space unexamined. In the movies, you see places ransacked; drawers scattered and broken in frustration, pillows slashed, objects literally swept off surfaces and left in pieces, everything that was in its place brutishly rearranged. The movies had come true. The kitchen was the worst. Every canister was dumped, the refrigerator rudely rifled. One can hide something in many places but with the celery and ice cubes would not have been my choice. Cellophane from ruined packages mixed with bread slices, flour, sugar, and left-overs coated the floor and cabinets. There was nothing to do but swab it all down a drain and start over.

I was thankful Audrey Louise never persuaded me to get that couch; there would have been nothing left of it judging from the remains of the unicorn pillow and my mattress. It had been sliced fore and aft, a total loss: the springs sprung and uncoiling out the edges and the backing hanging in shreds. I wandered through the wreckage, unable to laugh or cry, just feeling numb and not entirely surprised. Feeling grateful that they were gone and I had not been home to become any semblance of that massacred unicorn pillow. The mess in the kitchen was less offensive than the rubble of the bookcase. No respect for literature, these oafs. If I could have mustered any tears, they would have been for my first edition Fitzgerald with the broken spine and splayed binding.

Shoes were slung from the closet to the living room, with the heels literally ripped off of a pair or two. They weren't just sent to search for the letters, obviously. In some of their unnecessary abuse was the dark suggestion William Porter wanted me to have, perverse little payments for invading his family privacy.

My immediate worry after a general tour of the ruin was the desk. I was afraid to look, afraid they had put feet through the roll top and smashed those polished and carved drawers to smithereens. To my great relief, the only mark on the desk was a gouge made under the lock when one of the thugs had forced it open. Pencils and bank statements and every folder had been strewn wildly. What gave me a shiver of dismay was the wastebasket. Every piece of crumpled paper had been unfolded. So they had seen all my attempts at the announcement of murder. The drafts weren't in sight but I found them in the haphazard mess of other papers on the floor. I could only hope the intruders were just interested in finding W. Stone's letters and were, at the most, amused at what I was trying to write about the Saint.

I didn't make any immediate effort to restore order. I did deal with the kitchen, and simple respect made me return my shoes to their home in the closet. The rest I just shuffled into piles. The bed was beyond hope and so was sleep.

Porter's assault backfired in one way because a resolve came over me as I stood and looked at the damage in the apartment and realized there was no turning back for me, not from my trip to Jacksonville or getting into the Kinter Paint Company print shop, even if we had to scale walls and drive through barricades. I would have the truth and I would provide delivery of a letter and the telling of a murder. When it was all over, I would call the esteemed Dr. Julia Ramsey and tell her to write me a recommendation so I could pack bags for Oregon. William Porter had moved not only personal objects in my life but my purpose as well.

Instead of limping shell-shocked into the new day, I began putting on some figurative armor. I dressed to meet Steve Raymond with an eye to the stylish but a drift toward the sturdy. I looked high class casual, but the corduroys would keep me warm tonight and I could move quick in them if need be. The black satin cap didn't quite match so I added a black ascot. With a quick trip to the building incinerator, I burned all my crumpled declarations about the Saint. I typed the final copy, leaving space for Nikki's drawing, and put it in a large envelope in my purse. Then I treated myself to a hearty breakfast. I felt like eating. I was the chimera again, stoking my courage fires with the fuel of eggs and bacon, pancakes with lots of syrup. I might be nervous or scared or panicked before tomorrow came. I might be telling lies and scoping out door locks and making rendezvous, but I wouldn't be hungry.

No one was going to make me feel like a cat dancing on hot tin. I had a little time before I headed out for Kinter, but I wasn't going to get rattled. I read the paper after breakfast. I made a conscious decision to relax. I went window shopping, ambling around an outdoor mall, past toy shops and stationery stores and hairdressers. As I passed a short alleyway between a Woolworth's smelling of old popcorn and a lounge collecting early Friday drinkers, I was grabbed and pulled off the sidewalk.

"What the . . . !"

I didn't scream because the scent of lilac and woodruff clued me that I wasn't being manhandled. Sara was laughing as I pushed away from her in the alley.

"Daydreaming can get you into trouble, Wade." She was grinning at me; she put one booted foot up against the wall and struck a match on the brick to light a cigar.

"I thought I was meeting you at seven." I only feigned being disturbed by her unpredictable appearance. There was no one I wanted more to see.

"You still are. This is just an extra added treat."

I wondered if she knew how true that was. "You aren't so funny, Sara. I just missed being grabbed last night when I got home and slung up against the wall like all of my belongings."

Sara snapped the boot down off the wall. Her shoulders tightened.

"Did someone junk your place?"

"You got it."

She took a step toward me and put one hand on my shoulder. "But you're okay?"

"Yes. They must have been after the letters. I gave them to you just in time."

"They're safe. But I wonder about you." She didn't move away from me but drew me into her eyes again, just as she had at Bevo's. As we stood so close together, Sara having no idea she was in my heart or my dreams, a part of me knew that loving someone inaccessible might prove to be my toughest adversary. I put my hand on her arm, felt how cold my fingers were against her warm skin. "I'll be okay. I haven't seen anyone following me. Besides you, that is."

She nodded, then moved away from me to the sidewalk. She looked both ways. When she turned back to me, she asked, "Have you got it?"

"What? The one-pager?"

"What else?"

"Yes, I have it."

"Okay, give it to me. I'm going to strip it and get the plate burned this afternoon. I'll destroy the original so there will be no paper with prints on it anywhere. Now, when you check out this press, be sure to get the name that's on it. An offset can be slow but a web is too goddamned big to crank up without letting everyone in town know about it. What we really need is a Miehle but we'll make do. Just find out what they have exactly so I'll know how much time we need."

"You want serial numbers while I'm at it?"

At first she wasn't sure I was kidding. But her frown disappeared in seconds and she grinned that irresistible grin again. I was glad I was steps away from her because I wanted to grab her and not for an alleyway chat. I told her the musclemen had seen my drafts but I had since burned them.

"That wasn't what they were looking for anyway."

"Good. That was a smart move. Hey, I gotta split. See you at seven."

"Take care until then."

With a quick turn, Sara walked out of the alley shadows and into the sunlight. For a moment all I could see was the glowing outline of her body. Then I heard her say, "By the by, that's a pretty schnazzy cap you got on, lady."

Steve Raymond was set to surprise me at lunch when he introduced his press foreman. Her polyester pant-suit had been dug out of the back of a closet for just such an occasion: a fancy fruit salad with the boss. As she stood up and her napkin floated into oblivion, Raymond announced to me, "This is Betts Wattle, our press foreman." He kept his eyes on my face. "We're more progressive at Kinter than you thought, eh, Nyla?" If I'd been a man, no doubt Steve would have slapped my back or nudged me in the ribs. As it was, I smiled at him with tight, unforgiving lips and gave a nod to Ms. Wattle. She nodded back at me; she had short brown hair and broad shoulders. I was sure she was as unimpressed at being shown off to me as I was with the situation.

Betts didn't say much during lunch. Steve prattled to me about her prowess with various kinds of printing machinery. I kept an ear open for the mention of a Miehle press. I was antsy to get a look at the layout of the print shop and drop a hint or two on Betts that would clue me on closing time and security systems. Whenever I looked up from my plate, she looked up from hers. She didn't exactly smile but there was an acknowledgement in her eyes of something.

Just when I was sure I couldn't sit still another minute, Betts excused herself. She said she'd meet us shortly at the print shop. This opportunity to leave Steve and me alone had been previously arranged. As she left me she said, "I'm so glad we had a chance to meet, Nyla," and there was sincerity double-layered in her voice.

One thing I could give Raymond: he didn't beat around the bush. He wanted me to know a few facts. Namely that Kinter had originally tried to locate the warehouse site in the meadow. The Fleming city fathers faltered, claiming questions on zoning, but that was a cover-up for a split ownership of the meadow land between two quarreling brothers. Fleming needed the jobs at the warehouse. They saw Kinter as a sign of prosperity for their town. The graveyard seemed a small sacrifice for that hope.

"You made some pretty strong points for saving the graveyard in your article, Nyla. But you want *me* to keep the dozers from rolling. You want *me* to do all the work."

"You're Kinter's p.r. expert. Who better to halt the onslaught than you?"

"That's where you're wrong. I know the Board of Directors and what they want. They think they're going to return the dream of American industry to Fleming. The warehouse *will* go up. But there's a way to give them what they want and a way for you to get what you want too."

"How?"

"I have nothing to gain by contesting the destruction of the cemetery. But it seems to me that the state historical society might want to declare such a unique graveyard a historical site, with the accompanying benefits and protection."

"Do they have enough clout to go up against the dream of American industry?"

"If you take your story to them and they declare that site, we can't build there. I have a feeling if that were to happen, those quarreling brothers would get sufficient pressure to reconcile and sell the meadow from all those Fleming fathers with dollar signs in their eyes."

Steve tipped his glass to me and said, "I'll table this story for one issue if you want to make a case with the historical society."

It was heartening to know that even a hardened p.r. type couldn't always live with his own whitewash. But the graveyard was the last concern on my mind at the moment. I would pursue saving it but not immediately.

"I want to make a case, Steve. But I can't get on this for a week at least. I've got some other pressing matters to attend to first."

"One issue, Nyla. That's all I can stall. After all, I told the Board the article would appear in the one we're running now."

"Okay, Steve. Thanks for the tip."

"What tip? You didn't get the idea from me."

We understood each other as I tipped my glass at him.

The print shop was not part of the main building and I was thankful for that. We wouldn't have to worry about the front guard station or the main building's alarm system. We headed for a pre-fab metal building set along the back fence of the Kinter compound. There was no guard station at the back fence and there was a chained gate next to a through access road with an entry to the highway.

Betts was in her element when we entered the print shop. She had changed into a sweatshirt, overalls, and an ink-stained apron. She looked up and waved from the press she was leaning over as we came in. As she spoke to the man running the press, I noticed she had a way of standing, a certain command about her that made me realize she wasn't hampered here by the lack of accoutrements associated with the new professional woman. She had a matter-of-factness to her, an immediate willingness to leave her office and tear down a cantankerous press which clearly preceded any dress-for-success squeamishness. Administering a department in her case didn't keep her at a distance from the oil and ink.

Steve told me he'd let Betts handle the tour. I thanked him for lunch.

"Call me when you've handled that matter we discussed," he said and left me in the print shop.

Betts clearly knew her equipment as she patiently showed me the cutter, ink mixer, various sorting apparatus, and a portion of *The Brush Stroke* in the stripping stage laid out on a light table. I almost needed earplugs against the din of the rattling machinery operating around us, all with speed and efficiency, each part of the printing process smoothly connected to the next.

"That's the web," she shouted at me as we beheld a behemoth of motor movement in one corner, zipping huge sheets of paper around its gears. Sara was right; if we flipped on the switch for the web press, it would be the same as setting off an alarm to announce our presence. I had not noticed the usual small red alarm box near the door of the printing building—I would have to guess there was not one on it and hope Sara could tell for sure.

"Here's your smaller offset," Betts shouted again. And patting a machine next to it, she yelled, "This is the Miehle." Success or luck, when I heard the name of the press, I knew we would be in business tonight.

"What's the difference?" I yelled to her.

"The Miehle prints copies four up so it's faster. The web is best for large quantity, multiple-color runs. Having all three gives us good flexibility."

All I needed to know now was when they shut down for the day and what kind of a chain locked the entry gates outside.

"Your crew looks like they work well together. What's your printing load like? Do you have to work a lot of overtime?"

"Naw." Betts wiped a rag over one end of the Miehle. "We've got it all down to a system now. Everyone works real hard all day so we can all leave right on time at night."

I nodded. She kept her eyes on me.

"I love running the print shop here." I looked back at her.

"But I have a private life too, you know." She grinned at me as if she'd told a joke we both thought was funny. One she wouldn't have told to everyone else. I didn't understand so I made my gesture to leave.

"I better be on my way. So you can finish for the day, on time as usual."

"Sure." We walked back up from the bay of machines to her office where the noise decreased slightly.

"Anytime I can help you, Nyla," Betts said, "just let me know." Again she looked at me with that half-smile of private understanding.

"I appreciate your time, Betts. You really have this place running shipshape."

As I put my hand out to shake hers, I wondered what kind of a sign I was wearing that I didn't have on before. Something she saw and read and wanted me to understand. Betts took my hand in both of hers in a sure handshake that suddenly made everything clear to me. She was sure of herself and of me; we were two strong women just a little different from everyone around us. So that was it. Betts also knew what was what. I had been recognized only a few hours after I had recognized myself.

Heading home, I worried if Sara could pick the heavy padlock that was on the chain holding the back gate locked. If they had a truck, could they run the gate open? Would that alert the guard at the front gate, even though the main building blocked sight line from the guard station? I probably could have just asked Betts to meet me back at the shop later. Could have filled her in on the need for the press and asked her help. But again I thought about keeping as few people involved as possible and the need to stay untraceable. I would have to trust in Sara's ability to make decisions about the locks when we met at seven. I went back to my apartment, bolted the door, and had three belts of scotch. I was able to stretch out with my coat bunched up under my head since there was no mattress or pillow left to me. Now it was safe to sleep for a few hours.

Sara listened carefully back at Sivu's as I described the layout of the print shop, the back access road, and the padlock on the gate. Sivu worked quietly cleaning ice cream plates, his turban nodding as he washed.

"What about the press?" she asked me.

"Paydirt. They've got a Miehle."

"Perfect. I've got the plate ready to go. With a few extra hands on the cutter and doing the bundling, we ought to be able to do the copies in about six hours. What about windows? Were there a lot of them?"

I had to think about the print shop again. I'd been scouting locks, not windows.

"I think there are six. Three in front and three in back. More square than rectangular. Maybe two feet by three feet?"

"Okay. Now I need to make two phone calls and then you and I will get rolling. We have to get in by ten o'clock and out before daylight."

After Sara made her calls, we got into a truck instead of the car she usually drove. The cab of the truck smelled of her cigars. The night and the excitement of what was coming closed around us. As we left Sivu's, Sara asked me, "You nervous?" I couldn't see her eyes in the darkness.

"Sure I am."

"Well, don't be. You're safe. You're with me."

It took some nerve but I scooted over next to her, needing to be close, pressing our shoulders together. I held onto her arm. We drove. We pulled in outside the New Yorker Lounge off Colfax. Two honks. Someone piled into the back of the truck. One block off Josephine we took an alley next to a laundromat and stopped behind a carriage house. Two honks and more passengers. Before we hit the highway and headed for Kinter, we slid in next to a green Bonneville parked at a Mr. McChicken. All I saw was the flash of some gold jewelry before I heard yet another rider climb aboard.

"Sorority sisters?" I asked Sara, warm and close next to me.

"Uh huh," she answered. "Alpha Gamma Come-uh."

When we reached the access road that ran behind Kinter, Sara pulled the truck off onto the shoulder. "I bet they're freezing their asses," she said. She started to get out and then told me, "You and your cap walk up this road a little way. Not too far. There should be another truck waiting for us. They'll put their lights on you and when they see the cap, they'll go on up and deal with getting the gate open. As soon as they head out, you come back here." I did what she told me. I couldn't see the faces of any of the women in the back of the truck as I headed off down the road. Sara was talking to them and they were lighting up a cigarette or two.

Sara's truck was quickly out of sight. I couldn't tell how far down the road I walked before headlights went on and I stopped in my tracks. I took off the cap and waved it. The truck turned around and took off in the opposite direction, toward the back gates of the paint company compound.

"They have the tongs," Sara said as I got back into her truck. "You know, to cut the gate chain."

I nodded. She passed me her cigars. "You cold?"

"Nope."

"Want a cigar?"

"Nope."

"We'll give them ten minutes. Then we'll go down and have a look."

"I thought you were going to pick the locks."

"Padlocks have different construction than door locks. It takes more time with the heavy stuff. So Nikki got some cutting tongs. We just figured it would be faster. And safer, in case they have any kind of security patrol."

"I'm sorry I didn't get time to find all this out for you ahead of time."

Sara reached over and gave me a gruff hug.

"Hey, you got us a press on real short notice. Everything will be okay."

"Can I see the plate you made for the press?"

We had started up and were rolling roughly over the road back to the gate.

"I want to see what he looks like."

"You'll get to see his face plenty. All one hundred thousand copies of it."

I had the next eight hours to contemplate where one hundred thousand one-page flyers would go. The gate was pulled open when we arrived; Sara shut the lights off on her truck and killed the engine. We coasted to the far side of the print shop where the other truck was parked, out of sight of the access road. Before we were to the door of the shop, several figures ran back and closed the gate. They gave each other a few short spoken signals and then I heard the clank of chain. They had brought their own replacement for the chain they cut.

Sara was at the door; Nikki was at her side, holding a small flashlight on the lock. I had told Sara at Sivu's that I didn't see an alarm box that afternoon when I was in the print shop. She ran her hands around the edges of the door, especially over the top. Then she put a small blade into the lock.

"No wires?" Nikki whispered.

"I can't feel any so far."

I heard the lock mechanism snap. Slowly, Sara edged the door open. No alarm. She'd guessed lucky. Behind me, three women bustled into the door. Two of them carried coils of electric cord attached to Redi-lamps. The third carried what looked like a small battery. Five women from Sara's truck followed the three who had been with Nikki. They each had several pieces of heavy cardboard.

Once inside, the operations began. The battery was actually a small generator to run the Redi-lamps which were hung by the Miehle, by the cutter, and one by a large table where the bundling would be done. Their metal shields kept the light from being seen from the door. The cardboard went up over the three front windows so that even the limited light from the lamps wouldn't have a chance to give us away. Before she went down into the bay where the presses and other machinery sat, Sara stood with me by the door.

"Your job is the most important one, Wade. You get to be the lookout. If you see anyone or anything headed for the building, or if you see a patrol car, give a yell. We'll shut down and scramble."

She looked out the small window in the print shop door.

"It's gonna be a long time with no more scenery than that. But someone has to watch out for us." Then she smiled, her face close to mine and my return smile.

"You can count on me, Sara."

As I took up my post, Sara went down into the bay again and showed one of the other women how to use the cutter.

"Now you show Lannie," she instructed. "Trade off when you get tired. Four cuts to each stack. I'll have your first stacks in just a few minutes."

They were all quiet and took the positions Sara assigned them. Then she began her own work with the Miehle: putting the plate in place and watching the paper feed. She started up the press. The noise was startling at first but the clack-clack of the rollers as they pulled the paper through soon began a regular rhythm. Nikki stood in between the Miehle and the other offset press, smoking a cigarette and watching Sara.

By the time everyone was bundling stacks of flyers, the paper still warm from the press, I had memorized the yardage between the print shop and the back of the main building. Nothing was moving out there, though at one point car lights at the front gate reflected momentarily against the windows of the main building and my heart turned over in panic. It was only someone driving up to the main building and they would have no reason to circle back behind. I had never seen any patrol cars at Kinter. They would have no reason to suspect someone might take seige of their print shop and they were far enough out of the city to make common vandalism a rarity. I leaned my head against the small window; eventually I was dozing, almost lulled by the sound of the press. Only because luck was with us all night did my napping on the job not result in all of us being discovered. But no one noticed and I awakened immediately when the press stopped.

Down in the bay, the ten women were dusting over their trail: stubbing cigarettes and carefully pocketing the butts, wiping everything in sight with large rags. They formed a sort of bucket brigade line and handed the bundles of flyers from the table up to the edge of the bay. All the extra paper used had been stuffed into a duffle bag which they were going to drag out with them, as if they'd never been there at all.

One by one they disconnected the Redi-lamps, first at the table and then at the cutter. Sara's press lamp was the only one burning in the darkness of the print shop. "Just one last little piece of business here," she said, sliding partially around the press as if it were a car up on a lift. In a moment she was wiping her hands on one of the rags. "I had to reconnect their counter. Can't have anyone thinking we fiddled with their stuff."

Several of the women laughed. They came up the ladder from the bay and gathered at the door, each of them carrying bundles of flyers with them.

"All the flyers in Nikki's truck." Sara's face was in the lamp light for a second as we all waited for her. "All clear?" she called to me. I looked out across the compound.

"All clear."

The cardboard came off the windows as Sara and Nikki brought up the rear with the generator and the last lamp. I stood to one side as everyone went out with the bundles. They had to make two trips and the sound of their feet was the only noise breaking the darkness.

Everyone headed for the trucks after the second trip. Sara checked the door to be sure it locked behind us and then she wiped the handle with her rag. In the darkness, if anyone had seen us they might have thought the duffle bag full of paper was a body being hijacked by a hooker hit squad.

Nikki went out first; two women jumped out of her truck and pushed the gate open again. She turned right and kept her lights off until she reached the highway. We pulled out of the compound and several of our passengers closed the gate and replaced the chain. One of them hit the roof of the cab twice when they were back aboard. We turned left and went back down the access road.

By the time we had returned all our riders to their respective posts, my watch was reading five a.m. We had beat the sun by scant time. My car was still at Sivu's and the shop looked asleep with its green shades pulled down and the "CLOSED" sign sitting lopsided in the front window. Sara pulled the truck in next to my Mustang.

"Well, mission accomplished." She stretched and touched the roof of the cab. A twinge in my stomach signaled me that we would soon be parting company.

"Before I forget . . . " Sara handed me a white envelope from the glove compartment. "Here's your dough for doing the flyer. And there's a key in there. Your letters are in a locker out at the airport. I figured that would be handy whenever you decide to go. Not to mention it will keep them out of your place until you're ready for the trip. I would bet those guys won't come back though. Sounds like they were thorough. So don't worry."

186

I took the key but I wasn't ready to think about money or traveling anywhere, least of all away from Sara.

"How will you know if your mission was a success?"

She smiled her patient and protective smile, knowing I didn't really want details.

"You'll read about it in the funny papers."

We were both tired.

"I mean it," she said.

"I never did get to see a flyer. I was too busy looking out."

"Save the lament. I brought you one." She pulled the piece of paper out of her back pocket. I looked at the drawing.

"Nikki did a good job. I think even *I* could spot this guy."

Sara laughed.

"All I meant was I don't travel in his circle but I still might recognize him."

"I know, I know."

Then I was laughing too and we were hugging each other and I wanted to cry because she would disappear before I could begin to tell her all the feelings she'd brought out in me.

When Sara lit up a cigar, I tried to concentrate on the flyer again. I had tears in my eyes when I saw there was some handwriting on the back of the flyer.

"What's this?"

Maybe she was a poet and was leaving me a love sonnet for posterity. At that hour, I thought anything was possible. I never expected what was written on the back: "W. Stone, 6420 Leehigh Way, Jacksonville."

"Where did you get this?" I grabbed Sara by the arm.

"You called us a sorority, babe, and you weren't far wrong. I know people all over the country, see. Some have even gone legit. Well, I happen to know this friend of a friend . . . " Her eyes were sparkling at me. She knew she'd given me a great gift. And we both knew what was what.

"Anyway, she's a masseuse out there at one of those spas. You told me who you were looking for so I had her make a quick pass over their records. We got lucky."

"Oh, Sara!" I couldn't stop my tears and they were for a mixture of feelings. She held me again briefly. I thought of the comforting way she'd been with Nikki at Bevo's and I knew they must be lovers. I sat up, wiped my face, and looked at her, this woman I had come to love.

"It might not be the right W. Stone, you know?" she said, moving one hand up to my face as if to wipe off a tear and then letting the gesture slide away.

"It will be, Sara," I said, taking her hand. "You're good luck for me. Just like the cap." I reached up and took it off, not wanting to relinquish it now. It might be all I'd have to remind me of her.

"Put that back on. It looks better on you than on me."

I sighed, trying to figure out how to hold those precious moments and not let Sara leave me.

"Sorry Sivu's is closed. I'd treat you to a sundae."

"Ice cream this early in the morning, Wade? What do you take me for? A woman who works nights?"

We reached the same point we had at Bevo's only a few nights before. No more words to trade in an overloaded moment. The sun was coming up.

"I've got to meet Nikki," she said softly, still holding my hand. I began to cry again and I just let the tears come.

"Good luck in Jacksonville."

Then Sara leaned over and kissed me, soft and sweet, so that I tasted my own salty tears against her mouth.

"I hope I'll see you in the funny papers, Sara."

"You will."

It wasn't much but it was my own Spartan shore and I wanted it to be swept clean again. I spent the weekend meticulously rebuilding some order to my plundered apartment. The time moved slowly, a precious slowness that afforded me ponderous movement of the body and mind. As I hung up clothes that had been tossed about, I visualized them on hangers in another closet, one at the end of travel west to Oregon. I let myself think about the question of relocating.

I was sure that most of the moments missing Mike would disappear if I put miles between us. Partly because the only thing I was holding onto was a loneliness I only now understood, a loneliness not connected to him nor solvable with another man. And not solvable with Sara as my heart might have hoped, but sometime, in the future, that loneliness would disappear and a soul would appear: one that could mirror my own, rooted in the experience of a woman.

Writing full-time for a small paper would give me new roots, both inspirational and financial. Not the hit-and-miss of free-lancing, such a job would provide a daily progression of people and living tied to my creativity. But even as the excitement of possibility began to grow in my thoughts, I knew I would not be able to take my solace with me, that best friend who had seen me through so much chance and confusion. We had been within reach of each other since college days together and thinking about parting from Audrey Louise was quite painful. I had made a parting I never thought possible when I divorced, and made anoth-er those few hours ago when Sara left me. What could only make leaving Audrey Louise bearable was that she would convince me moving toward myself would never mean leaving her behind.

When I sorted all that had been dislodged from the desk, I tossed several old letters into a stack and all my outdated *Writers Digest* issues into the wastebasket. Everything was neatness and order again but there I sat on the floor in the afternoon shadow of the desk near a stack of old letters and realized what a maelstrom chance could whirl about a person. Audrey Louise had wanted to buy a blasted couch but I persisted with my "beacon to the artist" frivolity and my heart set on a desk—a desk sold by chance in Denver, by a rich boy too proud to tell his family he had money problems, a desk that held the secret of Cybil's letters, hidden there by chance only when some matter pressed her to get them out of sight.

Was chance accident, luck, or both? Was it chance that we went to The Gravy Boat and found the desk? Accident that the tape around the packet of letters finally aged and let them fall into my sight when the desk was accidentally jolted? Luck that Audrey Louise insisted I put up cards to advertise myself so that I could help, even in a veiled way, try to bring an eight year old murder to light? Luck that Sara knew a friend of a friend who came up with W. Stone's address? I hoped there would be luck for me in Jacksonville and the conclusion of delivering someone else's old letters, and no accidents along the way.

As I righted the bookcase and put my hands on each prized volume, placed them back on the shelves I had built and then ar-

189

ranged them in my peculiar order, a confidence burned in me. Some day my own titles would sit among these. I had a hand in writing that I must trust. No matter where it started, with a paint company newsletter, or where it might travel, between Burnton school board reports and articles on the meetings of the Water Commission, or features on parades and street bazaars, I was a writer. There was a definite move in all that chance toward my dream of a novel, built along the way by accident and luck, such as the one-page flyer no one would ever know I had written.

The trusty Mustang felt frisky on our Monday morning sprint to the airport; I picked up my ticket at a travel agency a few blocks from the apartment, located in the yellow pages to avoid last minute delays with my plane. I was wearing Sara's cap; I kept looking into the rearview mirror, wishing I'd see a red light flagging me down, a red light on the green Chevy she drove. She didn't appear, though, and most of the cars were going into town to start the work week. Traffic in my direction was sparse. But in looking for, wishing for, Sara in my mirror, I noticed a black Gremlin staying close on my tail. It joined me from the exit onto the highway at Colorado Boulevard. Two men wearing low-slung hats were in the car. They kept a precise distance behind me and changed lanes whenever I did. I was never out of their sight. Porter's thugs hadn't returned yet to Rochester? If they followed me into the airport, how would I get the letters out of the locker without being grabbed?

As we approached the parking area at the airport, there were lines of cars at each entry lane. I pulled into the lane for Small Car Parking. The Gremlin pulled in a car behind me. As the flag went up, a space cleared in the lane next to me for Upper Deck Parking and I pulled into that space, to the reaction of noisy honking all around me. Even if the Gremlin could follow suit, I was enough ahead of them to get into the airport and with any luck, to that locker. These guys could have figured I had the letters on me now, though, and I didn't want to meet them alone anywhere in the parking lot.

I was at Door Four of the Passenger Arrival stations when I heard the Gremlin screech up the ramp to the Upper Deck. My ticket desk was at the other end of the airport. I ran inside and then went to the far side of the counters, running along the shop fronts rather than the more crowded and obvious passenger lines. It would take them awhile to check each line even if they split up. I had only my carry-on bag so I got into the Express Check-Out line at the Continental counter to get a boarding pass. Chance was there waiting for me, all right, but not dressed as Luck. The agent had no record of the ticket for the woman in front of me.

"Did you go through a travel agency, Miss?"

"Yes, the one at the Brown Palace. They aren't supposed to make mistakes."

"Yes, Miss. I'm checking."

"Did they misspell my name? It's Levitan. L-E-V-I-T-A-N, Alicia."

"Yes, Miss. I'm still checking."

I didn't want to look down the counters to see if the two from the Gremlin were catching up. But surely they wouldn't try to mug me right in front of all these people. Yet from the total wreckage of my apartment, I couldn't be sure. They were probably taking the heels they'd snapped off my shoes back to William Porter as a prize.

"Apparently the reservation has been misplaced, Miss Levitan. But we have room on this flight. I'll have to ask you to step over to our regular check-out line and they will help you."

"Look, I have to get stamps and a gift for my daughter and do some errands before my flight. Can't you just punch me into the computer?"

I'll punch you myself in a minute, Alicia, if you don't move it. Still no sight of my heavy-footed pursuers.

"You'll have to step into the regular line, Miss. This is the Express Line."

"That line will take me an hour. It's not *my* fault the reservation didn't register."

"Nor mine, Miss. Now please, just step over into the . . . "

I took a quick scan of the crowd and then glanced across at the window outside the doors for Passenger Arrival. Garson must have had two brothers because there were two meaty hooligans with their hands against the glass, staring at me from outside Door Ten, which led directly to the Continental counter.

"Please, I'm in a hurry." I thrust my ticket on the counter and pushed Alicia Levitan aside. "Sorry, but I've got to meet someone and I'm late already." Alicia gave me a disdainful look and a petulant sigh.

"An aisle seat is fine. Non-smoking. But hurry!"

The agent barely got the boarding pass slipped into the ticket folder before I raced off from the counter. I headed away from the concourse in my panic and hit the escalator down to the baggage area. I heard footsteps clamoring behind me. When I realized I was going the wrong way and that my best safety would be to get to the concourse and the security station, I wasn't sure where to turn. Then I remembered a shoe shine station at the end of the escalator and a small office. If the office wasn't locked, I could run in there and ditch them. As they went around the corner and into the baggage area, I'd make a beeline for the Up escalator.

There are some things you can almost always count on at a shoe shine station. That two of the three seats will be occupied and that someone will have left their paper in the third seat as a courtesy to the next bored traveler killing time. My feet became an ordinary pair among two other sets and the newspaper offered a perfect hiding place in plain sight. My unfriendly fellows clattered by me and I was on the Up escalator in seconds.

I took off my coat as I half-ran, half-walked to the concourse. One sleeve was dangling and the airport security guard at the security station gave me a questioning look when I sent my bag through the X-ray machine and I nearly jumped through the metal detector. I could breathe a slight sigh of relief—my stalkers would make the detector bells burst their moorings if they were packing revolvers.

"By the way," I asked one of the guards breathlessly, "where are the airport lockers?"

He frowned and pointed back the way I had come. "On either side of the coffee shop, lady, just at the entrance to this concourse."

So they could lie in wait for me at the lockers. They wouldn't have to dump their heat after all. Once they figured out I wasn't carrying the letters. Unless ... unless I didn't go to the locker myself and they had to conclude that I was safe beyond the barrier of the security station. I walked down toward my gate trying to figure out where and how to find a cooperative soul willing to play retriever for me and accomplish that in the next twenty minutes. I stopped at the door to the Women's Room and looked back up the concourse. Garson's look-alikes stood ten paces from the security station with their eyes peeled on me.

I went into one of the stalls in the bathroom and sat down, put my head in my hands. Which stranger milling about would help me? A teenager willing to make a quick five-spot? A woman with a friendly face? And what if those bloodhounds sniffed my accomplice out? I needed someone with a good bluff in their natural posture.

"And then he says to me, 'Still checking, Miss. Still checking.' The nerve of those people, making me move into the other line. I just got through this minute. It's been nearly thirty minutes since I started. And all because they can't spell my name. I mean, *really!*"

Alicia Levitan's voice was unmistakable. I could spell her name and she spelled my ticket to a successful ruse of those thick-brained rogues.

"Miss Levitan?" I came meekly out of my stall. She was applying a new lip line and when she recognized me as the woman who had pushed her aside at the ticket counter, she offered no smile of welcome.

"I'm so sorry I had to be brusque with you at the counter but I too have been given the runaround by the airline people. You were lucky."

"Really?" She wasn't any too willing to hear her own troubles topped on any sympathy scale.

"Yes, you see my son is here on holiday from Choate. He had to go through customs and I got instructions to meet him precisely at eleven at the clearance office or he'd be detained and we'd miss our flight on to Florida."

Alicia's interest was piqued, as I hoped it would be, by someone who could afford to send a son to a top private school.

"Well, I was at the office right on time but they've hustled him all over this airport and we still haven't found each other. He's fit to be tied by this time, I'm sure. We just can't miss that flight. His father made a special effort to come back from business in the Bahamas. We're going down the coast to our beach home at Boco Raton. He'll be quite upset if we're late. He has so little time these days."

"Yes, I guess you have had quite a runaround, Mrs. . . . . "

Alicia was warming up to me, what with mention of the Bahamas and a beach house.

"Mrs. Steiner. Of Steiner Couriers, International. That's Albert, my husband's, business."

Alicia's eyes brightened. She closed her lipstick and offered me a smile.

"Well, your brusqueness is certainly understandable, Mrs. Steiner. You have an important passenger to collect today."

"Thank you, Alicia. *Levitan:* isn't that Levitan Manufacturers? Everything from luggage to industrial furnaces?"

She could just as easily have said, "No, you have the wrong Levitan," but Alicia wanted to play my game.

"Why yes, how kind of you to recognize Daddy's name."

"Albert knows your father. I think they met in . . . "

"At the capital, probably. Daddy spends most of his time up there."

"Yes, of course. Say . . . " I looked at my watch. "Alicia, could you do me a quick favor? I have a locker just up here at the end of the concourse with some of Albert's papers in it that he asked me to bring him. The last word that I had on my son was that he's being brought to the gate on one of those electric carts and I can't really leave until he gets here. We're just about to board; would you be so kind as to go to the locker and get me the papers? It will only take a few minutes and it would be ever so generous of you to help while I wait here and hopefully try to collect that boy of mine."

"No trouble at all, Mrs. Steiner."

"Do call me Cybil." I smiled in spite of myself.

"Cybil, then. This is my chance to be a courier for the courier!" We both laughed politely.

"Yes indeed! Here's the key. It's number forty-two."

When we were in the air, I had a laugh to myself. About the faces on those thugs as I left the restroom, waved to them, and walked without fear to my gate for the flight. Alicia passed them going toward the lockers, completely unsuspected. There was the look on her face too, when she handed me the envelope on the plane, expecting to see my son sitting beside me.

"Oh, I had hoped to meet your son," she said, looking at some of the other passengers as they stowed their coats and settled in around us.

I leaned over and said to her, "He's in the toilet just now."

"Oh, yes, well, I see." She blushed slightly.

"Thank you, Alicia, for retrieving these papers for me. And again, sorry I had to be so pushy at the ticket counter."

"So glad to be able to help you, Mrs. Steiner . . . uh . . . Cybil."

I chuckled to myself, sure she watched that airplane bathroom like a hawk. But what could she say, considering her own fictitious claim to the Levitan name, when she saw the man sitting next to me return. He had a head of white hair and was well over sixty.

If Sara's friend had not located the right W. Stone in Jacksonville, then my work would be cut out for me. I'd have to visit every spa in that city and then if I still turned up with nothing, I'd have to go to the county records office and see if I could turn up anything there on Stone. But Sara had been a lucky presence in my life and I felt sure I was headed in the right direction.

I wondered if Stone would know about the pen in the desk and why Cybil had had to hide the letters. I wondered how he had felt when he was unable to attend his beloved's funeral or her memorial ceremony. Perhaps having her letter finally after all these years would somehow help.

There was just one little detail nagging at me that I hoped Stone could explain. It had to do with that newspaper photograph that had fallen from Sheila Rush's photo album. Maybe it was the final picture she had of Cybil, placed at the back of the book after the formal portraits and probably taken on one of those last visits to Greenwood Spa. There had been a peculiar reaction in Sheila when I saw the picture and though it seemed a small detail now on the brink of possible finality to my mission of delivery, I still wanted that reaction explained. It might be a waste of time and Sheila Rush could have been nervous that day. Maybe she thought I would learn about her money dealings with William Porter. I wished I could figure a different explanation for that transfer. I didn't want to believe Rush could be paid off, much less to work in cahoots with William. There was also the possibility that Stone would not know about the picture of Cybil; I could only remember the caption: "Summerfest for Seniors." I could ask and hope he could provide the answer.

My cab headed me for Leehigh Way. When Stone answered the door, what would he look like? An aged poet, with curly white hair and pinkish skin, with the obvious lips of a romantic, even in his late seventies? Would he be short or heavyset, stooped or tall and elegant like Sheila Rush? I could not believe he would make only ordinary conversation, not a man who could write such love letters for so many years. He would no doubt be a wit, or perhaps somewhat of a dreamer with a little melancholy in his eyes. Within minutes, I would discover if I had unraveled a plausible story or if I was dead wrong.

Leehigh Way turned out to be a street bordering one side of Leehigh Acres, a retirement oasis approximately four blocks square. Within the development were several large, high-rise apartment buildings, as well as small three and four story, multiple dwellings. Then one block consisted of single dwelling homes of varying sizes, all built in brick. I got out on the corner of Leehigh Way and Progress Avenue. The address I sought was on the street of brick houses.

Sixty-four twenty had tan brick, a green roof, and green slats on either side of the front door that made it appear like an entry to a courtyard garden. There were two orange tile designs in the arch above the door, a chimney stack, and one of those small false attic windows in the center of the front roof. The curtains at the front window were pulled back; no fear of sunlight here. Now perhaps with my delivery, no fear ever again that William Porter would possess the letters hidden years ago. When I lifted the door knocker, I was quite surprised to find it was one that operated just like the one at Porterfield. When pulled upright, the knocker moved back into resting position with a sequence of chimes inside the house.

The melancholy poet's face of W. Stone at 6420 Leehigh Way was not forthcoming. More surprising to me was that a woman opened the door when I rang. She looked vaguely familiar, something about the shape of her chin. I couldn't place the acquaintance because I was taken aback at not being met by the man I expected. The woman took a quizzical but unfearing look at me and said, "Can I help you?"

"Yes. Well, I think so. I am trying to find W. Stone. Perhaps I have the wrong address."

She did not reply but looked at me more closely, with a careful scrutiny.

"You're probably wondering who I am. I'm Nyla Wade from Denver, Colorado. If W. Stone does live here, I have a letter for him. Actually, a number of letters that he wrote and one that was written to him but never delivered."

Again I was surprised after the woman's wary expression now to see her smile, not just with friendliness or courtesy but with a recognition I was not sure about. In that smile was again something unusual and somehow known to me. Maybe she reminded me of Sheila Rush; they were certainly of the same ilk — elegant, gracious women who had aged into a completely relaxed finesse and style.

"You have the right address. Do come in."

The woman showed me into the house and offered me a chair in a spacious living room.

"One thing," she said, sitting down across from me and with her voice just above a whisper. "We need to be a little quiet. My housemate is napping."

I assumed she meant Stone and hoped he wasn't a heavy afternoon sleeper. I had come so far with only an impression of him; I did not want to leave without meeting the eloquent poet of passion in person.

"Tell me about the letters."

"Well, I really should wait . . . "

Her manner was entirely reassuring when she leaned over to touch my arm and say, "How did you find them?"

There was nothing for me to do but wait for Stone to arise, and even if I had to repeat my story, the woman seemed interested and our visit would at least pass the time.

"Several months ago, I purchased a desk at an antique store. I'm a writer with aspirations to be more than a free-lance journalist. So the desk I wanted to buy was more to me than just additional furniture. It was to be a resource for my energy and inspiration, an environment and not just an object. It was that desk, which had previously been owned by a woman named Cybil Porter and her mother-in-law before her, Maye Della Porter, that I bought. A myriad of events since I purchased the desk have brought me here today."

The woman was all intent interest in my story. "Yes, go on."

"When my friends and I were moving the desk, we jolted it accidentally in the truck. Later, I discovered that jolt had dislodged a package hidden inside the desk. A package of letters written to Cybil Porter from W. Stone. And one Cybil wrote but for some reason never sent to Stone."

The woman sighed and clasped her hands together. Again I saw in her something recollected by unfocused; was it her face I knew or just something in her manner? When she looked me directly in the eyes, as I was about to ask if she was Stone's wife, sister, or companion, she startled me into utter silence.

"At last my letters are safe. I am glad you found me, Nyla. The fate of those letters that I wrote to Cybil has been a burdensome worry for many years. You have just lifted that burden."

I can only imagine my expression. The woman sitting across from me leaned toward me again and said, "I see that you were not expecting this information. I am W. Stone. My first name is Winona."

The poet of passion I had waited to meet sat before me: another woman. I was taken totally by surprise at her revelation. It had never occurred to me to see their eloquent exchange as other than heterosexual. I knew in that nearly painful moment what a victim I was of an ordinary and limited perspective. No wonder the letters had seemed like a storybook to me, something few men could write. *A woman had written them to another woman.* Cybil had thought of Winona when she was with Lawrence because her discovery of her true feelings of love, like my own, were a wonder to her. They had been acquainted for some time before their fateful "vacation" together had changed the fabric of their friendship. I knew how the closeness of friendship could spawn love; I thought of Sara. I hoped never again to be so small in my analysis of love. I hoped I could tell Winona before I left that she had helped pull off the blinders of my lifetime.

All the questions I held from the moment I discovered the letters seemed to fly out of my thoughts as I let Winona Stone's identity sink in. She realized my temporary shock and most perceptively did not try to get me to talk for a few minutes about the letters or the desk or Cybil. She sat with her hands relaxed in her lap, alternately watching my face and the sun where it feathered across the rug through the living room windows.

As I began to revive, I looked at Winona Stone with my own careful scrutiny. I realized suddenly why she had seemed familiar to me. She was one of the women in the newspaper photo that had made Sheila Rush so nervous. She was the one with the thin face and the sturdy chin. Her eyes were lively, even as she sat relaxed trying not to stare at me and to allow me some space to regain my composure.

"Would you like some tea, Nyla? Then we can talk some more."

"Yes, that would be wonderful."

"Or if you want something stronger, I have some scotch."

"Perfect! I am sorry to seem so unnerved, Ms. Stone . . . "

"Call me Winona. And don't apologize. I can imagine your complete surprise. If there had been a safe way to give you some warning, perhaps I could have spared you the shock."

She crossed into the open dining area adjacent to the living room and opened a cabinet, taking out two glasses and the scotch. J&B—it tempted me from clear across the room. I got up and walked over to her as she poured the scotch at the table.

"I thought maybe I recognized you at the door but I didn't know why. I saw your picture, only for a second, when I visited Sheila Rush just a few days ago."

"Yes, I know."

"You *know* about that visit? Then she *is* in contact with you and hasn't lost track of you as she told me. Why did she lie?"

Winona took a healthy drink of scotch before she answered.

"There is a great deal to tell you, Nyla, and Sheila's protective story is only part of it."

She opened a drawer in the bureau below the liquor cabinet and pulled out a folded newspaper. She looked at the paper and then at me with such an odd expression that it sent a tingling up my spine. I hadn't felt that sensation since I was in the left wing at Porterfield: surely the ominous orchid had departed! Audrey Louise's warning came to my mind: "You'll think you're sifting through ash and find a live fire." Winona handed me the newspaper and I recognized the photo I'd seen at Sheila Rush's house.

"Sheila was so nervous when I saw this picture. I wondered why at the time. I see that your names are listed here under the photo . . . 'long-time resident Winona Stone' . . . Sheila didn't want me to know you were a woman. That must have been why she snatched the photo away from me so quickly."

It all came over me, all these days of unknowing: the search, the tense graveyard chat and the airport chase, the pure chance of being in Stone's home because of Sara's tip from a friend. A desk that left New York and was abandoned in Denver gave up its secret to me and I passed it on to a hooker from Washington, D.C., who found the letter writer, a woman, in Florida. I never wanted to be such an obvious fool again in my life nor to be so manipulated by chance. All I could do in this rush of feelings, this release, was to laugh: loud, long, and hard. Winona seemed startled at first, but then she laughed with me, until we were both clutching at our glasses of scotch and each other, our broken phrases overlapping.

"Can't stop, sorry, but . . . didn't know, didn't guess . . . "

"So complex, wanted to get in touch . . . couldn't risk it . . . "

"The letters . . . so beautiful . . . I thought . . . "

"I know, I know . . . some crazy surprise for you . . . "

It was at the same moment that I was about to put the newspaper on the table that I heard a door open and footsteps in the hall. I noticed as I was putting the paper down that the date on the *Jacksonville Daily News,* carrying the photo of Winona Stone and Cybil Porter, was dated August 15, 1973: three years after Cybil's death.

"What's all this racket?" a woman's voice called as she came down the hall. The live fire that seemed to be ash finally burned bright in my brain.

"We have a visitor," Winona answered, turning toward the hall doorway. "Nyla Wade, the woman Sheila Rush told us about."

I could scarcely believe my eyes when she stepped into the doorway: Cybil Porter, alive and well.

If I could have read the clues a different way, I would have known Cybil was alive from her own letter when she wrote, "None of it is simple and all of it can seem impossible to understand." No wonder William Porter didn't want me to question a doctor and nurse in England. No wonder he didn't want to talk about the quickness of the memorial ceremony. What was it Sheila Rush said? "I prefer to think Cybil was finally allowed her own desires. She went on to circumstances she deserved after years of duty well-spent." So Sheila wasn't cosmic after all; she had been speak-

ing of Cybil's leaving but not by death. My visions of the orchid finally made sense; Sheila Rush told me William never liked Cybil's orchids because they reminded him of funerals. Mine must have been a symbol of the funeral that never was.

We went out into their back garden until dinnertime. They took their time to answer all my questions, sitting close together, often holding hands as one or the other of them spoke. Sheila Rush, they told me, had been their loyal friend for many years. She was the only person in Rochester who knew where they were and that they were together. The only person, that is, besides William. It suited him to be party to their intrigue although the road to his agreement in the scheme had been a rocky one.

Tanned, dressed in a grey leather coat and mauve shirt, grey tweed pants and with a diaphanous lavender scarf at her neck, Cybil began the story she had been concealing with Winona Stone and Sheila Rush for more than a decade. As she spoke, there was a certainty in her movements and her tone of voice, her inquisitive and confident regard for me, that confirmed the bearing of one who had gracefully managed an empire.

"You have no idea how close our paths came to crossing sooner when Sheila found out from Randy that my desk had ended up in Denver. She obtained the name of the antique store and volunteered to try and purchase it for us. Randy was sure there was no hope of it still being unsold; we hoped whoever found the letters would either destroy them or keep them lost in anonymity. By the time Sheila called the store, you had already purchased the desk. Apparently the fellow she spoke to did not want to reveal your name. Sheila said he was most suspicious and quite protective of you."

"That would be Thomas. He's somewhat of a seer, I think. He seemed to sense that there was more to the desk than initially appeared. Perhaps because of the flaw."

"What do you mean by the flaw?" Cybil gazed at me with slight discomposure; Winona squeezed her hand and asked, "This is the first I've heard of a flaw. What was wrong with the desk?"

I remembered those anxious moments when I dug the pen point out of the desk to find the emerald eye, when those few inches of pen barrel had seemed unretrievable. I described to them what had been embedded in the golden oak. They looked at each other, then after a moment, Cybil nodded, affirming her memory to me.

"I had forgotten about the pen. That happened just before my hurried trip to England. Winona, you'll remember too, I think, because of a harried phone call over the trans-Atlantic cable after I arrived there. But first, I have to give you some background, Nyla.

"The year after Lawrence died was an unbearable period for

me. William and I warred in a thousand subtle ways during my marriage to Spencer but when the buffer, my son, was gone, he let out the complete vehemence of his soul upon me. I was trying to decide how to leave Porterfield and join Winona here. There was some . . . "

She paused and touched the scarf at her neck. My memory stirred to the comments Winona had made in a letter about Cybil's reluctance to let out her feelings.

"I had some difficulty in leaving all those years at Porterfield behind me. The familiarity, the control and security. To change my life again, totally, even though love awaited me here, was not easy.

"William didn't know about our affair until 1970. The circumstances of his discovery amaze us to this day."

"Oh, we didn't have the luck that year, to say the least," Winona offered.

"William was never a party-goer," Cybil continued. "He surprised both Sheila and me by showing up unannounced at her New Year's Eve gala. Knowledge of my meetings with W. Stone was not widespread but was known to a small circle of friends who had sympathy for our situation. Apparently two rather intoxicated fellows were trading tales of their visits to Greenwood Spa. It was not just a spa in those days, you see, but something of a resort as well, with dancing and drinking and availability for discreet entertainment to select clients from all over the country. These fellows were unaware of William's presence; he gathered clearly from their conversation and their mention of Winona and me as part of the Jacksonville group, what we were all about. The men didn't mean to break our confidence. William was simply in the right place at the right time for discovering a secret of nearly thirty years."

Cybil sighed; Winona patted her arm.

"Want to rest a minute, honey?"

"No, I am all right. And Nyla has waited a long time to know the whole story. For a few weeks after the party, William had his secretary, Simon Gant, intercept my letters. Our mail had been previously unsuspected because our friendship was accepted at face value. When William had confirmed from the letters the gist of the conversation he'd overheard at Sheila's party, he confronted me about the affair. He was so righteous, so indignant, literally suppurating moral outrage. He sermonized to me that he would not allow me to damage the Porter name. At first I denied his accusations. He grew angrier, shouted that I had fouled his prestigious family's honor and history. He had warned Spencer not to marry me and now his early distrust of me had been borne out. In his rage, he went to the desk, vowing I would never use it again to write my 'improper sentiments.' He slung my papers across the room and in a final act of fury, drove the pen into the desk."

I was trying to imagine that cold and grey little man roused, exhilarated even, with the fire of fury, when Cybil and Winona surprised me with their laughter. Winona had remembered about the pen also.

"When Cybil called me after it was all over, we laughed about poor William because he was madder still when he realized in the midst of his lecture that he'd marred Maye Della's precious desk. More than that, he'd ruined her favorite pen as well. Didn't Bernard give her that pen when Spencer was born, Cybil?"

"Yes, that's what Spencer told me years ago. William went on like that anyway, raging. Said he wanted me out immediately. As you know from your visit, he is more like a pressure cooker than a feeling person with possible emotions. I was afraid he would become violent. I left immediately for England, to give myself time to think and him time to calm down. I had been planning to go anyway and so most of the arrangements had already been made."

"But why did you hide the letters? Why didn't you take them with you? And why didn't you go directly to W., that is, Winona?"

"I had only fifteen minutes alone in the study after William's tirade. He told me he wanted all of Winona's letters and would find them before I left. He planned to keep them and said that I could never again make claim to any of the Porter wealth. He knew I would bring no scandal down upon the memory of Spencer or Lawrence. While he went to get Simon, I quickly hid the letters in the desk. It seemed such an obvious place to me that he would never think of it. When he returned, Simon began to search the study, the desk drawers, everywhere in the house. They were men obsessed. William stood in my bedroom while I packed, vowing to me again that he would find the letters. Until I was on the plane to

England, I was escorted by either Simon or William. I'm sure they hoped I would make a mad grab for the letters wherever they were hidden."

I imagined her panic in those frantic moments alone in the study. If only the men and the eras had been reversed, she would have had an ally in Simon's nephew, Peter, the gentle soul who played the piano in the dusty private ballroom.

"I went out of the country partly because I needed a way to break all ties. I had no friends in England to complicate the plan I was forming. And also I was afraid if I came here directly, William might follow and burst in on us still in that wild frame of mind. I thought the trip was the best protection for all concerned."

"So it was in England that you decided on the mock funeral? William could have his empire unencumbered by any resistance from you, and you could begin your life in Jacksonville?"

"Yes. I contacted Winona and we agreed it was probably the only thing that would work to keep William at bay. When I called William, he still hadn't found the letters but wanted to be rid of me once and for all. He was slightly more composed by that time and he agreed to my plan. Unfortunately, I never returned to Rochester or to Porterfield so I had no chance to retrieve my letters."

"What about Sheila Rush? Was there no chance for her to get them for you?"

"She didn't ever go to Porterfield after I left for England. And it would have been too risky for her anyway."

"So you and William agreed to the faked death for a cool million?"

There was a flutter of defensiveness in Cybil's expression. Winona's eyebrows shot up. I hadn't meant to embarrass them.

"Forgive me, that is certainly your business. I became aware of the transfer while I was looking into the matter of delivering the letters. I thought at first that Sheila Rush had been paid off by William to keep Winona's whereabouts a secret."

Winona said, "Sheila was simply acting as our agent. She held the funds for us and then eventually got them to us here."

"Did any of your other friends know you were not dead, Cybil?"

"It was only those people that William valued to whom I wished to appear dead. As well as to the other Porters, for whom I had no great loyalty. We were extremely careful, and then, of course, we moved out of the Greenwood Spa circle into a quieter life centered here once we had our home together."

For several quiet moments, the three of us concentrated on points of abstraction: the fading light of day, the chip in tiles on the terrace, the taller grass above one brick near the back gate—anything but each other's faces. Then I asked Cybil, "Why was your letter to Winona never sent?"

She seemed to be thinking, sifting, remembering, before she answered.

"If I recall correctly, there is no date on that letter. The reason for that is because I was writing on it periodically the same week that Spencer died so unexpectedly. He had kept his heart problems from me, from everyone in the family, because of his pride."

"That was always his weakness," Winona added. "He was too proud for his own good."

"Yes," Cybil agreed. "I loved Spencer; while we had a distance between us partly due to that pride, we also had love and respect for each other. The feelings seemed to balance over the years and make a successful partnership possible. Not, perhaps . . . " She paused again, this time to hold Winona's eyes for a moment. "Not the partnership of my inner spirit, but certainly one that allowed for happy times. And our son. Anyway, when I reread the letter after Spencer's funeral, I felt the timing for expressing those senti-ments was not entirely appropriate. So that letter was forgotten after awhile and eventually bundled in with the rest."

They talked awhile about Lawrence then, as if he was their son, even though Winona had never met him.

"We thought it best, even when I made occasional visits to Rochester, for me not to see him. It would only have made things worse. Cybil's letters let me know him through the years."

"I was sure once Winona laid eyes on Lawrence, he would cap-ture her heart. We could have raised him together, but . . . "

I could tell that Cybil's years with Winona had made it easier for her to open herself to others but now she needed some help. Winona completed her thought.

"That would have been too great a breach of values that neither of us could bear at the time. I got pictures of Lawrence so I could see him change and develop. In a way that was better for me, less painful not being so close to his growth. He separated us through no fault of his own, but still, we felt it."

When it became too cool to sit outside, Winona insisted that I see Cybil's paintings. Cybil tried to avoid the tour, but Winona caught her hand and playfully tugged at her.

"No artistic modesty, my dear. You have a right to be proud of your work so come along with us."

Cybil's canvases were in one of the back bedrooms, a large and cluttered space. The clutter of inspiration, I guessed.

"It's difficult to show strong texture and diversity in water colors, you know," Winona told me as I looked at each painting. "But Cybil can do it well."

Leaning against the door frame, Cybil told me, "I've taken a few classes here. They tell me I have a 'masculine line' in my work."

Winona squeezed my arm and winked. "We find that comment very amusing."

The paintings clearly featured the only love in Cybil's new life: Winona paused in morning light, holding a bright green vase; Winona seated within a park full of flowers, her hands holding a seashell; Winona's face studied for countless expressions but all one mood: a much returned and devoted love.

The three of us shared supper and they told me animated and tender stories about their clandestine meetings. In thirty years, there were few tricks they had not tried, nor disguises used. They laughed and interrupted each other: "My word, Winona, do you remember . . . " and "Oh, Cybil, don't forget that time we . . . " I asked them about their friends in Leehigh Acres.

"There are other Lesbians here. We're not so much of a peculiarity anymore. At first, a few of our neighbors wondered if we were sisters."

Winona reached over and took Cybil's hand.

"Yes, we know one couple who say they're cousins, but most of us know they've been lovers for thirty-four years."

"You *can* gain more tolerance with age instead of less," Cybil observed.

"We occasionally see a few of our old crew, some of them still trying to relive their former escapades. Sheila comes here at least once every three or four months. Then we have wild times."

Cybil's eyes dazzled a look toward Winona.

"We play backgammon fiercely, and charades. Winona is a devil at charades."

I was more audience than participant in their evening conversation, party to their release of a tiresome burden. Though they had their life, a zestful one when some people are ready to acquiesce and stop living, there had still been a nagging doubt about the letters. There was the possibility of William's somehow getting them and playing his own depraved havoc with their cherished messages. I had brought them delivery indeed, the closing of that final door to conclude their unsettled past. I was glad to have that chance to feel involved in their lives.

When Cybil and Winona offered me their guest room for however long I might want to stay, I felt strong temptation to linger in their world. I would have enjoyed hearing Cybil's version of the stories Sheila Rush had told on her. I resisted, trusting that the weariness I wore next to every bone was a sign to get back to my own home. Because I had brought the past with me, a past when these two women lovers were separated, sensitivity demanded of me that I not ask them to dwell in that time for my own curiosity, even for a short time. They were due their undisturbed life together in the present.

Cybil insisted on driving me to the airport herself, even though it was late. She let Winona and me out close to the ticket counter and then went to park the car. While we had a few brief moments alone, Winona put her hand on my arm.

"You know, Cybil may seem somewhat impenetrable and since you saw only one of her early letters to me, you don't have a whole picture of her. But the truth is, during all those years, *she* was the persistent one. She had more to lose, both in terms of her family and her lifestyle. For so long, there was no end in sight to that life. I knew my own orientation early in my life. I knew I loved Cybil when we met and I would continue to do so for a lifetime. There were so many down times for me. I often thought we would never have our life together. But Cybil kept the dream alive. Her passion did not flow into words the way mine did, but in many ways, hers was the real sustaining energy."

My two new friends stood at the concourse window and I could see them even when the plane rolled away and they became smaller and smaller. My bond with them was by chance, but strong, even if we never met again.

My relief came gradually in a red-eye flight out of Florida and back toward the Rockies. Nearly everyone was trying to sleep, shifting into all manner of positions around those airplane pillows that have always been too small. I was wide awake, my own thoughts still restless, rambling around the last vestiges of the completed puzzle. Clear in my mind was the expression that Cybil and Winona exchanged when I handed them the package that held their letters.

I had been so unaware. I thought about standing at Cybil's grave and asking, as if she could hear me, if her letters were a strange legacy I would some day understand. "As if you were a season yourself . . . " Winona had described Cybil. She had borne her season of duty and one kind of love. She was lucky enough to find another with Winona Stone. I was meant to find their letters, to observe what sacrifice they made for their life together: a life that worked, one made by two women who were lovers and willing to do the hard work of resisting difficult circumstance.

Times have not changed so much. Love between women is still claimed under difficult circumstances. I can think of it no longer as some abstraction because it is my choice too, made luckily before too much unhappy time within the conventions of my era. Maybe it won't be simple, and for many who know me, it will seem impossible to understand. They may not be able to know that I have Sara within me, Sheila and Yolanda, Betts Wattle, and now too, Cybil and Winona. I am alive and will be alive in a new way for the rest of my life because of them, understanding a season that is a part of nature and human love. We've been around since time began and we're still ahead of our time.

Despite the groan from the man across the aisle, I put on my reading light. Someone had left a paper in the seat pocket in front of me. It was the *New York Times*. The national scourge of flagging economics assailed me on the front page so I leafed toward the entertainment section. A headline mid-way through the paper caught my attention: "SCATTERED BY STEALTH—LITTER REVEALS MURDER."

The article with the headline detailed a strange phenomena that had police in more than eight major cities baffled. Thousands of flyers had appeared in these cities on the streets habited by prostitutes; no one knew how the flyers got there. No one had seen anything. They might as well have been dropped from the sky. The winter wind had whipped the flyers for several blocks in Philadelphia. They had blown into the snow in Detroit and some stuck out of the drifts downtown. In Times Square and on the docks near the Westside Highway in the Village, hookers were wading through flyers. The same was reported on Bourbon Street in New Orleans, on Turk and Powell Streets in San Francisco, in Boston's "combat zone," where the heaviest concentration of flyers was reported, and in L.A., Atlanta, Chicago, and St. Louis. Tenderloin strips were flooded with this unusual litter, written on one page with a drawing and anonymously citing a pimp known as the Saint for the murder of a hooker some eight years previous. While police in no one city would comment as to whether the Saint's true identity or whereabouts were known, one cop in Boston was quoted as saying, "Whoever he is, wherever he is, he's out of work now."

Publications of
THE NAIAD PRESS, INC.
P.O. Box 10543 • Tallahassee, Florida 32302
Mail orders welcome. Please include 15% postage.

Mrs. Porter's Letter by Vicki P. McConnell. A mystery novel.
224 pp. ISBN 0-930044-29-0 $6.95

To the Cleveland Station by Carol Anne Douglas. A novel.
192 pp. ISBN 0-930044-27-4 $6.95

The Nesting Place by Sarah Aldridge. A novel. 224 pp.
ISBN 0-930044-26-6 $6.95

This Is Not for You by Jane Rule. A novel. 284 pp.
ISBN 0-930044-25-8 $7.95

Faultline by Sheila Ortiz Taylor. A novel. 140 pp.
ISBN 0-930044-24-X $6.95

The Lesbian in Literature by Barbara Grier. 3rd ed.
Foreword by Maida Tilchen. A comprehensive bibliog.
240 pp. ISBN 0-930044-23-1   ind. $7.95
inst. $10.00

Anna's Country by Elizabeth Lang. A novel. 208 pp.
ISBN 0-930044-19-3 $6.95

Lesbian Writer: Collected Work of Claudia Scott
edited by Frances Hanckel and Susan Windle. Poetry. 128 pp.
ISBN 0-930044-22-3 $4.50

Prism by Valerie Taylor. A novel. 158 pp.
ISBN 0-930044-18-5 $6.95

Black Lesbians: An Annotated Bibliography compiled by
JR Roberts. Foreword by Barbara Smith. 112 pp.
ISBN 0-930044-21-5   ind. $5.95
inst. $8.00

The Marquise and the Novice by Victoria Ramstetter.
A novel. 108 pp. ISBN 0-930044-16-9 $4.95

Labiaflowers by Tee A. Corinne. 40 pp. $3.95

Outlander by Jane Rule. Short stories, essays.
207 pp. ISBN 0-930044-17-7 $6.95

Sapphistry: The Book of Lesbian Sexuality by
Pat Califia. 195 pp. ISBN 0-930044-14-2 $6.95

Lesbian-Feminism in Turn-of-the-Century Germany.
An anthology. Translated and edited by Lillian Faderman
and Brigitte Eriksson. 120 pp. ISBN 0-930044-13-4 $5.95

(continued on next page)

A VOLUTE BOOK
NAIAD PRESS, INC.
P.O. Box 10543
Tallahassee, Florida 32302

All Naiad Press Books listed in this book can be purchased by
mail, as well as Valerie Taylor's three titles.

**Journey to Fulfillment, A World without Men and Return to
Lesbos**
$3.95 each plus 15% postage and handling—minimum 75¢.

NAME _____

ADDRESS _____

CITY _____ STATE _____ ZIP _____

BOOK(S) _____

_____

TOTAL ENCLOSED $ _____